Realist Critiques of Visual Culture

Edward Barnaby

Realist Critiques of Visual Culture

From Hardy to Barnes

Edward Barnaby
University of Virginia
Charlottesville, VA, USA

ISBN 978-3-319-77322-3   ISBN 978-3-319-77323-0   (eBook)
https://doi.org/10.1007/978-3-319-77323-0

Library of Congress Control Number: 2018935419

© The Editor(s) (if applicable) and The Author(s) 2018
This work is subject to copyright. All rights are solely and exclusively licensed by the
Publisher, whether the whole or part of the material is concerned, specifically the rights of
translation, reprinting, reuse of illustrations, recitation, broadcasting, reproduction on
microfilms or in any other physical way, and transmission or information storage and retrieval,
electronic adaptation, computer software, or by similar or dissimilar methodology now
known or hereafter developed.
The use of general descriptive names, registered names, trademarks, service marks, etc. in this
publication does not imply, even in the absence of a specific statement, that such names are
exempt from the relevant protective laws and regulations and therefore free for general use.
The publisher, the authors and the editors are safe to assume that the advice and information
in this book are believed to be true and accurate at the date of publication. Neither the publisher nor the authors or the editors give a warranty, express or implied, with respect to the
material contained herein or for any errors or omissions that may have been made. The
publisher remains neutral with regard to jurisdictional claims in published maps and institutional affiliations.

Cover illustration: Zoonar GmbH / Alamy Stock Photo

Printed on acid-free paper

This Palgrave Macmillan imprint is published by the registered company Springer International
Publishing AG part of Springer Nature.
The registered company address is: Gewerbestrasse 11, 6330 Cham, Switzerland

ACKNOWLEDGMENTS

Material from Chap. 1 originally appeared in an article titled "Literary Realism as Meta-Spectacle," published in 2008 by the *Journal of Narrative Theory* (volume 38, issue 1, pages 37–59).

Material from Chap. 5 originally appeared in an article titled "Airbrushed History: Photography, Realism and Rushdie's *Midnight's Children*," published in 2005 by *Mosaic, an interdisciplinary critical journal* (volume 38, issue 1, pages 1–16).

I wish to thank Michael Hatt for many formative and enjoyable discussions during the early stages of this project. I also extend my appreciation to Ned Cooke for the opportunity to workshop several chapters with his Material Culture Colloquium at Yale University.

I express my deepest gratitude to John Maynard for his sustained guidance, support and critical engagement over a period of many, many years. One could not find a more generous mentor.

Finally, love and thanks to Hannah for sharing my fascination with the spectacle and to my parents, Howard and Peggy, for countless hours of conversation and encouragement about the writing of this book.

Contents

1 Introduction: Literary Realism as Meta-Spectacle   1

2 "Pugin was wrong, and Wren was right"—Architectural
Revival as Spectacle in Thomas Hardy's *Jude the Obscure*   31

3 "The true Italy is to be found by patient observation"—
Tourism as Spectacle in E.M. Forster's *A Room with a View*   57

4 "You've stirred in me my unacted part"—Historical
Pageantry as Spectacle in Virginia Woolf's *Between the Acts*   81

5 "Pressed against the screen"—Cinema and Photography
as Spectacle in Salman Rushdie's *Midnight's Children*   115

6 "The law of white gloves"—The Museum as Spectacle
in Edward Carey's *Observatory Mansions*   141

7 Epilogue: "Those old *soixante-huitards*"—Debord
as Spectacle in Julian Barnes' *England, England*   167

Index   183

CHAPTER 1

Introduction: Literary Realism as Meta-Spectacle

Visual technologies that produce and circulate images are not unique to contemporary society or even to modernity. Neither is critical discourse about the nature or meaning of images. However, the concentrated proliferation of these phenomena during the industrial age has contributed to a uniquely modern experience of spectatorial distance from the real. The study of visual culture emerged in response to this unprecedented consolidation of the influence that images and mediation exert collectively upon everyday existence. Commentators on early industrial-era visuality identify the *camera obscura*—a room within which an isolated observer inspects projected images of the outside world—as emblematic of a distinctly modern paradigm for comprehending reality through rationalist separation and visual abstraction. Other developments in post-Enlightenment visual culture—such as the looking glass, the microscope, the refracting telescope, linear perspective in painting, the science of optics, documentary photographs, and popular visual entertainments such as the stereoscope, panorama and magic lantern—fundamentally transformed the modern individual's encounter with reality by artificially reconstructing spatial depth, warping the scale of human perception and advancing claims to objectivity (Crary 1990; Jay 1993; Armstrong 1999).

A more contemporary emblem of this spectatorial model for interacting with reality is the screen. Beginning with the advent of cinema and now penetrating all sites of social interaction and solitude, screens make it possible for individuals to consume the wealth of images produced in our

© The Author(s) 2018
E. Barnaby, *Realist Critiques of Visual Culture*,
https://doi.org/10.1007/978-3-319-77323-0_1

1

post-industrial culture. The science of image display strives for literality through increasingly larger screens of finer resolution, yielding 70-foot screens in IMAX theaters and 110-inch ultra-high-definition home television screens that dominate the physical scale of the viewer. At the same time, increasingly smaller screens facilitate the portability of images through the use of various pads and pods. All categories of screen-based interaction—including photography, cinema, television and interpersonal communication—have been amalgamated into hand-held devices that generate images and display an inexhaustible archive of films, shows, music videos, home movies, advertisements and other visual internet content. These devices are networked to social media channels that enable individuals to participate directly and continuously in the mass production, captioning and circulation of images. The crowd has been successfully sourced for an unceasing stream of representations.

The realist impulse materialized in mid-nineteenth-century fiction alongside this intensifying spectatorial distance from an increasingly objectified world. One witnesses at that moment a discernable shift in literary production toward unembellished depictions of contemporary, quotidian situations. Novelists sought to render lived experience with authentic social complexity and psychological depth, portraying the convergence of multiple individual perspectives against the context of the societal, political and economic conditions that would lead them to intersect in a particular manner. As such, realist novels typically reference extant social discourses, material culture and built environments with greater specificity than other literary forms. They are often set in cities (or in rural locales threatened by encroaching urbanity) and reflect the displacement of traditional agrarian and feudal social relationships within the alienated "mass" character of industrial society. Conceived of as an iconoclastic break from idealized literary conventions that falsify the real, realist narration sometimes theorizes its own validity relative to other acts of representation and at other times exhibits an ironic awareness of its limitations.

Realist fiction is thus uniquely capable of giving shape to the modern condition of spectatorship because it depicts a commonly inhabited material environment, various individual perceptions of that environment, and elements of industrialized visual culture that mediate those acts of perception. Heightening the capacity to recognize our own immersion within objectified representations of the real, literary realism remains a vital discourse in contemporary society, particularly one that is so deeply invested in visually reproducing and archiving lived experience. However, the per-

INTRODUCTION: LITERARY REALISM AS META-SPECTACLE 3

sistence of realism's critique of post-industrial visual culture in twentieth-century fiction has been largely obscured by the stylistic innovations of modernism and postmodernism. A post-war meta-fictional arms race has led some critics to engage in a presentist dismissal of classic realism. Such critics posit the naïve pursuit of pure verisimilitude by authors whose alleged confidence in the possibility of unmediated representation fueled their deluded attempts to reproduce the dimensionality of space and time through words.[1] I share the view of those who reject such reductive caricatures of classic realism and who argue instead that a systematic critique of the limits of representation has always been a defining trait of realist fiction.[2] I contend that literary realism is not fundamentally an aesthetic form, but an ethical gesture; that this gesture is motivated by and primarily expressed as a critique of the spectatorial distance from reality wrought by industrialization; and that this critique has evolved continuously since the classic realism of the nineteenth century and remains operative in contemporary fiction.

Articulating this ethical relationship between art and society has long preoccupied Marxist critics. Suggesting, however, that "aesthetics is Marx's blind spot," W.J.T. Mitchell points to the difficulty that Marx and his critical successors have experienced in applying the concept of commodity fetishism with sufficient nuance to the field of cultural production (1986, 202). In addition to Marx's own tendency to idealize art and redirect his strongest critiques toward other sectors of capitalist transformation, the Marxist tradition has struggled in general to locate a middle ground between, on the one hand, allowing art to persist as a mystified rationalization for the contemporary image-making industry and, on the other, engaging in the dismissal of all aesthetic objects and mediated experiences as uniformly alienated false consciousness (203). Mitchell seeks a discourse in which the fetishized and commodified aspects of art and media are recognized alongside the reality that "the museum is (sometimes) the site of authentic aesthetic experience, the media (sometimes) the vehicle of real communication and enlightenment." He uses the phrase "mutual embarrassment" to describe a productive relationship between Marxism and aesthetics that keeps both perspectives honest and prevents the "rhetoric of iconoclasm" from devolving into a one-note "rhetoric of exaggerated alienation." This productive tension exists when Marxist criticism itself is rigorously historicized and self-critical, when "notions like fetishism and ideology" are understood to be "historically situated *figures*" and not deployed formulaically in what Mitchell describes as a "theoretical exercise, with all options predetermined" (204). Mitchell reminds us that Marx selected the term *fetishism* precisely to address an enlightened nineteenth-century audience bound up in imperial chauvinism, such that equating his readers with the primitive object-worshipers whom they were in the process of Westernizing was a poignant rhetorical move. What, then, is the paradigm that would best convey to contemporary society its same ironic act of forgetting—the same blindness to the fact that we have endowed objects with arbitrary value and allowed them to abstract our social relationships, our experience of time and the manner in which we organize and inhabit physical space?

Guy Debord's theorization of a post-industrial *Society of the Spectacle* provides a particularly useful vocabulary and framework for understanding the uniquely modern visual culture to which literary realism responds and the source of the alienated false consciousness that realist fiction often depicts.[3] As with Marx's trope of fetishism, Debord reorients the concept of "spectacle" to transform what could be popularly regarded as two defining achievements of our era—namely, the precipitous rise of media technologies and the democratization of mass consumer goods and entertainments—into the epitome of society's blindness to its own utter disenfranchisement. He envisions the modern individual as "imprisoned in a flat universe bounded on all sides by the spectacle's screen" and subjected by "figmentary interlocutors [...] to a one-way discourse on their commodities" ([1967] 1995, 218). Debord traces the legacy of fetishism within celebrity worship, tourism, urban planning and the culture industry, while also turning the critique of ideology onto various fetishized manifestations of Marxist political thought that had themselves become iconic and ended in failed revolutions. In precisely the manner that Mitchell recommends, Debord continuously scrutinized his critical stance for signs of iconoclastic hypocrisy and abandoned his collective when he sensed that it was degenerating into a spectacle of intellectual chic.

Debord was a founding member in 1957 of the Situationist International, an organization of artists, social theorists and political revolutionaries that was heavily influenced by Marx, Dadaism, the Surrealists and the Frankfurt School and which played a significant role in the civil unrest in France of 1968. The group's name refers to its development of experimental "situations" to facilitate the analysis of everyday life. The Situationist practice of *dérive*, for example, encourages an individual to "drift" through a city without recourse to the political, historical, commercial and touristic meanings that have been mapped onto it by various authorities, establishing instead an alternate "psychogeography" that is informed only by individual encounter and personal associations. Through a process called *détournement* (which Debord describes as the "antithesis of quotation"), verbal and visual discourses that have taken on "theoretical authority" are restated in new contexts that allow alternate meanings to subvert canonical ones (Debord [1967] 1995, 208). Works of art, political slogans and corporate advertising have all served as fodder for these Situationist "pranks." The Situationists intended that such exercises would bring the participants to a greater consciousness of their authentic desires and motivations, which had become suppressed by the alienated labor of producing and consuming surplus commodities in post-industrial culture.[4]

Arguing in *Society of the Spectacle* that the capitalist division of labor is accompanied by a corresponding division of the senses, Debord describes a modern visual economy that reduces the individual to a mere spectator of ideologies and identities which are represented to him as his own, but which he cannot authentically inhabit. Key to this visual economy is the refashioning of the built environment through a "technology of separation" that suppresses the political consciousness of "the street" and facilitates the circulation and consumption of commodities (Debord [1967] 1995, 171–2). The urbanist reorganization of space atomizes the public sphere and reconstitutes it as a false community of shared dependency on one-way communication from the mass media. Also central to this visual economy is a robust culture industry in which representations of lived experience are recirculated as commodities and fetishized as a false substitute for historical knowledge and identity. Debord blames the technology of image diffusion for collapsing the distinction between public and private life and inspiring a fundamentally voyeuristic disposition in modern culture toward the real. Under such conditions, he argues, consciousness is reduced to an "illusion of encounter" between individuals, who in turn develop a pathological need for representation within the spectacle in order to regain their sense of agency (217–9).[5] Debord's insights anticipated current trends in social interaction whereby one documents lived experience in real-time and exhibits it to others by posting brief tweets and captioned photographs to social media sites. The shared experience of authentic encounter is delimited to the act of viewing and commenting on the posts of others within this abbreviated reality of the spectacle.

It is not simply these layers of mediation themselves that produce the experience of spectacle, but the state in which our immersion within these layers of mediation and their underlying ideological filters becomes invisible

6   E. BARNABY

to us. This is the double act of forgetting that underlies Marx's original use of the figure of the fetishist to describe commodity culture (Mitchell 1986, 193). Debord conceives of the spectacle not as a particular image or even as a set of images, but the environment in which images and their captions take on an objectified authority that subjects the individual to spectatorial distance and psychological division. The dominant experience of reality in such a culture shifts from the ethical sphere of interaction to an aesthetic sphere of contemplation. In some cases, this alienation stems from the revival and commodification of cultural products that are foisted upon a resistant spectator. Other times, an individual clings to the role of spectator, perhaps because he has come to rely upon the spectacle for his sense of identity and agency. Literary realism is uniquely suited to depicting these effects of the spectacle because it traces the most subtle alterations of consciousness—active, passive, manipulative or spontaneous—wrought by the discourses in which an individual character is immersed.[6]

Debord's analysis in *Society of the Spectacle* is doubly important to this study of realism in that he highlights the limitation of various critiques of spectacle—political and artistic movements alike—that fail to escape the logic of spectatorship. Debord cautions that literary and artistic critiques of the spectacle are themselves highly susceptible to commodification as cultural products. In this sense, the greatest threat to literary realism is its reduction to a canonical aesthetic trope. Realist fiction is particularly resistant to recuperation as spectacle, however, when it is recognized as a Situationist exercise that subjects the spontaneous experience of everyday life to critical scrutiny through whatever technical means best achieve that end. Unlike many other attempts to analyze realism through the aesthetic categories that Debord pejoratively associates with the culture industry, this study will demonstrate that literary realism is not ultimately reducible to a particular moment or style in literary history, but is defined by an ethical commitment to foreground its own role in mediating reality.

Realist novels habitually confront the reader with the role of spectator that he or she is forced to play, often by advancing a discursive restatement of the characters' socially conditioned acts of seeing. Some locate realism's consciousness of the act of seeing in the trope of the *flâneur* who strolls city streets and chronicles urban material culture (Rignall 1992, 2), a spectatorial figure that has been theorized by Walter Benjamin as a product of industrialized society and which I explore further below in connection with Edward Carey's novel *Observatory Mansions*. Others point to the presence within realist novels of Victorian travel apparati such as panoramas, guidebooks and non-fiction travel guides that "incorporated a layer of self-reflexivity into their narratives" about tourism's influence on the practice of seeing (Byerly 2013, 3; Buzard 1993), a phenomenon that informs my analysis of spectatorship in E.M. Forster's *A Room with a View* that follows. Alison Byerly notes the frequent "aesthetic cross-referencing" in realist fiction of other artistic media and specific works of art that enables novelists to depict the "moral and political dimensions" of their characters' aesthetic judgments (1997, 2, 8, 9). This capacity to advance a reader's ethical consideration of aesthetic interactions is precisely the achievement of literary realism that this study elucidates.

Realist fiction does not simply picture reality for the reader, but enables the reader to re-experience the conditions through which reality is pictured. The original connotation of the Greek term *mimesis*—or *imitation*—described the function of art not simply as a literal and transparent copy of the real, but a performance and re-enactment that enables the audience to undertake the characters' perceptions and experiences as a conscious process (Furst 1995, 188–90). William Stowe invokes Claude Levi-Strauss' concept of art as miniature to argue, similarly, that literary realism does not "create a substitute for life or a faithful reproduction of life" in the form of "an object to be contemplated" or "a project ready for consumption," but crafts "versions of actual phenomena" which "the perceiver of a work of art is invited to retrace and in effect to relive" (1983, 9–11). Further shifting the notion of literary realism from a still-life to a performance, Esther Leslie describes such fiction as *enstaging* reality instead of merely "mirroring its external contours," thus "making explicit the aspects that fetishized existence and ideology submerge" (2007, 129).

Building on Debord's particular use of the term "spectacle," I contend that literary realism functions as "meta-spectacle" by making visible the various processes through which individual consciousness becomes distorted by a visual culture that objectifies reality. This framework allows one to recognize that Thomas Hardy's *Jude the Obscure*, E.M. Forster's *A Room with a View*, and Edward Carey's *Observatory Mansions* do not simply rehearse detailed descriptions of recognizable buildings and cities, but depict how architectural revival, the Grand Tour and urbanism aestheticize the individual's relationship to the built environment and transform inhabitants into permanent tourists within a "museum-as-habitation."[7] As instances of meta-spectacle, Virginia Woolf's *Between the Acts*, Salman Rushdie's *Midnight's Children* and Julian Barnes' *England, England* do not merely document social customs and material culture with the literality of a photograph or newsreel, but portray a pageantizing mindset and curatorial impulse to objectify, possess and even colonize the real as a set of images.

A preoccupation with particular stylistic and thematic differences between classic realism and modern and postmodern fiction has diverted critical attention from what makes realist fiction realist. It is instructive to examine respective attempts by Hardy, Forster and Woolf to position their realist ethos within an evolving modernist aesthetic. Hardy took great pains to distinguish his fiction's critique of industrialized life from the naturalistic practices of his contemporaries, yet he unwittingly contributed to the conflation of ethics and aesthetics by appealing to the authority of classical tragedy and satire. In comparing his novels to Greek drama and poetry, Hardy sought to underscore their shared ethical concern for the conflict between individual consciousness and externalized universal forces, but instead he drew criticism for failing to maintain Aristotelian unities. Forster lamented the emergence of an intemperate historicism that led fellow critics to isolate texts within narrow periods of production and disregard the continued influence of literary tradition—including nineteenth-century realism—on modernist authors. Forster's description of such criticism as *pseudo-scholarship* anticipates the language of Debord's critique of the culture industry for restricting the meaning of individual works of literature and art within a positivist progression of aesthetic forms. Virginia Woolf avoids Hardy's pitfall of relying on classical aesthetic categories by articulating in her essays a new vocabulary to discuss his novels and her own. She distinguishes between the naturalistic reproduction of material reality in some modern fiction versus the realist portrayal of individual consciousness struggling to inhabit a commonly perceived material reality. Woolf also escapes the pigeonholes of periodization of which Forster warns by distancing herself from her modernist contemporaries and identifying instead with Hardy. I will elaborate on these critical perspectives toward realism advanced by Hardy, Forster and Woolf in the chapters that follow.

Certain novelists who fall historically within the modern and postmodern eras cite realism as an ethical stance that motivates them to achieve a more authentic engagement with the real in their fiction. This ethical stance transcends literary styles and periods. Woolf suggests that there is, in fact, no single method for achieving the realist perspective, as long as it enables the author to "come closer to life" and the reader to come "closer to the novelist's intention" ([1925] 1984, 150, 152). Salman Rushdie echoes Woolf's notion that realism is not a specific method of representation, but an ethic that compels an artist to "attempt to respond as fully as possible to the circumstances of the world in which the artist works" (1991, 210). He compares himself with Dickens as writing fiction in which "details of place and social mores are skewered by a pitiless realism [...] against a scrupulously observed social and historical background." Noting the presence of certain "highly fabulated" scenes in *Midnight's Children*, Rushdie explains that what some have misinterpreted as magical realism or imperialist exoticism are simply realist accounts of the narrator's neuroses that stem from his lifelong exposure to the spectacles of European chauvinism and nationalist idealism (2002, 64, 72). Julian Barnes, too, has urged critics to forgo the variety of labels that are applied to twentieth-century fiction. For Barnes, fiction is simply "the best way of telling the truth [...] about society or the way in which emotional lives are led." When a novel achieves this level of truth, it is inherently, he contends, a "realist form" (Guppy 2000).

In these and other examples, authors reassert their commitment to a realist ethic that has been obscured by aesthetic considerations.[8] A similar dynamic has threatened the legacy of Bertolt Brecht's "epic theater," through which Brecht sought to transform theatrical audiences from passive spectators of tragic fate and melodramatic plots into vigilant critics of contemporary social conditions in which they feel compelled to intervene. Brecht himself recognized the risk that the so-called "alienation effects" which he employed to jar his audience into social awareness could ultimately brand Brechtian consciousness as an aesthetic style instead of an ethical stance.[9] Despite their shared antagonism toward spectacle, epic theater and literary realism have each suffered what Debord would describe as a similar encapsulation within the history of literary form through which they are recuperated and redeployed as fetishized artifacts within the culture industry. A play is Brechtian, however, because it challenges the audience to take issue with the acts depicted on stage and not because of various stylistic gimmicks that Brecht himself regarded as a provisional and temporary means of producing consciousness. Similarly, a novel is realist because it depicts the various verbal and visual discourses that form a character's consciousness of the real at a particular moment in time. Traits that have come to be associated with realism as a genre, such as a certain density of material detail or plots that reach beyond the aristocracy for their subject matter, were the provisional gestures of realist consciousness in the novel and its initial registers of industrial transformation. This study

10   E. BARNABY

explores how literary realism continues to produce consciousness of false reality. It counters a reductive view of realism that has led not only to a misreading of specific texts and authors, but also to a muddled sense of literature's relationship to the real.

The significance of literary realism has thus evolved beyond a technique of nineteenth-century fiction to what Fredric Jameson has described as "an epistemological category framed and staged in aesthetic terms" (2007, 261). That is to say, the turn in literary production toward an unembellished depiction of contemporary, quotidian experience has spawned a critical discourse that analyzes the very claims about reality made by such fiction. Certain authors have identified themselves as realists based on their depiction of individual consciousness in negotiation with the observable world, and certain literary critics have evaluated the effect on the reader of these fictional representations of consciousness. Among those critics, some credit works of literary realism with bringing the reader to a greater awareness of social conditions that have become objectified as natural and unchangeable. They argue that literary realism disrupts the spontaneous hold exerted on the reader by hegemony and ideology, thereby collapsing spectatorial distance and restoring the individual's ethical consciousness and agency. Other critics, arguing precisely the opposite, indict literary realism for objectifying the present social order as an aesthetic image to be contemplated by the reader. In this alternate view, literary realism contributes to the reader's abstraction from reality and susceptibility to false consciousness, thereby reinforcing hegemony, ideology and the reader's role as spectator.

These contradictory appraisals of literary realism demand reflection on what is at stake in the act of mediating the real through fiction. This study distinguishes realist fiction that restates reality for our critical inspection from realist-*ic* fiction that reproduces reality to be consumed as an aesthetic product. This is not simply a matter of discerning authorial intention. The act of reception can cause slippage between these two modes of mediating the real through fiction. The visual detail through which the realist novel stages its ethical challenge to spectatorship can be misappropriated within post-industrial culture by readers who seek the purely aesthetic experience of realistic effect, or who have been trained in the classroom to understand realism as a naturalistic literary style of the late nineteenth century. If the role of visual description in a novel is merely to catalog material culture so as to invoke a recognizable time and place for the reader, then such fiction reinforces the very acts of consumption that it might otherwise reveal. I propose, however, that the realist novel's engagement with visual culture must come to be understood as fully as Hayden White, for one, has explored the influence of narrative form on historiography. In particular, White (1975) argues that realist writing is embedded with ironic discursive elements that enable readers to recognize how their understanding of reality is shaped by rhetorical structure. I argue that realist fiction is also embedded with ironic visual elements that enable readers to recognize how their understanding of reality is shaped by visual culture. In this manner, the realist novel achieves *détournement* by resituating its characters' limited reality within the "overall frame of reference of its period" and the "precise option that it constituted within that framework" (Debord [1967] 1995, 208).

James Joyce's *Ulysses* ([1922] 1986) is a potent, even extreme example of this function of realism, as well as of the emphasis on narratology over iconology in criticism of the novel. Joyce immerses his main character, Leopold Bloom, in a spectacle of commercial jingles, popular music, tabloid headlines, political slogans, legal jargon, Christian apologetics and academic scholarship. These verbal discourses constitute communities of shared consciousness, but also introduce layers of mediation that reinforce Bloom's role as a marginalized spectator of those communities. Joyce re-enacts this experience of spectacle for his readers through the pageant of narrative forms that comprise the novel. In one chapter the diction pro-gresses through a history of English prose styles; another is scripted as a stage performance; another adopts the question-and-answer format of religious catechism; and the final chapter manifests as stream of conscious-ness. On a meta-fictional level, Joyce confronts the spectacle of cultural commodity head-on by conceiving of the novel as a massive classical allu-sion to Homer's *Odyssey*, which not only serves as the organizing principle for plot and characterization in Joyce's novel, but also broaches the prob-lem of spectatorship as a threat to epic heroism.

Ulysses functions as a grand *dérive* whereby Joyce records Bloom's radi-cally subjective encounter with industrial-era Dublin through Joyce's own radically subjective appropriation of a canonical text. The novel consoli-dates the geographic scale of Odysseus' twenty-year journey into Situationist psychogeography, mapping Bloom's physical ramblings across Dublin during a twenty-hour period against his mental ramblings across the greater part of the Western cultural tradition, both high and low. Visual culture plays an important role in Joyce's realist (and fundamen-tally Situationist) gesture. The verbal discourses that Joyce invokes are complemented by a spectacle of visual discourses that contribute to Bloom's abstraction. Cosmopolitan eclecticism contributes to Bloom's speculative stance as a *flâneur*, voyeur and culturally literate connoisseur. Joyce depicts Bloom in the act of gazing upon the city from the inside of a drawn carriage, spying lasciviously on women bathing at the beach, witnessing religious services of a denomination other than his own, anonymously contemplating the behavior of strangers at pubs, and stopping at a museum to look at an exhibition of classical sculpture. Joyce appeals at various moments to sounds, smells, tactility and even scatology to puncture the bubble of images and words that insulates Bloom. While it is arguable whether Bloom himself ultimately transcends the role of spectator, Joyce's novel makes the dynamics of spectacle unmistakably visible to the reader.

Along these lines, certain major critics have identified realist fiction as a restatement of reality that exposes the false consciousness of ideology, laying bare opportunistic constructions of history and stripping them of their compelling internal coherence. Written in the late 1930s, Georg Lukàcs' study of the historical novel praises Walter Scott's fiction for providing an alternative to the epic model of heroism, which tended to mystify social forces as the workings of an heroic individual's will ([1937] 1983, 270). Lukàcs regards the "full political effect" of realism as the "literary unmasking of the pseudo-hero of Fascism," which the novel achieves through its "social-historical and not merely individual-biographical standpoint" (341). According to Lukàcs, the heroes of Scott's novels serve as a "neutral ground" on which social forces in conflict are rendered on a human scale and made visible through the "concrete historicism of all the details" (36, 151). Philip Rahv employs similar language to contend that the "pseudo-context of a political speech or editorial" is made apparent when it is "injected into the real context of a living experience" through fiction ([1939] 1978, 303). Enlarging upon this idea of realist literature's ability to make ideology visible, Pierre Macherey later argued in *A Theory of Literary Production* that although the substance of the realist novel is rooted in historical reality, the text is mediated by a literariness that disrupts any possibility of mistaking the novel as an attempt to achieve an objective reflection of the real ([1966] 1978, 118). As a fictional environment comprised of "partial reflections" and often presenting the very "improbability of reflecting," the realist novel makes it possible, according to Macherey, for the reader to move beyond the "domain of spontaneous ideology" into a "state of consciousness" (132, 133). The novel thus "establishes myth and illusion as visible objects" from which the reader can achieve a critical distance (133). Such fiction generates the consciousness of industrial and post-industrial visual culture that I call "meta-spectacle."

Hardy, Forster and Woolf have each expressed a similar commitment to pursuing this realist restatement of the formation and distortion of consciousness. Hardy portrays the persistence of archaic social institutions and visual forms that no longer correspond to the present reality of human experience, but which nevertheless continue to influence—and sometimes stunt—individual identity and aspiration. Anticipating the public outcry against *Jude the Obscure*, Hardy declared in his preface to the first edition that his fiction advances no ideological or even practical agenda for social reform. Instead, he makes his characters' troubled relationship to reality visible by providing "shape and coherence to a series of seemings, or personal impressions" and leaving aside "the question of their consistency or their discordance, of their permanence or their transitoriness" ([1895] 1965, 3). Forster, too, identifies the unique capacity of fiction to make visible the "secret life" of individual consciousness that is not otherwise accessible in the everyday ([1927] 1954, 99). He suggests that the novel is capable of achieving a "parallel in our perception of life" by depicting characters that exhibit the "incalculability of daily life" and experience the "intermittent knowledge" to which consciousness is prone (123, 118). Woolf similarly argues that realist fiction reconstructs the complexity of an individual's interaction with an external world by "trac[ing] the pattern, however disconnected and incoherent in appearance, which each sight or incident scores upon the consciousness" ([1925] 1984, 150). Woolf locates herself centrally on a realist spectrum bounded by Arnold Bennett's naturalism at one extreme and James Joyce's experimental modernism on the other. She faults Bennett for reproducing a veneer of material reality that is uninhabited by human consciousness and Joyce (particularly, one suspects, the Joyce of *Finnegan's Wake*) for reproducing a radical interiority with little referent to a world outside the individual mind (147, 151).

As Peter Brooks observes in *Realist Vision*, modernist literature like Woolf's is not a rejection of the realist premise that the novel can trace human experience within the world, but represents a shift in emphasis toward representing the "selectivity of consciousness applied to the phenomenal world, and the establishment of a perspective resolutely within consciousness as it deals with the objects of the world" (2005, 211).[10] This notion of literary realism as a restatement of the process through which consciousness is formed persists in contemporary fiction by Rushdie, Edward Carey and Julian Barnes. Their novels, particularly those treated here, address a post-industrial visual culture in which the false consciousness of spectacle has achieved what Debord calls "material form" ([1967] 1995, 216). Noting that "ideological entities have never been mere fictions," Debord argues that the influence of ideology is exerted through "a distorted consciousness of reality" that becomes a "real factor [...] producing real distorting effects" (212). In this respect, realist fiction is particularly suited to reveal the workings of spectacle. Rushdie demonstrates in *Midnight's Children* how conflicting ideologies of European chauvinism and nationalist idealism are false realities that take on material form through a variety of visual media. Reflecting on the blend of history, fantasy and irony in his autobiographical narrative, Rushdie's narrator concludes that its "metaphorical content [...] does not make it less real," but instead alerts readers to the various agents that intervene in his understanding of the real ([1981] 2006, 230). Carey demonstrates in *Observatory Mansions* how conflicting ideologies of antiquarian revival and urbanism take on material form by shaping a built environment in which his characters' tactile connection to their city is supplanted by a predominantly visual relationship that is more appropriate to a tourist. Carey (n.d.) has noted that he routinely consults architectural guidebooks while drafting his novels and even built a model of the city in which his second novel is set—not to achieve greater naturalistic detail, but to think through how his characters are either connected to or disconnected from the environments they inhabit. Barnes credits the "psychological complexity and inwardness and reflection" of realist fiction with modeling authentic consciousness to the reader and serving as a corrective to ideologies that fail to "reflect the fullest complications of the world" (Guppy 2000).

Realistic—as opposed to realist—fiction, on the other hand, reproduces the visible veneer of reality for the reader, but does not overtly challenge the reader to move beyond the role of spectator or to engage critically with the act of representation. Like much "reality" television programming, realistic fiction is primarily a mass-market commodity that drives consumption by cultivating the reader's voyeuristic impulse to observe the present or re-inhabit the past from a position of aesthetic detachment. In an essay titled "Raffles and Mrs. Blandish," George Orwell examines how popular fiction of his time reduced the consciousness advanced by literary restatement (the "political effect" of which Lukàcs writes) to sensationalistic reproductions of modern culture that objectify and naturalize a dysfunctional industrialized world for the reader. Describing a dime-store crime novel titled *No Orchids for Miss Blandish*, Orwell writes:

> Several people, after reading *No Orchids*, have remarked to me, 'It's pure Fascism.' This is a correct description, although the book has not the smallest connection with politics and very little with social or economic problems. It has merely the same relation to Fascism as, say, Trollope's novels have to nineteenth-century capitalism. It is a daydream appropriate to a totalitarian age. ([1944] 1981, 146)

The *realistic* novel fails to circumscribe ideology within literary language and subjectivity, but instead provides the very material form through which ideology falsely defines the real for the reader. Visual culture exists in realistic fiction as the unscrutinized backdrop of a "daydream," or what Debord describes as spectacle's ambient capitalist *décor* ([1967] 1995, 169). Of particular concern to Orwell is the presentation of violence in industrial culture as "normal and morally neutral," sometimes even aesthetically compelling when achieved on a mass scale ([1944] 1981, 146). The shift from realist to realistic fiction thus entails a corresponding shift from ethical engagement with the problem of representation to an aesthetic appraisal of representation, the very same spectatorial stance that undermines the reception of Brecht's epic theater. Forster describes a similar transfer from ethical engagement to aesthetic appraisal when he differentiates between the "round" characters of realist fiction who exhibit the full possibilities of human consciousness and the "flat" characters of realistic fiction who function as mere embodiments of a static worldview and which invite analysis as "art objects" ([1927] 1954, 123).

Several of the realist novels discussed in this study feature examples of realistic fiction. In each case the realist narrator critiques the depicted realistic text, thus reinforcing the primary novel's overall claim to authentic literary realism and its function as meta-spectacle. A minor character in Forster's *A Room with a View*, for example, writes a sensational novel about a group of British tourists in Italy. She makes various "calculations in realism" to introduce "local colouring" to her narrative, but otherwise replicates the conventionally titillating and superficially exotic details of an affair abroad ([1908] 1986, 317). In another example, the narrator of Woolf's *Between the Acts* notes the increasing number of "shilling shockers" shelved alongside literary, historical and scientific works in the library at Pointz Hall, observing that they are consumed by visitors during the train ride from London and discarded after a single use ([1941] 1970, 16). Rushdie's narrator in *Midnight's Children* directly criticizes realistic fiction in general for advancing "matter of fact descriptions of the outré and bizarre, and their reverse, namely heightened, stylized versions of the everyday." Echoing Orwell's concern that literary realism not be confused with an amoral, quasi-journalistic naturalism, the narrator contends that although realistic fiction bears a superficial resemblance to material reality, it reproduces "a picture of the world of startling uniformity" in which literature's capacity to elicit an ethical response is displaced by a "terrifying, nonchalant violence" ([1981] 2006, 250).

These moments of proximity between realist and realistic fiction are effective in bringing their fundamental disparity into relief, but without such context there remains the possibility that the two genres could be confused, perhaps even by skilled literary critics.[11] When confronted with the distinction between a realist restatement of reality and a realistic reproduction of reality, Jameson's critique of realism in *The Political Unconscious*, for example, begins to appear misdirected. On the one hand, Jameson acknowledges the success of literary realism in "estranging commonplaces against some expected 'real'" and "foregrounding convention itself" as the basis of our understanding (1981, 151). However, he also suggests that realist fiction merely displaces one static vision of the real with another reality that is made to appear equally as natural and unchanging, namely, "life and work in the new world of market capitalism" (152). Thus, for Jameson, although the impulse toward realism is revolutionary in character, it ultimately leads the author to enact numerous "containment strategies," as Jameson calls them, that objectify "impulses of desire and other transformational praxes [...] as naturally occurring feelings, psychological attributes, [and] representable forms of being instead of agents warping totality itself" (193).

This ease with which realism can slip into repressing the reality of historical change leads Jameson to criticize Lukàcs for failing to see his own imprisonment within the "ideological expression of capitalism" constituted by realism's "reification of daily life" (1981, 229, 236). Jameson calls instead for a "progressive or critical realism" that does not merely "reflect or express the phenomenology of life under capitalism" (134). He disparages fiction that reproduces reality in an objectifying manner and seems to disallow the possibility that fiction can restate reality for the purpose of critical scrutiny. His concept of the "political unconscious" is aptly applied to *realistic* fiction, namely, novels that function as the spontaneous daydreams of their age and which reinforce and naturalize the verbal and visual discourses in circulation at that moment. However, when applied to *realist* fiction such as the novels treated in this study, Jameson's critique encourages readings of these texts that fail to recognize their critique of the industrial transformation of visual culture. In this sense, Jameson not only falsifies literary realism in order to discredit it, but also participates as an agent of the culture industry in realism's recuperation as spectacle. This study reasserts realism's function as meta-spectacle in order to liberate it from such false reception.[12]

Since its inception, realist fiction has functioned as meta-spectacle by tracing the influence of industrialization on visual culture. Balzac's figure of the *flâneur* observing urban life from the margins, George Eliot's portraits of a vanishing rural agrarian society, Charles Dickens' accounts of the material texture of industrializing cities, and Henry James' depiction of American consumers of European culture all participate in a realist consciousness of the emerging social paradigm of spectatorship in the nineteenth century. Each novel I consider in the chapters that follow exemplifies realist fiction's sustained critique of industrial and post-industrial visual culture across the twentieth century. Because I seek in particular to clarify the ethical function of visual detail in realist fiction, my analysis will focus on their portrayal of an industrialized visual culture that has been warped by the intensified production and consumption of images. My selection of texts could well be expanded to other works by these writers and their contemporaries. However, this particular grouping is advantaged in two respects. First, this selection identifies the most poignant examples of realist fiction's engagement with the problem of spectatorship, so as to bring into relief more subtle treatments of spectacle that are nevertheless equally informed by the realist ethos. Second, the diachronic scope of this selection emphasizes the shared realism of novels and authors that are typically treated in isolation within the discrete aesthetic and historical categories of Victorian, modern, postmodern and post-colonial.[13]

Writing across the span of one hundred years, the authors treated here describe their literary perspective in realist terms, and their fiction restates the alienated verbal and visual discourses of industrial and post-industrial culture. Hardy's characters in *Jude the Obscure*, for example, struggle to internalize identities derived from the revival of Gothic and neo-classical art and architecture, and their alienated relationship comes to embody a critical debate between art critics John Ruskin and Walter Pater. Forster's *A Room with a View* reveals a link between the visual consumption of Italy by tourists and their infection with a cosmopolitan detachment that alienates their domestic lives after they return to England. Juxtaposing deliberate and unconscious acts of spectatorship in *Between the Acts*, Woolf connects the popularity of pageants in England at the turn of the century with her characters' feelings of belatedness and historical disinheritance as bystanders at a post-agrarian ritual. In *Midnight's Children*, Rushdie's narrator loses his connection to the real amid the competing iconographies of British colonialism and Indian nationalism that are mediated to him by architecture, urban design, the visual arts, photography, cinema, political symbols and commercial advertising. Epitomizing the spectacle's substitution of images for tactility, the protagonist of Carey's *Observatory Mansions* practices an "art of stillness" in his work as a human dummy in a celebrity wax museum and as a performance artist who impersonates statues in a local park (2000, 14). His sole form of social interaction is to be observed by others, and he internalizes this spectatorial distance by curating a private collection of personal objects that he calls the "Exhibition of Myself." Barnes draws collectively upon the visual discourses of architectural revival, tourism, pageantry, post-colonialism and museum culture in *England, England* to critique both the simulacrum of British culture marketed as a commodity by the heritage industry and the reconstructed folk culture through which some seek to escape from industrial society.

Even these most avant-garde works of art and literature, however, seem destined for respectability and antiquarian devotion as specimens of a period or an author's *oeuvre*, their iconoclasm repackaged as iconicity and, in Benjamin's words, their "cult value" exchanged for "exhibition value" ([1935] 1969, 224–5). How can the realist novel *defamiliarize* the act of perception—the purpose of all art according to the Russian formalist critic Viktor Shklovsky ([1925] 1990)—when the genre itself has become what Shklovsky would call *habitualized*? Faced with the process of literary realism's recuperation within a class-consolidating cultural literacy, one wonders whether realist fiction can effectively critique the dynamics of spectacle, or if perhaps the novel—as a commodity produced by and circulated within industrial and post-industrial culture—is itself an irretrievably alienated medium.[14] Debord provides examples from politics and art in which the critique of industrial capitalism unwittingly conforms to the very logic that it aspires to transcend and ultimately reinforces spectatorial distance and false consciousness instead of overcoming them. He observes that the various socialist and anarchist movements which sought to overthrow the capitalist order evolved into alienated ideologies that became untethered from historical reality and reduced the proletariat to an abstract image within the spectacle. One is reminded, for example, of the corporatization and franchising of the anti-spectatorial "Fight Club" by the conclusion of the eponymous novel and film.

Similarly, Debord explains that the Dada movement asserted a temporary disruption of the established meaning of representational art, but not a new mode of expression or way of seeing. Rejecting but not displacing the structuralist aestheticism at the foundation of the modern culture industry, Dada would eventually be affixed to its spot on the gallery wall in testament to its failed revolution. In this sense, Debord anticipated quite presciently the Dada exhibit at Paris' Centre Pompidou in 2005, in which the "anti-art movement" was itself anthologized for general consumption and circulated as cultural capital to New York's Museum of Modern Art and the National Gallery in Washington. While touting Dada's "raging contempt for existing values" that led its practitioners to engage in a "voracious interrogation of modernity itself," this exhibit sets out to put the "entire Dada period on parade" by tracing chronologically and geographically the work of numerous "icons of modernism." The promotion of this event exemplifies a deep contradiction between the premise of Dada and curatorial practice. It is difficult to imagine what would have been more offensive to Dadaists: being referred to as "icons," having their gestures staged as live performance pieces enacted by art historians during an event called the "Zapping Dada Evening," or seeing their critiques of gallery culture distilled into discrete "works" in an exhibition funded by global retail and e-commerce conglomerates Yves Saint Laurent and PPR ("Dada," n.d.). Such an exhibit not only transforms Dada into a cultural commodity, but inscribes it within the very historical and aesthetic meta-narratives that Dadaists sought to negate.

Like Dada mummified within the museum, realist fiction is vulnerable to similar recuperation when a novel is fetishized as a cultural artifact from which one can derive objective knowledge of an historical moment. Instead of enabling one to experience critically an instance of alienated consciousness in modern industrial society, the novel thus comes to resemble the fragment masquerading as a worldview that is central to Debord's concept of spectacle. The works treated here are not immune to this vulnerability. Hardy received many invitations to adapt his novels as popular stage entertainments, including one from the famed pageant-master, Louis Napoleon Parker, whom Woolf satirizes in *Between the Acts* (Parker 1928, 213). Although Hardy resisted these offers for many years, he relented late in his career and drafted several scripts for productions staged by the Dorchester Players. Perhaps most notable is his adaptation of *The Dynasts*, from which Hardy removed all critical commentary on historical representation and reduced the plot to a pageant of pastoral tableaus that made no demand on the audience other than to be consumed out of nostalgia for the vanishing English countryside (Wilson 1995, 88). Numerous film adaptations of Forster's and Woolf's novels inscribe their critique of spectacle within lavishly produced period pieces of the Merchant-Ivory ilk that curate and market Victorian and Edwardian visual culture for post-imperial consumption. Most recently, a film adaptation of *Midnight's Children* was released in Toronto which reproduces the very spectatorial distance that Rushdie's narrator attempts to overcome in the novel, with one reviewer commenting that "We look at the unfolding spectacle with our eyes wide but our emotions closed—so much to see, so little to feel" ("Toronto" 2012). Rushdie's critique in the novel of the extremes of Bollywood exoticism and the plot-less literality of socialist propaganda films was neither featured nor heeded by the film, which has been described as "an epic, panoramic look at the history of India and Pakistan over a 50-year period" that is "ambitious and often sumptuous to watch but not always dramatically satisfying" ("*Midnight's Children* Telluride" 2012). The soul of the novel—its consciousness of spectacle's effects on the individual—is not reincarnated in the film.

Brecht conceived of his theater for the "scientific age" as a process of training the audience to adopt a sociological mood toward performance ([1929] 1964, 26). Realist fiction similarly demands the reorientation of its audience, and as Macherey has noted, the critical explication of realism plays an important role in framing this process ([1966] 1978, 128). In his preface to *The Picture of Dorian Gray*, Oscar Wilde evokes the Shakespearean figure of Caliban to describe the savagely uncultivated sensibilities of his audience. He writes: "The nineteenth century dislike of Realism is the rage of Caliban seeing his own face in the glass. The nineteenth century dislike of Romanticism is the rage of Caliban not seeing his own face in the glass." Through this seeming contradiction, Wilde locates authentic realism at the intersection of two axes—one bounded by the extremes of naturalism and romanticism, the other bounded by the extremes of materialist externality and stream of consciousness. Fiction that exists on the margins of these quadrants frustrates the reader with various falsifications of the real. Wilde suggests that this audience seeks inarticulately for literature that engages with the problem of modern con-

INTRODUCTION: LITERARY REALISM AS META-SPECTACLE   21

sciousness, but finds no satisfaction in the taxidermic naturalism or escapist antiquarianism presented by the fiction of its age. In *Dorian Gray*, Wilde responds with a novel that stages a violent reassertion of the ethical capacity of art in the form of a portrait that adopts an increasingly monstrous appearance as its subject commits acts of degeneracy. Wilde's novel is a satire of moralistic readings imposed onto works of art, but also a reflection on the outcome of applying the principles of aestheticism to life in society. Noting that "it is the spectator, and not life, that art really mirrors," Wilde regards realism as capable of making the reader's consciousness visible and thus accessible to critique ([1891] 1969, 235–6).

In restating visual discourses, realist fiction reveals the extent to which individuals are often reduced to salvaging identities out of the competing and contradictory representations of life that circulate within the spectacle. At the same time, fiction that employs such mimicry risks literal association with the discourses that it restates. In that case, any critical distance from the spectacle that the novel achieves would collapse and the text would simply reinforce those discourses to the reader. The failure to maintain this distinction between *restatement* and *reproduction* has led to confusion between realist fiction's ethical challenge to the culture of spectatorship and realist-*ic* fiction's aesthetic flattening of lived experience. A critical dialog between the concepts of realism and spectacle, however, enables the literary gesture of restatement to remain visible to the reader, provides a vocabulary and framework for the reader to recognize the alienated industrial visual culture to which the realist novel points, and deters the reader from engaging the novel solely on aesthetic grounds from a spectatorial standpoint. The realist novel brings into relief the visual discourses in which its characters are situated; from which the characters derive, often dysfunctionally, their sense of self; and on which the characters depend, in a manner Debord would consider symptomatic of spectacle, for their sense of reality and presence. I advance the concept of meta-spectacle as a corrective to the trajectory that the theorization of literary realism has taken and will demonstrate the value of this perspective in the readings of key twentieth-century realist texts that follow.

NOTES

1. Beaumont (2007, 3–4), Shaw (1999, 8–30) and Tallis (1988, 14–5) each note this tendency among theorists of postmodernism to define realism negatively against postmodernism itself.

2. See, for example, McGowan (1986, 21–4), Shaw (1999, 8, 20–1, 30), Levine (2008, 189), Schehr (2009, 6) and Smith (1995, 3).
3. Quotations from *Society of the Spectacle* are from Donald Nicholson-Smith's translation. Citations refer to the numbered paragraphs in the original as opposed to the page numbers of the 1995 Zone edition, in order to facilitate comparison across various translations and editions.
4. Sadler (1998) and McDonough (2009) provide useful overviews of the history of the Situationist movement and its critical vocabulary.
5. Debord attributes this association between ideology and schizophrenia to the French Marxist sociologist and philosopher Joseph Gabel, particularly his 1962 work titled *False Consciousness*.
6. Other than Bulson's brief discussion of the Situationist practices of *dérive* and psychogeography to describe how fiction orients and disorients the reader through its production of space (2007, 121–4), I am not aware of explicit applications of Debord's concept of spectacle that comprehend literary realism as a critique of visual culture. Olson's work on the depiction of the ordinary in modernist fiction alludes to Debord and the Situationists, but she maintains that their perspective is not relevant to fiction before the Second World War (2009, 13–4). Dewey uses the term "spectacle realism" to describe a strain of American fiction in the 1980s that re-enchants the reader's experience of the everyday by "co-opting"— but not critiquing—the dynamics of spectatorship (1999, 15, 29). Although they do not establish a particular connection to Debord, Shonkwiler and La Berge advance a framework called "capitalist realism" that, like my concept of "meta-spectacle," considers whether fiction is a suitable medium to "interpret and historicize" our experience "as consumers, producers, as debtors, and as spectators and as casualties" (2014, 7). In addition, Morris' (2013) category of "metonymic realism" to describe fiction that critiques "normative universalism, imposed uniformity and closure of identity" intersects with my claims regarding the realist critique of spectatorship.
7. Kuhns uses the phrase "museum as habitation" to describe the social condition of the contemporary city primarily as place to exhibit and be exhibited (1991, 261).
8. This impulse to identify an ethic of realism that transcends the particulars of aesthetic form is echoed in literary criticism. Tallis identifies a "persistent tendency to confuse the *aims* of realism with certain techniques used to achieve those aims," noting that the narrow understanding of realism as a set of aesthetic conventions incorrectly defines modernist and postmodernist literary experimentation as external to it (1988, 3). Levine identifies a "strong moral impulse" among realists to replace "false representations with authentic ones" that renders the aesthetic practice of realism "ambivalent and often self-contradictory" (2008, 188). He regards realism as ethi-

cally "consistent in its determination to find strategies for describing the world as it was" by performing "close observations of the details of society and the context in which characters move," but aesthetically "inconsistent [...] because every artist's conception of what the world was differed and the world changed from moment to moment, generation to generation" (208). Feldman invokes William James' philosophy of pragmatism to affirm the ethical constancy of realism in light of its aesthetic variability, contending that realism is "not so much a method of finding the truth as an openness to various methods, a reactive tendency; a pluralist and changing set of positions" (2002, 5). This ethical pragmatism among realists is borne out by Arata's study of the extensive critical and public response to realism by the close of the nineteenth century, which, as Arata demonstrates, "tended to move rapidly away from [...] narrative strategies and conventions in order to take up the more general question of literature's role in effecting social change" (2007, 181).

9. Brecht regarded his initial "alienation effects," such as displaying the titles of scenes on stage, as a "primitive attempt at literarizing the theater" ([1931] 1964, 43). Brecht abandoned his theoretical terminology when he sensed that it was distilling into formal aesthetic concepts ([1956] 1964, 276; Willett 1964, 281) and warned those who pursued epic theater that "temporary structures have to be built, but the danger is that they will remain" ([1949] 1964, 215).

10. Olson makes a similar observation that Woolf is "sometimes stylistically less radical than her essays on the modern novel would have us believe," suggesting that Woolf "transforms, but does not reject, the literary realism of the past" and that Woolf's "most successful works render ordinary experience and do depend upon facts and fabric" (2009, 66).

11. Studies of realism are often muddled by an interchangeable use of the terms *realist* and *realistic* and would benefit from a consistent terminological distinction between what one might call "serious," "high" or "literary" real-*ism* and "pulp" or "mass-market" realist-*ic* fiction. Arata points to Oscar Wilde's distinction between works of "imaginative reality" and "unimaginative realism," although Wilde might be gesturing more toward the difference between realism and naturalism as opposed to the difference between literary fiction and derivative commercial fiction (2007, 183). Smith invokes the unsatisfyingly vague phrase "influential realist novels" in reference to literary realism, which fails to account for the fact that non-literary realistic fiction can itself exert a powerfully normalizing influence (1995, 2). Dewey gets closer to the heart of the matter when he describes "realistic" consumer literature that "invoke[s] the trappings of realism" but "deliberately dispense[s] with the unsettling nuances of the immediate," pointing to the example of "disposable realistic narratives brought to our living rooms by cable technologies" (1999, 28). Shonkwiler and La

24   E. BARNABY

Berge develop particularly precise language around this issue, distinguishing between fiction in which "struggles of representation" are "informed by the literary" versus fiction that is "an aesthetic afterthought to a political and economic ideology" and "a localized application, in the literary realm, of the more generalized market-driven 'realism'" (2014, 7).

12. Ermarth's (1983) *Realism and Consensus in the English Novel* and Armstrong's (1999) *Fiction in the Age of Photography* are versions of Jameson's critique of realism as a "containment strategy" that warrant similar scrutiny.

Ermarth transforms the familiar trope of emotional "sympathy" between novelist and reader into one of rational "consensus" that forces the reader into a "middle distance" from the real. This homogenized and flattened sense of time is coordinated by the narrator in the same way that the idealized focal point of a realist painting is coordinated by an "implied spectator" (25, 37–40). This consensus, Ermarth argues, falsifies the real by implying "a unity in human experience which assures us that we all inhabit the same world and that the same meanings are available to everyone [...] however refracted [they] may be by point of view and by circumstance" (65).

Armstrong similarly inverts realism's mimetic relationship to the real, arguing that "visual culture supplied the social classifications that novelists had to confirm, adjust, criticize or update" (3) and that "fiction helped to establish [visual representations] as identical to real things" (3, 5). She faults realist fiction for concealing the reader's spectatorial distance from a "so-called material world" which was constructed "chiefly through transparent images" that reinforced the reader's illusion of "conceptual and even physical control" of the real (4–5). Armstrong contends that "together fiction and photography produced a spatial classification system specific to their mutual moment and class of consumers," with fiction "pointing to certain images as if they were chunks of the world itself" in a self-affirming tautology (28).

This Jamesonian perspective, however, "demotes the powers of the reader," according to Shaw, by reducing the encounter with realist fiction to the "contemplation of the already achieved typicality of figures" instead of "an evolving participation in a set of mental processes that promises to help us grasp the typical determinants of the historical situation" (1999, 19, 35). As Novak has argued, far from colluding with photographs to objectify the world, realist fiction was scrutinized alongside photography by the nineteenth-century reader-viewer as image-texts that exhibited "anonymity, interchangeability, and abstraction" and which relied on "the effacement of particularity" for their claims to reality (2008, 30). Byerly also notes a Victorian-era obsession with preventing the artwork's representation of reality from substituting for the reality of the artifact (1997, 2).

13. A number of critics have disputed the generic separation of realism from modernism and postmodernism. Shaw argues that merely because an ethos

of realism "reached maturity during the nineteenth century in close association with the rise of historicist thinking," one need not adopt the expression of realism in the nineteenth century as a "universal yardstick" by which to measure subsequent fiction as anti-realist (1999, 7). Baker similarly recommends "reading, in relation to realism, texts often seen as the others of realism"—such as "magical-realist or postmodern works"—in order to "recognize the 'mixed conditions' of the realist texts as inclusive of modernist and postmodernist revisions of the form" (2010, x, xi, xii). Rignall traces the figure of the *flâneur* across realist, naturalist and modernist fiction (1992, 6–7), and Olson connects nineteenth-century realism and twentieth-century modernism through their mutual representation of "ordinary experience" and "everydayness" (2009, 17–9). Others blame the false distinction between realism, modernism and postmodernism on a misleading critical travesty of realism that portrays it as the attempt to achieve a total and direct reproduction of reality. Armstrong contends that modernism was "no less dependent on a visual definition of the real than Victorian realism," but merely attempted to "lay claim to [...] greater realism beyond the conventional" by advancing a "caricature" of realism as "a futile attempt at documentary fidelity to the object world" (1999, 11). Commenting on contemporary trends in "experimental realism" and "meta-realism," Julia Breitbach observes that what is now being touted as a "new realist mode" only appears new in relation to the "straw man of nineteenth-century bourgeois representationalism," which prompts the common disclaimer that contemporary realist fiction is not a "regression into a 'naïve' or 'innocent' realism" (2012, 8–9).

14. The issue of realism's recuperation as spectacle is central to the concept of "capitalist realism" advanced by Shonkwiler and La Berge, through which they seek to theorize the "point at which realism simultaneously records and undergoes the economic processes of commodification and financialization" (2014, 16). Recognizing that "'capitalism' as a system cannot exist apart from modes of representation" and that "the realist mode (however else it is defined) is invested in an economically situated conception of history," Shonkwiler and La Berge seek to ensure that literary realism is not afforded a "naïve authority to demystify capitalist processes of accumulation, or to de-reify the real" (17). Rignall points to the figure of the *flâneur*—itself a consumer of visual commodities—as a trope that allows realist fiction to explore "imaginatively and critically this central aspect of contemporary culture in which it is itself so deeply implicated" (1992, 4). Smith's discussion of the "life cycle of the realist paradigm" during which realism variously "occupies both traditionalist and innovational roles" is also useful in parsing "the relation of individual works to a system of literature" and analyzing the novel's status as a commodity vis-à-vis its capacity to "defamiliarize" the culture of commodity (1995, 7–9).

REFERENCES

Arata, Stephen. 2007. Realism. In *The Cambridge Companion to the Fin de Siècle*, ed. Gail Marshall, 169–188. Cambridge: Cambridge University Press.

Armstrong, Nancy. 1999. *Fiction in the Age of Photography: The Legacy of British Realism*. Cambridge: Harvard University Press.

Baker, Geoffrey. 2010. Introduction to *Realism's Others*, ed. Geoffrey Baker and Eva Aldea, ix–xiv. Newcastle upon Tyne: Cambridge Scholars Publishers.

Beaumont, Matthew. 2007. Introduction to *Adventures in Realism*, ed. Matthew Beaumont, 1–12. Oxford: Blackwell.

Benjamin, Walter. (1935) 1969. The Work of Art in the Age of Mechanical Reproduction. In *Illuminations*, trans. Harry Zohn, 217–251. New York: Schocken.

Brecht, Bertolt. (1929) 1964. A Dialogue About Acting. In *Brecht on Theatre: The Development of an Aesthetic*, ed. and trans. John Willett, 26–29. New York: Hill & Wang.

———. (1931) 1964. The Literarization of the Theater. In *Brecht on Theatre: The Development of an Aesthetic*, ed. and trans. John Willett, 43–47. New York: Hill & Wang.

———. (1949) 1964. From the Mother Courage Model. In *Brecht on Theatre: The Development of an Aesthetic*, ed. and trans. John Willett, 215–222. New York: Hill & Wang.

———. (1956) 1964. Appendices to the Short Organum. In *Brecht on Theatre: The Development of an Aesthetic*, ed. and trans. John Willett, 276–281. New York: Hill & Wang.

Breitbach, Julia. 2012. *Analog Fictions for the Digital Age: Literary Realism and Photographic Discourses in Novels After 2000*. Rochester: Camden House.

Brooks, Peter. 2005. *Realist Vision*. New Haven/London: Yale University Press.

Bulson, Eric. 2007. *Novels, Maps, Modernity: The Spatial Imagination, 1850–2000*. New York: Routledge.

Buzard, James. 1993. *The Beaten Track; European Tourism, Literature, and the Ways to Culture, 1800–1918*. Oxford: Oxford University Press.

Byerly, Alison. 1997. *Realism, Representation, and the Arts in Nineteenth-Century Literature*. Cambridge: Cambridge University Press.

———. 2013. *Are We There Yet?: Virtual Travel and Victorian Realism*. Ann Arbor: University of Michigan.

Carey, Edward. 2000. *Observatory Mansions*. New York: Vintage Books.

———. n.d. *Interview with Edward Carey*. Harcourt Books. http://www.harcourtbooks.com/authorinterviews/bookinterview_carey.asp. Accessed 25 Feb 2005.

Crary, Jonathan. 1990. *Techniques of the Observer: On Vision and Modernity in the Nineteenth Century*. Cambridge: MIT Press.

"Dada" Press Release. Centre Pompidou. http://www.centrepompidou.fr/
Pompidou/Communication.nsf/docs/ID36434B2EE77F4DF9C125707C0
0546878/$File/cpdadaanglais.pdf. Accessed 18 Jul 2006.

Debord, Guy. (1967) 1995. *The Society of the Spectacle*. Trans. Donald Nicholson-Smith. New York: Zone Books.

Dewey, Joseph. 1999. *Novels from Reagan's America: A New Realism*. Gainesville: University Press of Florida.

Ermarth, Elizabeth. 1983. *Realism and Consensus in the English Novel*. Princeton: Princeton University Press.

Feldman, Jessica. 2002. *Victorian Modernism: Pragmatism and the Varieties of Aesthetic Experience*. Cambridge: Cambridge University Press.

Forster, E.M. (1908) 1986. *A Room with a View*. New York: Signet.

———. (1927) 1954. *Aspects of the Novel*. New York: Harcourt, Brace & Company.

Furst, Lilian. 1995. *All Is True: The Claims and Strategies of Realist Fiction*. Durham: Duke University Press.

Guppy, Shusha. 2000. Julian Barnes, The Art of Fiction No. 165. *The Paris Review* 157. https://www.theparisreview.org/interviews/562/julian-barnes-the-art-of-fiction-no-165-julian-barnes. Accessed 6 Aug 2017.

Hardy, Thomas. (1895) 1965. *Jude the Obscure*. Riverside edition. Boston: Houghton Mifflin.

Jameson, Fredric. 1981. *The Political Unconscious: Narrative as a Socially Symbolic Act*. Ithaca: Cornell University Press.

———. 2007. A Note on Literary Realism in Conclusion. In *Adventures in Realism*, ed. Matthew Beaumont, 261–271. Oxford: Blackwell.

Jay, Martin. 1993. *Downcast Eyes: The Denigration of Vision in Twentieth-Century French Thought*. Berkeley: University of California Press.

Joyce, James. (1922) 1986. *Ulysses*. Ed. Hans Walter Gabler, Wolfhard Steppe and Claus Melchior. New York: Vintage.

Kuhns, Richard. 1991. The Last Manifesto. In *City Images: Perspectives from Literature, Philosophy and Film*, ed. Mary Ann Caws, 261–269. New York: Gordon and Breach.

Leslie, Esther. 2007. Interrupted Dialogues of Realism and Modernism. In *Adventures in Realism*, ed. Matthew Beaumont, 125–141. Oxford: Blackwell.

Levine, George. 2008. *Realism, Ethics and Secularism: Essays on Victorian Literature and Science*. Cambridge: Cambridge University Press.

Lukàcs, Georg. (1937) 1983. *The Historical Novel*. Trans. Hannah and Stanley Mitchell. Lincoln: University of Nebraska Press.

Macherey, Pierre. (1966) 1978. *A Theory of Literary Production*. Trans. Geoffrey Wall. London: Routledge.

McDonough, Tom, ed. 2009. *The Situationists and the City: A Reader*. New York: Verso.

McGowan, John. 1986. *Representation and Revelation: Victorian Realism from Carlyle to Yeats.* Columbia: University of Missouri Press.

Midnight's Children: Telluride Review. 2012. *The Hollywood Reporter*, September 2. http://www.hollywoodreporter.com/review/midnights-children-telluride-review-deepa-mehta-salman-rushdie-367491. Accessed 10 Feb 2013.

Mitchell, W.J.T. 1986. *Iconology: Image, Text, Ideology.* Chicago: University of Chicago Press.

Morris, Pam. 2013. Making the Case for Metonymic Realism. In *Realisms in Contemporary Culture: Theories, Politics, and Medial Configurations*, ed. Dorothee Birke and Stella Butter, 13–32. Berlin/Boston: De Gruyter.

Novak, Daniel. 2008. *Realism, Photography and Nineteenth-Century Fiction.* Cambridge: Cambridge University Press.

Olson, Liesl. 2009. *Modernism and the Ordinary.* Oxford: Oxford University Press.

Orwell, George. (1944) 1981. Raffles and Mrs. Blandish. In *A Collection of Essays*, 132–147. San Diego: Harcourt, Brace & Company.

Parker, Louis Napoleon. 1928. *Several of My Lives.* London: Chapman and Hall.

Rahv, Philip. (1939) 1978. Proletarian Literature: A Critical Autopsy. In *Essays on Literature and Politics, 1932–1972*, ed. Arabel J. Porter and Andrew J. Dvosin, 293–304. Boston: Houghton Mifflin.

Rignall, John. 1992. *Realist Fiction and the Strolling Spectator.* London/New York: Routledge.

Rushdie, Salman. (1981) 2006. *Midnight's Children.* New York: Random House.

———. 1991. *Imaginary Homelands: Essays and Criticism, 1981–1991.* London: Granta.

———. 2002. *Step Across This Line: Collected Nonfiction 1992–2002.* New York: Random House.

Sadler, Simon. 1998. *The Situationist City.* Cambridge: MIT Press.

Schehr, Lawrence. 2009. *Subversions of Verisimilitude: Reading Narrative from Balzac to Sartre.* New York: Fordham University Press.

Shaw, Harry. 1999. *Narrating Reality: Austen, Scott, Eliot.* Ithaca: Cornell University Press.

Shklovsky, Viktor. (1925) 1990. *Theory of Prose.* Trans. Benjamin Sher. Elmwood Park: Dalkey Archive Press.

Shonkwiler, Leah, and Clare La Berge. 2014. Introduction: A Theory of Capitalist Realism. In *Reading Capitalist Realism*, ed. Leah Shonkwiler and Clare La Berge, 1–25. Iowa City: University of Iowa Press.

Smith, Mark. 1995. *Literary Realism and the Ekphrastic Tradition.* University Park: Pennsylvania State University Press.

Stowe, William. 1983. *Balzac, James and the Realistic Novel.* Princeton: Princeton University Press.

Tallis, Raymond. 1988. *In Defence of Realism.* London: Edward Arnold.

Toronto International Film Festival Movie Review: *Midnight's Children*. 2012. *The Globe and Mail*, September 9. http://www.theglobeandmail.com/arts/awards-and-festivals/tiff/tiff-reviews/tiff-movie-review-midnights-children/article4530111/. Accessed 10 Feb 2013.

White, Hayden. 1975. *Metahistory: The Historical Imagination in Nineteenth-Century Europe*. Baltimore: The Johns Hopkins University Press.

Wilde, Oscar. (1891) 1969. Preface to *The Picture of Dorian Gray*. In *The Artist as Critic*, ed. Richard Ellman, 235–236. Chicago: University of Chicago Press.

Willett, John. 1964. 'Dialectics in the Theatre': An Editorial Note. In *Brecht on Theatre: The Development of an Aesthetic*, ed. and trans. John Willett, 281–282. New York: Hill & Wang.

Wilson, Keith. 1995. *Thomas Hardy on Stage*. New York: St. Martin's.

Woolf, Virginia. (1925) 1984. Modern Fiction. In *The Common Reader*, ed. Andrew McNeillie, 146–154. San Diego: Harcourt Brace & Company.

———. (1941) 1970. *Between the Acts*. San Diego: Harcourt Brace & Company.

CHAPTER 2

"Pugin was wrong, and Wren was right"— Architectural Revival as Spectacle in Thomas Hardy's *Jude the Obscure*

Thomas Hardy recognized the link between industrialization and an emerging spectatorial separation from the real in modern society, and he employed literary realism to make this transformation visible to his readers. Hardy was uninterested in performing technical feats of naturalism that reproduced the material texture of reality in still-life. Instead, his fiction restates the experience of alienated consciousness in a manner that demands an ethical response from the reader and confounds a purely aesthetic appraisal of his style. Hardy's characters routinely suffer the displacement of their vestigial feudal perspective within an industrial environment characterized by destabilizing geographic and class mobility, dehumanized labor, nostalgic distance from folk traditions, and a sense of isolation within mass culture. Of all his so-called "Wessex novels," Hardy's final work, *Jude the Obscure*, takes a particularly visual turn that anticipates Debord's concept of spectacle. The characters in *Jude the Obscure* struggle to inhabit a world that is mediated to them by layers of falsely captioned images, including the aesthetic transformation of their built environment by Gothic and classical revival, the theorization of the revival movement by cultural critics such as John Ruskin and Walter Pater, and the advent of photographic literality as a surrogate for the real.

Just as Brecht sought to rehabilitate the nineteenth-century theatergoer from catharsis junkie to social critic through his theater for the "scientific age" ([1929] 1964, 26), Hardy believed that nineteenth-century fiction had not yet achieved maturity "in its artistic aspect, nor in its ethical

© The Author(s) 2018
E. Barnaby, *Realist Critiques of Visual Culture*,
https://doi.org/10.1007/978-3-319-77323-0_2

31

or philosophical aspect; neither in form nor in substance" ([1888] 1997, 246). He acknowledges literary naturalism as an impulse on the part of certain "intellectual adventurers" to advance the novel's critical engagement with modern life. Nevertheless, he regards this impulse as yielding only "crude results" ([1890] 1997, 256). Hardy's primary challenge in reorienting the novel as a venue for depicting the industrial transformation of consciousness was to distance his practice of literary realism from any association with naturalism. This required that he re-legitimize the term *realism* itself, which Hardy describes as "an unfortunate, ambiguous word" that had been "taken up by society" as connoting either artless "copyism" or sensualist "prurience" ([1891] 1997, 262). He contends that the naturalists had, in their reaction against romantic idealism, "overleapt" a truthful depiction of lived experience and arrived instead at the opposite extreme: an "artificiality distilled from the fruits of closest observation" (263). He denigrates the naturalistic writer as a mere collector of the "scientific data" of fiction whose "powers in photography" conjure a merely realistic effect—not an artist but a *technicist* and "automatic reproducer of all impressions" (261). Hardy's pejorative association of naturalistic fiction with photography features in another of his essays, in which he derides naturalism as a form of "photographic curiousness" in life's "garniture" as opposed to the "true exhibition of man" in fiction that penetrates "further into life" ([1888] 1997, 245).[1] By establishing this dichotomy between photographic naturalism on the one hand and the "mental tactility" and "sympathetic appreciativeness of life" that characterize his own practice of realism on the other, Hardy casts naturalistic fiction as a visually dominated abstraction that contributes to the reader's spectatorial distance from reality ([1891] 1997, 263)—the very condition that Debord would later describe as spectacle.

Hardy must do more than discredit naturalism, however, if he seeks to address the modern condition of spectacle in his fiction and not merely reinforce it. Recall for a moment Debord's analysis of the cycle of iconoclastic critiques enacted by avant-garde movements such as Dada and Surrealism. Debord argues that these gestures of "negation" momentarily disrupt the culture industry, but ultimately take on their own iconicity and exhibition value within the spectacle. Hardy identifies naturalism as an iconoclastic negation of romanticism that exchanges one distortion of the real for another (the vacillating "rage of Caliban" in Wilde's formulation). He positions his own practice of realism as a "third something" which breaks this dialectical cycle of negation by pursuing a new relationship between fiction and reality ([1891] 1997, 263). In *Jude the Obscure*, Hardy does not merely reproduce the material trappings of late-nineteenth-century Oxbridge, but portrays the struggle of two individuals to discern the real amid the proliferation of images and discourse about images in which they are immersed. As such, visual description in this novel routinely transcends the passive function of a naturalistic backdrop to exhibit the dysfunction of industrialized visual culture to Hardy's readers.

Hardy unwittingly muddled the initial reception of *Jude the Obscure* by invoking classical aesthetic categories to describe his motivations as a realist. He looks to Greek drama and satire as genres that "reflected life, revealed life, criticized life" by elaborating the "collision between the individual and the general" ([1890] 1997, 256). However, the characters in *Jude the Obscure* do not bring about their tragic fate through *hubris* and *hamartia*, but are confronted instead with their lack of agency as marginalized spectators of industrial transformation. Jude complains at various moments in the novel that he feels satirized, but Hardy replaces the ethical function of classical satire to effect moral improvement with Jude's existential resignation in the face of mass culture. The tragic hero actively, yet blindly, arranges the circumstances that shape his demise, whereas the realist hero, like Jude, is a passive "neutral ground," in Lukàcs' words, onto which colliding social forces "can be brought into a human relationship with one another" ([1937] 1983, 36). Indeed, Jude more closely resembles the "thinker" or "wise man" that Benjamin describes as the modern theater's decisively "untragic hero" who is "nothing but an exhibit of the contradictions which make up our society" ([1939] 1969, 149). The realist hero is acted upon and paralyzed by external and impersonal forces that allow the past and the future to be, as Jameson has argued, "grasped as hostile but somehow unrelated worlds" (1975, 158). Under these conditions, recovering historical difference becomes the realist hero's dilemma, as opposed to the recognition of a universal tragic fate. Consequently, the immediate popular response (and even much of the early critical response) to *Jude the Obscure* rejected it as philosophically inconsistent and aesthetically immature. Those seeking tragic insight from this novel find no catharsis; others seeking satirical insight find only caricature; and those seeking a naturalistic slice of life find cumbersome intrusions of allegory and symbolism, speculative narration and pedantic diction.

Recent criticism, on the other hand, has reinterpreted this lack of aesthetic unity in *Jude the Obscure* as evidence of Hardy's avant-garde insights about the capabilities of realist fiction. One school regards *Jude* as a form of total satire that turns inward against the very claims of literature to represent the real, after which Hardy leaps from the burning platform that remains of the genre and returns to poetry (Widdowson 2004; Matz 2006). Other critics focus on structural disruptions within the text, contending that Hardy introduces them deliberately to underscore the narrator's struggle to assemble the characters' disparate perceptions into an objective point of consciousness (Sumner 1995; Rogers 1999; Pyle 1995). A third category of critics suggests that the awkward, hyper-intellectualized exchanges between Jude Fawley and Sue Bridehead are not bad writing, but moments of mimicry through which Hardy foregrounds the inadequacy of cultural literacy as an alienated language (Musselwhite 2003; Mallett 1995; Garson 2000; Timko 1991). Finally, a fourth strain of criticism analyzes Hardy's characters in relationship to iconography. Drawing upon W.J.T. Mitchell's concept of the *imagetext*, Alison Katz (2006) describes Jude and Sue as embodiments of Hebraism and Hellenism that Hardy assembles out of various statements and visibilities from those traditions. Sheila Berger observes "tensions between external matter and subjective perception" in Hardy's novels that derive from "collisions of images within metaphoric constructions" (1990, 15). Like Katz, Berger regards Jude and Sue as typical of Hardy's characters in that they "create icons as expressions of themselves and engage in idolatry" (144).

These critical assessments lack a coherent sense of the underlying motivations of Hardy's realism, and as a result the individual findings of these critics are not without their inconsistencies. Matz, for example, disregards the context of industrialization when he associates *Jude the Obscure* with a vague hyper-satirical pessimism also found in Hardy's poems[2]; Garson's gendered reading suggests that only Sue, as a woman, is subject to the dynamics of spectacle, as if Jude's medievalism is entirely authentic[3]; and Katz reduces Hardy's characters to icons and symbols, instead of individuals struggling to inhabit real-world conditions. Regarded cumulatively, however, recent criticism of *Jude the Obscure* gestures toward Hardy's critique of the extent to which the production and consumption of images and discourse about images in modern society had come to establish an alienated, surrogate reality. He makes visible to his readers the process through which ideology achieves material form and warps individual consciousness of the real. Hardy's depiction of this process closely anticipates Debord's description of the spectacle as "a social relationship between people that is mediated by images" and a "world view transformed into an objective force" ([1967] 1995, 4–5). Understanding Hardy's realism as a form of meta-spectacle reveals insights that Hardy himself was unable to articulate critically, but which he discerned intuitively and strained literary convention in the attempt to convey.

The novel traces the life of the eponymous Jude Fawley from his lonely childhood in an agrarian village to his alienated adulthood as a self-educated classicist struggling to succeed in the university town of Christminster. As a young boy Jude develops a fixation on the distant Gothic spires of Christminster, from which he derives the false conception that the city and its scholarly community are a bastion of feudal ideals that persists into industrial-era England. Misunderstood by pragmatic village folk, entrapped into marriage by a conniving country girl, slowed in his studies by his day-job as a stonemason, advised by university deans to keep to his own class, disillusioned by his intellectual role model, and thwarted by the vacillating affections of his progressive cousin, Jude shuttles endlessly between town and country in search of work and companionship. When he finally manages to secure a relationship with Sue and a job in Christminster restoring its crumbling architectural facades, a combination of economic pressures and social marginalization lead their prematurely cynical eldest child to hang himself and his two siblings in a grotesque Malthusian gesture. Sue abandons Jude, his first wife returns from Australia to manipulate him into remarrying, and he dies from consumption listening to the sounds of the university's graduation festivities outside his window.

One encounters a variety of Debordian themes in *Jude the Obscure*. Jude is nostalgic for the cyclical rhythms of agrarian community, which have been disrupted by the mobility that accompanies industrialization. He grows disillusioned with the mechanical production of knowledge at universities and his inability to overcome class boundaries that are reinforced by cultural literacy. Jude's constant geographical displacements transform him into a commodity that circulates within the engineered uniformity of industrialized space. Jude is regarded by the villagers as a "returned purchase" when his urbane intellectual venture fails and he is forced to roam the countryside seeking work as a stonemason (Hardy [1895] 1965, 103). He is ultimately reduced to exploiting the public taste for Gothic kitsch by selling "Christminster cakes" modeled after the city's architecture.

Particularly relevant to understanding Hardy's realism as a form of meta-spectacle is the section of *Society of the Spectacle* titled "Negation and Consumption in the Cultural Sphere." Here Debord describes culture as "representations of lived experience" that have become detached from their historical context through an "intellectual division of labor" and an "intellectual labor of division" ([1967] 1995, 180). As separate scholarly disciplines elevate their partial vantage points to assert a positive knowledge of the world, discourse about culture—"a dead thing to be contemplated"—comes to replace lived experience, and language itself comes to serve as the "illusory representation of non-life" (184, 185). The result is a falsely objective sense of historical reality that is mediated by cultural authorities who peddle "unilaterally arrived-at conclusions" about "what had been experienced" (187). The living sense of possibility at stake in the original cultural moment is supplanted by what Debord calls an "immobilized spectacle of non history" (214). The Situationists sought to reverse this process through the practice of *détournement*, an exercise in which "a fragment torn away from its context, from its own movement, and ultimately from the overall frame of reference of its period and from the precise option that it constituted within that framework" is restated within a "fluid language" that relocates interpretative power from cultural authorities to individuals (208).

Hardy performs *détournements* on two competing cultural histories in circulation in the late nineteenth century: John Ruskin's *Stones of Venice* and Walter Pater's *The Renaissance*. In *Stones of Venice*, Ruskin calls for a revival of the Gothic form of architecture as a means to counteract the dehumanizing effects of industrialization in modern-day England, which Ruskin traces to the neo-classical rationalism of the Renaissance. In contrast, Pater points to the Renaissance itself as a revival of humanism that had been suppressed during the Middle Ages, touting the return of a Hellenic appreciation for the continuum of physical and intellectual beauty. Hardy's characters attempt to internalize the symbolic value of their visual culture as theorized respectively by Ruskin and Pater. The competing visual and discursive elements of Gothic and classical revival do not function as a naturalistic backdrop that situates Hardy's characters in a given time and place. Instead, the Gothic revival deludes Jude into believing that retreating to the medieval city of Christminster will enable him to escape the transformations wrought elsewhere by industrial culture, and the classical revival inspires Sue with a false sense of liberation from feudal piety and chauvinism. Jude and Sue struggle to comprehend their own desires and achieve an authentic relationship in an environment that is saturated with images and mediated by conflicting ethical readings of those images. Hardy astutely identifies this dysfunctional social dynamic that Debord would later diagnose as spectacle.

The courtship of Jude and Sue occurs almost exclusively in the context of producing and consuming images. Their private spaces and public encounters are dominated by photographs and religious iconography with a density that substitutes spectatorial distance for tactile experience and emotional encounter. Jude first encounters Sue in a photograph, and later in the novel, Sue's estranged husband, Mr. Phillotson, "kisses the dead pasteboard" of her photograph in a moment of alienated affection (Hardy [1895] 1965, 128).[4] Jude's room at Melchester has been decorated by his landlord with architectural photographs of rectories and deaneries, and Jude attempts to personalize this space by adding his own photographs of ecclesiastical stonework that he has carved. Sue lives and works in a shop dedicated to selling devotional images and icons, and her room, too, is furnished by her landlady with "Gothic-framed prints of saints, the Church-text scrolls, and other articles" that had become "too stale to sell" (77). Jude follows Sue into an educational exhibit featuring a scale model of Jerusalem and later proposes dates at a cathedral, a ruined castle and a gallery. Even their domestic squabbles manifest as iconoclastic debates. They argue over whether "Pugin was wrong, and Wren was right" (242), whether the classical empires are more relevant to modern education than Judaism, whether the fact that Sue prefers the railway station to the cathedral makes her "modern" or "more ancient than medievalism," and whether to visit Corinthian or Gothic ruins. On the occasion of their visit to the galleries at Fonthill, Jude lingers among "the Virgins, Holy Families and Saints," his aspect growing "reverent and abstracted." Sue waits for him at a distance by "a Lely or Reynolds," a detail through which Hardy reinforces her association with a secular classical perspective. She watches Jude look at the paintings, stealing "critical looks into his face [...] as one might be interested in a man puzzling out his way along a labyrinth from which one had one's self escaped" (109).

This juxtaposition of Jude's solitary communion with medieval devotional paintings and Sue's observation of him from the modern wing of the gallery captures the visual culture of industrial society in all of its complexity. Hagiography stands alongside secular portraiture, cult worship has been transferred from the temple to the museum, and a condescending modern iconoclasm that is blind to its own fetishes perpetuates an endless cycle of avant-garde negations. Jude may be trapped in a labyrinth of false medievalism, but one must question whether Sue's self-proclaimed Hellenism is any more authentic. Were Hardy actually to suggest in this scene that Sue had escaped the spectacle to which Jude is subject, he would fall prey to Jameson's critique of realism as demystifying one ideology only to replace it with an equally false objectification of the real. Hardy, however, does not privilege Sue's neo-classicism, which manifests the same voyeuristic and spectatorial stance as Jude's medievalism.[5] Jude and Sue interact primarily through their consumption of images and derive a false sense of encounter and agency from the cultural discourses that mediate those images. Their dysfunction exemplifies Debord's disparagement of the culture industry in which "the language of real communication has been lost" and "a new common language has yet to be found" ([1967] 1995, 187). Mere references to Ruskin and Pater are not what makes Hardy's fiction realist. His realism lies in the depiction of both Jude's and Sue's failed attempts to internalize prescribed meanings of medieval and classical culture. Hardy does not set out to replicate a naturalistic slice of life that features art historical debates of the day. Instead, he dramatizes a society in which individuals are consigned to live, as it were, in revival.

Architectural revival and restoration contribute to the experience of spectacle by severing the historical connection between the built environment and lived experience. Victor Hugo's meditation in *Notre Dame de Paris* on the historical character of architecture warrants a moment's diversion, insofar as it anticipates much of Ruskin's thought on the Gothic and is itself an early instance of meta-spectacle in the novel. Hugo describes architecture as the "deposit left behind by a nation; the accumulation of the centuries; the residue from the successive evaporations of human society" ([1831] 1978, 129). This layering of cultural deposits provides a visual legibility to history, such that Hugo's narrator can observe the "Romanesque stratum" underlying and mingling with the "Gothic stratum," a Roman stratum that occasionally "still showed through the thick crust of the Middle Ages," and a Celtic stratum "that no longer turned up even when wells were being dug" (148). The process of social transformation is visually present, Hugo argues, in hybrid constructions such as Notre Dame that were completed across two architectural periods, as well as in the scars on a building left by political revolution and the passage of time (128, 126).

With the advent of architectural revival in the nineteenth century, Hugo contends, an historically illegible eclecticism emerges in the modern cityscape that alienates the city's inhabitants. The "ever more foolish and grotesque fashions" visited upon architecture by the academies have, according to Hugo, "killed the building, in its form as well as its symbolism, its logic as well as its beauty" ([1831] 1978, 126). The once visible parallel between social and architectural transformation gives way to an aestheticized city *qua* gallery that one experiences as a "collection of specimens from several centuries" and which flattens architecture's participation in the historical process (150). Hugo observes that the societal values embodied in architecture are re-captioned within industrial society so that, for example, the solemnity of the Greek temple is applied to the stock exchange (151). The abandonment of stone in favor of plaster introduces the concept of planned obsolescence to the cityscape, rendering it cheaper to fabricate and easier to demolish—with similar implications for collective memory itself. Architecture in revival has exchanged its "cult value" for "exhibition value," to use Benjamin's terminology, inserting an alienating and disorienting spectatorial distance between urban space and its inhabitants.

This dislocation of historical consciousness by the anachronistic redeployment of architectural form reinforces the experience of "pseudo-cyclical" time that Debord associates with the spectacle. Hardy portrays this aspect of the spectacle at work in the Wessex countryside through the dismantling of country churches and their replacement with neo-Gothic structures that were "unfamiliar to English eyes." Similarly to Hugo, Hardy vilifies the architect responsible for this travesty as an "obliterator of historical record" who is dispatched from London to impose the latest urbane fashion onto rural England ([1895] 1965, 12). It is in the context of this visual dispossession that Jude first lays eyes on the Gothic skyline of Christminster, its gleaming towers emerging dramatically before him one afternoon from behind an overcast sky in a moment of apocalyptic transfiguration. Adrift within an emerging industrial culture, Jude fetishizes the spires of Christminster as a "new Jerusalem" in which a venerable medievalism has been preserved from historical change. Visible traces of industrialization are reassigned sacred functions by Jude's "painter's imagination," such as the smoke from burning coal to which Jude ascribes the "mysticism of incense." He returns ritualistically to the spot of his first glimpse of Christminster, maintaining a voyeuristic vigil with the hope of occasionally being "rewarded by the sight of a dome or spire" revealed in strip-tease through the parting clouds. We are told that this view of the skyline "acquired a tangibility, a permanence, a hold on his life" (20). Jude's obsession with Christminster is a literalization of Ruskin's fantasy that through a revival of Gothic architecture, "the London of the nineteenth century may yet become as Venice without her despotism, and as Florence without her dispeace" (1851, vol. 3, 197).

While one might excuse Jude's idealization of Christminster when practiced from a distance, his spectatorial relationship to the city persists well after his arrival there. Jude exhibits the "trancelike behavior" that Debord attributes to inhabitants of the society of the spectacle, for whom "the real world becomes real images" and "mere images are transformed into real beings" (Debord [1967] 1995, 18). Jude prefers the company of "the saints and prophets in the window-tracery, the paintings in the galleries, the statues, the busts, the gargoyles," and even "the corbel-heads" to interacting with the city's inhabitants (Hardy [1895] 1965, 69). The narrator notes that the dilapidated structures "moved him as he would have been moved by maimed sentient beings" (68). As he walks the streets of Christminster during his first night in the city, Jude imagines a spectral pageant moving through the deserted campus populated with phantasms of renowned scholars with whom he attempts to converse. Although Jude eventually recognizes that the "town life was a book of humanity infinitely more palpitating, varied, and compendious than the gown life," and that the "reality of Christminster" was constituted by the "struggling men and women before him" among the city's working class, he comes no closer to engaging with them than "gazing abstractedly at [...] groups of people like one in a trance" (95). Indeed, we are told that the "active life of the place [...] was largely non-existent to him" and that "the one thing uniting him to the emotions of the living city" turns out to be a photograph of his cousin Sue, not even Sue herself (69).

Jude's true homelessness within the spectacle is apparent from his very first day in Christminster when he sets out to "read" the buildings around him as "architectural pages" and "historical documents" (Hardy [1895] 1965, 67, 68). In this passage, Hardy mimics Ruskin's directive in "Nature of the Gothic" that "the criticism of the building is to be conducted precisely on the same principles as that of a book" by any "reader" who has expended the "industry and perseverance" to educate himself (1851, vol. 2, 230). The narrator notes, however, that Jude approached architectural structures "less as an artist-critic of their forms than as an artisan and comrade of the dead handicraftsmen whose muscle had actually executed those forms" (Hardy [1895] 1965, 67-8). Having sought out virtual community the night before among specters of scholars whom he knows only through their books, Jude now asserts a vicarious solidarity with medieval guildsmen that is mediated by the material traces of their labor. Thus engaged in a marvelously ironic instance of the "pathetic fallacy" that Ruskin denounces elsewhere in his writings, Jude personifies objects in an

ARCHITECTURAL REVIVAL AS SPECTACLE   41

attempt to populate his lonely world, but merely reinforces the profound separation that Debord identifies as the fundamental experience of spectacle. An abstracted "common mental life" that Jude presumes to share with the students at the university does not grant him access to its Gothic facades (69). Jude's presence in the city is not one of an inhabitant living among people, but a cultural tourist encountering a collection of images and objects. Indeed, Jude envisions his aspirations in spectatorial terms as the possession of a privileged view, hoping for the day that he can inhabit the Gothic buildings as a member of the university and "look down on the world through their panes" (70). Just a short time later, however, recognizing the futility of his plans, Jude mounts to a glass chamber atop a theater and surveys the panorama of university buildings—the skyline view typically sought out by the tourist and not an inhabitant. He describes the sheer invisibility of his own quadrant of Christminster, the "shabby purlieu" of the laborers, which possessed no value within the cultural economy and thus went "unrecognized as part of the city at all by its visitors and panegyrists" (94).

Whatever his capabilities as a reader of architecture, Jude is unable (or perhaps unwilling) to recognize the extent to which the act of restoration is at odds with Ruskin's principles of "Gothicness." Stopping at the Christminster stone yard in search of employment, Jude is confronted with the visual disparity between the "keen edges and smooth curves" of the restored pieces of Gothic ornament and the "broken line" of the original specimens that still hung "abraded and time-eaten on the walls" (Hardy [1895] 1965, 69). Ruskin argues that the "mental tendencies of the builders" are "legibly expressed" in the "material form" of the Gothic (1851, vol. 2, 154). How, then, does Jude reconcile the respective "precision, mathematical straightness, smoothness, exactitude" of the restored pieces with the "jagged curves, disdain of precision, irregularity, disarray" exhibited by the "broken lines of the original idea" (Hardy [1895] 1965, 69)? At this moment in the text, Jude's intellectual justification for his need to perform manual labor, namely, that he is participating in a venerable tradition of medieval artisanship, comes under great strain.

First, Jude obscures the ontological difference between original and copy within a universalizing romanticism, suggesting that the machine-like processing of the restored piece expresses in "modern prose" the same timeless Gothic ideal that the hand-hewn original presents in "old poetry." Musing that "some of those antiques might have been called prose when they were new" and "had done nothing but wait, and had become poetical" (Hardy

[1895] 1965, 68), Jude confuses the historically legible effect of time on architecture with the effects of fashion and the culture industry that produce an inauthentic replica. Collapsing Ruskin's metaphor of reading architecture as a text, Jude performs an ahistorical structuralist reading of both architectural forms and literary genres that fails to recognize change in the conditions of production between the feudal and industrial eras. Jude's unwitting association of machined restoration with "modern prose" is a not-so-subtle swipe on Hardy's part at the literary naturalists' excessive materialism. In describing the Gothic principle of "naturalism," Ruskin similarly criticizes the "men of facts" who seek only to imitate and replicate material details in their art with no sense of arrangement, composition or design (1851, vol. 2, 185). Ruskin would argue that the respective visual characteristics of the original and restored specimens of stonework indicate a shift in emphasis from medieval humanism to neo-classical rationalism and participates in two fundamentally opposed relationships between the laborer and his product.

The second false conclusion at which Jude arrives is that restoration and academic scholarship are both noble intellectual pursuits. The manner in which his insight is narrated—"here in the stone yard was a centre of effort as worthy as that dignified by the name of scholarly study within the noblest of colleges"—allows for an ironic literal reading in which both are regarded as equally worthless (Hardy [1895] 1965, 68). Jude is not, as the narrator tells us, an "artist-critic" like Ruskin, but a simulacrum that one might call a "sophist-copyist." He is a pseudo-intellectual trafficking in the ideas of others and a pseudo-artisan trafficking in the craftsmanship of others. Jude finds himself torn between two divided and alienated forms of labor—stone cutting and scholarship—both of which, Hardy implies, had taken on the aspect of factory work.

Anticipating Debord's motif of "separation" to describe alienated labor within the spectacle, Ruskin argues that the division of labor in industrial culture results in the political and psychological division of men and leads to a society in which manual labor is denigrated because it has become separated entirely from intellect (1851, vol. 2, 165–6). Ruskin recognizes the extent to which divided labor produces the generalized abstraction and dehumanized exchangeability to which the society of spectacle is prone, noting that only when "mathematically defined" can "one man's thoughts [...] be expressed by another" and warning that the "spirit of touch" is not translated from one man's idea to another's execution of that idea (169). Jude travesties this "spirit of touch" in the false solidarity with the feudal laborer that he asserts when running his fingers along the transoms, stroking them "as one who knew their beginning" (Hardy [1895] 1965, 68). This same degradation of tactility in industrial culture through the production and consumption of images is what leads Debord to characterize modern culture as a society of spectacle.

Ruskin further analyzes the phenomenon of alienated labor in his discussion of Gothic "savageness," where he distinguishes between the "servile" character of classical ornament and the "constitutional" character of medieval ornament. He argues that Greek, Assyrian and Egyptian architects developed geometrical designs so that lesser trained slaves could execute them repeatedly with precision, whereas the medieval Gothic form, motivated by a Christian sense of humility and human imperfection, permitted the worker greater artistic liberty and a unique role in executing design. Ruskin compares the ethos of manufacturing in modern England to the classical servile mentality due to its mania for precision that reduces men to machines which carry out repeatable and specialized tasks (1851, vol. 2, 160–1, 171–2). Several times Hardy's narrator alludes to Jude's insulation from this aspect of industrial culture, describing Jude as an "all-around" type and noting that in London, by contrast, "the man who carves the boss or knob of leafage declines to cut the fragment of moulding which merges in that leafage, as if it were a degradation to do the second half of one whole" ([1895] 1965, 62, 78). Raised in rural Wessex, Jude has no prior experience with the hyper-specialized industrial labor that Ruskin describes and is thus unable to recognize that the modern-day stone worker who has been consigned to recreating Gothic ornament with geometrical precision is not an artisan, but a slave. Nevertheless, Jude still hopes that his work as a stonemason is a temporary diversion from his goal of becoming a professional thinker—enacting the very separation of idea from execution that Ruskin and Debord both regard as alienated labor within the spectacle.

By the end of the scene in the stone yard, Jude arrives at the vague suspicion that "at best only copying, patching and imitating went on" there. However, he fails to apply this insight to the practice of revival and restoration in general, nor does he recognize that the same dynamics inform the work of the university. The extent to which the academy, like the stone yard, had taken on the aspect of a factory is concealed from Jude by its Gothic facades. Adopting Ruskin's belief that the moral code of the preindustrial age could be shored up with flying buttresses and ribbed vaults against the evolving ethics of consumer culture, Jude's faith in the continued relevance of medieval visual discourse remains unshaken. Hardy leaves the only clear articulation of historical consciousness to the narrator. It is the narrator, not Jude, who recognizes that "medievalism was as dead as a fern-leaf in a lump of coal" (an allusion to Ruskin's analysis of sculptured leaves in Gothic and Renaissance ornament),[6] and who is attuned to the reality that "other developments were shaping the world around him." The narrator points to a new social order "in which Gothic architecture and its associations had no place" and where there was, instead, a "deadly animosity of contemporary logic and vision towards so much of what [Jude] held in reverence" (Hardy [1895] 1965, 69). This passage is among the most poignant examples in the novel of Hardy's attempt to make the industrial transformation of visual culture apparent to his readers.

The density of allusions to Ruskin's writings on the Gothic and Jude's consistent misapplication of them positions Hardy's readers to observe the circulation of discourses about visual culture and their distorting effect on individual consciousness. Hardy contends that realism is "not a tract in disguise" and that an author such as himself might voice through his characters a philosophy "as full of holes as a sieve" in order that he more accurately portray the "reality of humanity" ([1888] 1997, 246). Ruskin's interpretation of Gothic art and his nationalistic pride in the feudal values embodied therein inspires Jude's irrational faith in Christminster and fails to prepare Jude for the reality of the rigid class hierarchy that lingers intact behind the university's Gothic walls. Further, the persistence of medieval form blinds Jude to the extent to which those same Gothic walls had allowed the logic of the industrial economy to permeate the profession housed within. Architectural historian and theorist Catherine Ingraham has observed that "architecture cannot in any direct sense embody any of the things that we have traditionally thought it could embody, such as nobility, the spirit of the age, social well-being, grandeur, harmony, the grotesque, or fascism." Ingraham finds it telling that this myth of embodiment is only ever visible in its dysfunction, namely "when the embodying act fails in some way" (1998, 137). Ruskin's reification of medieval labor in *Stones of Venice* is a mirage that Jude believes he can inhabit vicariously through his own work with the stones of Christminster. However, Ruskin's neo-feudalism is an uninhabitable image, similar to numerous other failed attempts to extricate labor from the logic of capitalism that Debord describes in a section of *Society of the Spectacle* titled "The Proletariat as Subject and Representation." Not until the end of the novel does Jude come to the realization that "one can work, and despise what one does"

(Hardy [1895] 1965, 242). Jude's acceptance of the alienated condition of labor signals his failure to translate Ruskin's idealization of the Gothic form into lived experience.

Sue's self-proclaimed Hellenism bears the similar stamp of a failed attempt to inhabit an ideology. Compared with the modern humanists whom Pater profiles in *The Renaissance*, Sue's Hellenism is more of an iconoclastic reaction against medieval chivalry that she expresses almost entirely through her preference for one set of icons over another. While Sue believes that she has opted out of the Judeo- Christian moral tradition by adopting a Hellenistic one, in truth she merely vacillates between asceticism and libertinism within a single Christian cultural logic that she fails to transcend. As such, the narrative of Sue's life comes to resemble the very cycles of negation that Debord identifies with the inability of avant-garde art to communicate outside the discourse of consumption. Sue herself says as much when, in response to Jude's comment that she is a "creature of civilization," she retorts that she is, indeed, a "negation of it" (Hardy [1895] 1965, 116, 117).

Sue's purchase of pagan idols from a peddler on the outskirts of Christminster speaks to the superficiality of her Hellenism and her susceptibility to the spectacle. From the ubiquitous Gothic architecture of the city to the interior of her room above the religious shop, Sue's visual sphere is saturated with Christian iconography. Seeking relief from this relentless display, Sue takes an afternoon walk in the countryside. The skyline of Christminster looms above the trees and her solace is broken by the repeated cry of "images" from a street vendor who seems to have pursued her from the center of town. She is struck by the incongruity of the peddler's collection of plaster pagan figures glowing in the setting sun in relief against the Gothic skyline of Christminster. The idols undergo a hypnotizing visual transfiguration that parallels Jude's first glimpse of Christminster (Hardy [1895] 1965, 75). Sue experiences a momentary sense of liberation in purchasing the idols, but the thrill of her transgressive purchase is quickly overshadowed by her decidedly un-Hellenic "nervous temperament" as she finds herself in public view saddled with two large, naked statues. She resolves in a "trembling state" to smuggle them back to her room (76). Once home, she sets the statues atop a chest of drawers, where a print of a Gothic crucifix hangs behind them flanked by candles. Having erected this relativistic altar, Sue conducts a secularized liturgy, reading not from scripture, but from Gibbon's account of Julian the Apostate, the last non-Christian Roman emperor and an advocate of the Empire's return to traditional pagan religious practices. In place of a psalm, she then reads from Swinburne's "Hymn to Proserpine," a meditation on the banishment of the gods on the day of Rome's official conversion to Christianity. Sue's paganism is a distinctly post-Christian paganism. We are told that she sleeps fitfully that night, awakening numerous times to the spectral image of the plaster idols framed in half-light against the cross. At that very moment in a chamber across town, Jude practices his Greek until dawn by reading Paul's epistle to the Corinthians, the letter in which Paul attempts to reinvigorate the Corinthians' eroding monotheism that had fallen under the influence of their pagan environment (77–8).

Pater's essay on Renaissance philosopher Pico della Mirandola suggests that the authentic humanist response to the conflicting discourses of paganism and Christianity is to "adjust these various products of the human mind to one another" and to recognize their simultaneous existence in the present moment ([1893] 1980, 23). Pater contrasts this holistic understanding of cultures in dialog across time with the historicist tendencies of the nineteenth-century intellect to rationalize all human experience into narratives of progress or decline. This shift that Pater describes is a symptom of spectacle in which the cyclical experience of time that allows the past to inform the present becomes marginalized by a linear, irreversible experience of time that Debord associates with industrial culture. According to Pater, Pico exhibits the authentic Hellenic spirit of the Renaissance insofar as he "seriously and sincerely entertained the claim on men's faith of the pagan religions" (33). Pico's work participates in the ethos of the classical world that he studies and is not alienated from it by the antiquarian motives or iconoclastic reactions against of his own era. Countering Ruskin's argument that Gothic humanism risked imperfection to afford the laborer an intellectual stake in his work, Pater points to the freedom exhibited by Renaissance thinkers like Pico to "reconcile forms of sentiment which at first might seem incompatible" with an exuberance that was often pursued "imperfectly or mistakenly" (23, 25). Pater adopts Pico's synthesizing impulse in his own argument that the roots of the Renaissance extend backward into the Middle Ages, as opposed to the oppositional narrative of decline with which Ruskin connects these two periods. Pater argues that the pagan gods were not entirely absent from the Middle Ages, but "still going to and fro on the earth, under all sorts of disguises," a fact "for the most part ignored by those writers who have treated [the time] preeminently as the 'Age of Faith'" (19).

Sue does not exhibit this humanist motivation to synthesize or reconcile cultural discourses. Her behavior resembles instead Pater's descriptions of the era's excessive historicism, which "by an imaginative act, throws itself back into a world unlike one's own, and estimates every intellectual creation in its connection with the age from which it proceeded" ([1893] 1980, 26). Sue denigrates any attempt to see continuities between Roman and Gothic art, observing that "under the picturesqueness of those Norman details one can see the grotesque childishness of uncouth people trying to imitate the vanished Roman forms, remembered by dim tradition only" (Hardy [1895] 1965, 243). As if in response to Ruskin's call to revive the Gothic design as a means of reuniting "the church, the palace, and the cottage," Sue rejects the premise that Gothic architecture expresses anything relevant to modern society. She describes the recuperation of authentic intellectual pursuit at the university as placing "new wine in old bottles," declaring that the "medievalism of Christminster must go" or it will be nothing more than "a place full of fetichists and ghost-seers" (119–20). She taunts Jude with the idea that the railway station has usurped the Church's place at "the centre of the town life," noting that "the cathedral was a very good place four or five centuries ago; but it is played out now" (107). She later suggests to Jude that he only take on restoration projects such as "railway stations, bridges, theatres, music-halls, hotels" in which architectural style is reduced entirely to ornament and "has no connection with conduct" (243).

Sue manifests Hellenism solely through intellectualized allusions to the classical world, a cultural literacy that finds little, if any, spontaneous existence in her emotional life. As an alternative to this spectatorial relationship with Hellenism cultivated by antiquarians, Pater provides the example of eighteenth-century classicist Johann Winckelmann, who genuinely embraced the Hellenic principles he studied. "Reinforcing the purer emotions of the intellect with an almost physical excitement," Winckelmann is free of the intoxication typically exhibited by one who approaches the pagan world from the standpoint of Christian asceticism (Pater [1893] 1980, 152). Whereas Winckelmann, Pater tells us, is serenely steeped in sensuousness, Sue, by contrast, is alternatively giddy with defiance and then guilt-ridden over her transgressions. She never stops looking over her shoulder in fear of society's disapproval of her unconventional relationship with Jude. Consequently, she never achieves the true liberty of the Hellenic mindset to become, like Winckelmann, "at unity with himself, with his physical nature, with the outward world" (Pater [1893] 1980, 177). Indeed, Sue's physical nature is repeatedly suppressed. On a number of occasions, Sue is present in the novel as a disembodied photograph that is kissed and embraced. Jude compares Sue to classical statuary from the Parthenon's frieze (Hardy [1895] 1965, 114), a compliment that nevertheless reduces her to a lifeless, half-dimensioned image in *bas relief*. Sue is repeatedly referenced as a "hologram" and a "phantasmal bodiless creature," and Jude apostrophizes her as "you spirit; you disembodied creature, you dear, sweet, tantalizing phantom – hardly flesh at all; so that when I put my arms around you I almost expect them to pass through you as air" (205, 194). The most honest conversation Sue has with Jude about her desire for intellectual comrades instead of lovers occurs while she is dressed in men's clothing (116–22). Sue comes to Jude's apartment after traversing a river while fleeing from a women's academy, and she wears Jude's suit while her own garments are drying, convincing Jude's landlady that he has a male friend visiting for dinner.

Just as Jude is unable to internalize Ruskin's image of the unalienated Gothic laborer, Sue is unable to internalize Pater's image of the liberated Hellene. In spite of her self-asserted "curiosity to hunt up new sensations" (Hardy [1895] 1965, 138)—a phrase drawn directly from Pater's demand that the "aesthetic critic regard all the objects with which he has to do [...] as powers or forces producing pleasurable sensations" ([1893] 1980, ix)— Sue is unable to live the part of the pagan. She thinks and speaks in a Paterian language with no fidelity to the ideal that he describes. Sue touts the "literary enormity" of the Song of Solomon, for example, chastising the bishops for their "attempt to plaster over with ecclesiastical abstractions such ecstatic, natural, human love as lies in that great and passionate song" just moments after defending herself to Jude against past accusations of being "cold-natured" and "sexless" (Hardy [1895] 1965, 121, 118). During a visit to an agricultural fair, Sue declares that she has achieved a moment of "Greek joyousness," a claim that is all the less convincing when she laboriously explains how this requires her to have "forgotten what twenty-five centuries have taught the race" (235). On another occasion in which Sue momentarily feigns disregard for the judgment of Christian society, Sue's Hellenism is projected onto her by Jude as a heap of classical allusions in the manner of an epic catalog, reproduced here in its entirety so as to convey the full extent of the grotesque narrative intrusion that Hardy pursues:

ARCHITECTURAL REVIVAL AS SPECTACLE 49

> You seem when you are like this to be one of the women of some grand old civilization, whom I used to read about in my bygone, wasted, classical days, rather than a denizen of a mere Christian country. I almost expect you to say at these times that you have just been talking to some friend whom you met in the Via Sacra, about the latest news of Octavia or Livia; or have been listening to Aspasia's eloquence, or have been watching Praxiteles chiseling away at his latest Venus, while Phryne made complaint that she was tired of posing. (214)

All of this is said of the same woman whom the narrator elsewhere describes as "so strictly proper and so lifelessly spoken that [her words] might have been taken from a list of model speeches in 'The Wife's Guide to Conduct'" (125, 150). Sue renounces Hellenism entirely toward the end of the novel after the death of her children, mocking herself for believing that it is possible to "make a virtue of joy" and attempting to access the "instincts which civilization had taken upon itself to thwart" (268). Reverting entirely to the vocabulary of medieval asceticism, she explains to Jude, "Our life has been a vain attempt at self-delight. But self-abnegation is the higher road. We should mortify the flesh—the terrible flesh—the curse of Adam" (273).

Reviews and criticism of *Jude the Obscure* have expressed dissatisfaction that the dialog between Jude and Sue is often stilted and self-conscious, particularly during moments in which a realistic sensibility would demand that they be stripped to an emotionally raw state. I contend that Hardy has opted for realism over the realistic in these moments, keeping the spectacle of revived culture squarely before the eyes of the reader at the expense of naturalism. Disrupting the consumption of his novel in the manner of Brecht's epic theater, Hardy's stylized diction prevents the reader from becoming emotionally invested in the suffering of his characters and participating in an illusory catharsis that validates their fate as timeless and inevitable. Hardy confers seriousness upon his literary project by referencing the classical tragic form in his critical writings, but in *Jude the Obscure* he points to the unmistakably contemporary problem of spectacle. His characters experience a profound unrest in their own time that the narrator describes as a "modern vice" (Hardy [1895] 1965, 68). Pater notes that the modern individual is incapable of experiencing a "naïve, rough" sense of freedom because the threat to self-determination is no longer an externalized figure "with whom we can do warfare," but is experienced in modernity as "penetrating us with a network, subtler than our subtlest nerves, yet bearing in it the central forces of the world" ([1893] 1980, 184, 185). Pater seeks from modern art a representation of the "bewildering toils" of real men and women struggling to free themselves from "entanglement" in a "magic web woven through and through us" (185). Jude and Sue are these bewildered men and women in Pater's formulation, and the spectacle is the web that has penetrated their consciousness. Hardy's realism portrays this network of forces that has been internalized within modern culture right down to the level of perception and speech. Through novels like *Jude the Obscure*, the modern subject can come to an understanding of the alienation wrought by spectacle.

Literary realism's effectiveness in generating an awareness of spectacle is ultimately, however, an issue of reception. Hardy recognizes that there are readers in search of escapist relief who resent fiction that "sets [their] serious thoughts at work," as well as those who misinterpret realism as engaging in a polemical "attack on religion, morals or institutions" ([1888] 1997, 253–4). He identifies a third abuse of realism among the "keen hunters of the real" who comb his novels looking for references to actual "landscapes, prehistoric antiquities and especially old English architecture" ([1911] 1997, 234). Hardy insists that any archaeological value of his fiction in preserving a "fairly true record of a vanishing life" stems from his ethic as a novelist to critique the displacement of "country customs and vocations" by the spectacle of industrial progress ([1911] 1997, 234). However, one cannot overlook Hardy's own cultivation of a Wessex "brand" that participated in a growing nostalgia-driven market for England's agrarian culture. As discussed below in connection with Woolf's critique of historical pageantry, Hardy consented later in his career to adapt a number of his novels for the stage, gutting their ethical dimension to present popular scenes of rural life (Wilson 1995, 4–5). Similarly, in spite of his initial disparagement of photography as artless copying, Hardy eventually collaborated with a photographer to capture various of his Wessex scenes on film (Boylen 2006), many of which needed to be staged because, as the opening of *Jude the Obscure* reminds us, they had mostly been obliterated. We see in these examples certain inroads of iconicity that gnaw at Hardy's ethic of meta-spectacle.

Inscribed as they are within the conventions of a given medium, gestures that critique the spectacle of revived culture through parody and mimicry are liable to become complicit in the very consumption of culture that proliferates the spectacle. Take, for example, Augustus Pugin's attempt to harness a mass event in order to gain exposure for the anti-industrial movement when he contributed a model of a "Medieval Court" to London's Great Exhibition in 1851. It is possible that Pugin's exhibit was immediately recognized, at least by some viewers, as an ironic attempt to disrupt the narrative of technological progress embodied in the Crystal Palace. Perhaps it even sparked discussions akin to the one between Jude and Sue regarding the authenticity and educational value of the scale model of Jerusalem that they go to see. Some have argued, however, that Pugin's very participation in the Great Exhibition inscribed the revival movement "within the very logic of commodification it opposes" (Crosby 1992, 109–10). One could say the same of Hardy's publication in serial of the story of Jude Fawley, naturalizing for the reader what Jameson has described as "that immense process of transformation whereby populations whose life habits were formed by other, now archaic, modes of production are effectively reprogrammed for life and work in the new world of market capitalism" (1981, 152).

I contend, however, that *Jude the Obscure* (and arguably any number of Hardy's other novels) disrupt their own reception as popular fiction despite their mass-market form. Whereas popular fiction relies for commercial success on an appeal to realistic familiarity, Hardy routinely estranges the real in order to stir in his reader a critical disposition toward the social conditions presented. Unlike Pugin's exhibit, Hardy deconstructs the production and consumption of images so thoroughly in *Jude the Obscure* that he produces what Macherey has called a "determinate image of the ideological" and advances the reader's consciousness of spectacle by "revealing it as an object rather than living it from within" ([1966] 1978, 132). In this sense, *Jude the Obscure* functions similarly to the installation piece "Prada Marfa" that was constructed in 2005 on a desert highway roadside in Marfa, Texas. The piece consists of a life-sized, freestanding Prada store that displays actual Prada merchandise. However, the entryless structure attracts the consumer and then forces him to stand outside the shop window to contemplate its performance of consumer culture from a critical distance. Citing the 1965 Highway Beautification Act, Texas lawmakers threatened to remove the structure in 2013 as an illegal outdoor advertising sign after Playboy commissioned its own similar exhibit a few miles away to take advantage of the tourist traffic generated by the Prada Marfa (Mari 2013). In a perfect example of how Situationist gestures are continuously recuperated as spectacle, the Department of Transportation was placed in the awkward position of having to distinguish between two replicas of commercial icons that both claimed to be art—one commissioned as a realist gesture but sanctioned by a corporate entity and the other commissioned by a corporate entity but masquerading as a realist gesture.

The recurring motif of consumption in *Jude the Obscure* achieves similar literality when Jude is forced to exploit his knowledge of Gothic architecture by selling "Christminster cakes" complete with "traceried windows and cloisters" which he models in the likeness of the college (Hardy [1895] 1965, 247). Having become "sickened of ecclesiastical work" and marginalized from the morally conventional lifestyle required to conduct business in rural villages, Jude must turn to the anonymity and amorality of mass culture in order to survive. Sue proposes that they sell Jude's Christminster cakes at "markets and fairs, where people are gloriously indifferent to everything except the quality of the goods" (243). Jude exploits his knowledge of Gothic architecture as a visual commodity within an economy of cultural revival, and Sue arrives at the cynical corollary that the unprofitable aspects of the past are disposable. It is this attitude taken to its logical extreme that prompts little Father Time to kill himself and his siblings when he learns that his mother Sue is pregnant again. As he states so succinctly in his suicide note, "Done because we are too menny." The novel makes visible "the outcome of new views of life" through its depiction of these "boys of a sort unknown in the last generation" (266). The narrator's comments echo Hardy's critical writings on realism, which he identifies as a "sincere school of fiction" that "expresses truly the views of life prevalent in its time, by means of a selected chain of action best suited for their exhibition" ([1890] 1997, 255). Regardless of certain late-career schemes to transform the Wessex novels into his own version of Christminster cakes, Hardy makes no attempt in *Jude the Obscure* to exploit the consumer's appetite for the picturesque. This novel foregrounds the dynamics of spectacle by portraying how revived visual culture conceals historical change and alienates the modern individual to the point of a fatal disconnection with the real.

NOTES

1. Green (1991) has noted the influence on Hardy of Ruskin's critique of photography as a mechanical and artless process that does nothing to reveal the inner life of the individual.
2. To demonstrate connections between Hardy and the tradition of satire, Matz parallels the chapter headings in *Jude* ("At Marygreen," "At Christminster," "At Melchester," etc.) with the titles of the poems in

Hardy's later cycle *Satires of Circumstance* ("At Tea," "In Church," "On the Death-Bed," etc.), effectively reducing the underlying premise of both efforts to the rather undifferentiated notion that "to be located in some place, to take up space [...] is already to fall into the error that draws the wrath of an elusive cosmic satire" (2006, 527). The enumeration of a localized "circumstance" in the title of each poem, however, creates an entirely different rhythm within the verse cycle than the chapter titles produce within the novel. From the novel's very first line—"The schoolmaster was leaving the village, and everyone seemed sorry."—and in the opening landscape in which an historic church had been replaced with a "new building of modern Gothic design, unfamiliar to English eyes, [...] by a certain obliterator of historic records who had run down from London and back in a day" (Hardy [1895] 1965, 12), *Jude the Obscure* is concerned quite specifically with the individual experience of displacement and exchangeability in an industrial society that was becoming increasingly uniform in appearance and dependent upon a nomadic labor force. Noting the presence of a similar hyper-satirical stance in Hardy's earlier novels *A Laodecian* and *Two on a Tower*, Matz overlooks the fact that these novels also share in common with *Jude* something more historically specific: they each depict forms of spectatorial distance in industrial culture that alienate the modern subject.

3. Garson argues that Jude's engagement in scholarly discourse is authentic, whereas Sue parrots intellectual speech in a shallowly eclectic and subversive manner, using cultural signs "the only way one can in the post-Christian age posited by Hardy—to define, express and defend herself rather than to transcend oneself" (2000, 189). This reading neglects to consider Jude's marginalization from the intellectual community at Christminster and his own failed attempts to inhabit Ruskin's concept of "Gothicness."

4. Boylen has noted that Jude first encounters Sue as a photographic image and that Sue remains throughout the novel as a projection of Jude's idealization of that first encounter with her image (2006, 80).

5. See Mitchell (1986, 186–208) for a particularly lucid critique of Marxism's blindness to its own iconoclastic cycles of negation that applies equally to Sue's attitudes towards medievalism.

6. Analyzing relief sculpture in the Ducal Palace in Venice, some of which was produced during the Gothic period and some during the Renaissance, Ruskin points to two symptoms of the erosion of medieval humanism. The first is the shift in subject matter from images of human frailty to those that exhibit the hubris of modern rationalism. While the Gothic artists opted to represent the "Fall of Man" and the "Drunkenness of Noah," the panel dating from the Renaissance depicts the "Judgment of Solomon" (Ruskin 1851, vol. 2, 305). Secondly, Ruskin compares the decorative foliage sculpted on the panels from each period. He finds that the Gothic artist lavished great effort to effect the natural appearance of the veins running

through each leaf, whereas the patterns in the leaves on the Renaissance panel lack a corresponding vitality and are, in Ruskin's view, excessively schematized and repetitive. Hardy's metaphor of "a fern-leaf in a lump of coal" suggests the obsolescence of medievalism. The fern leaf is a metonym for Gothic humanism that has been enveloped by the lump of coal, an emblem of the utility and consumption that powers the industrial economy.

REFERENCES

Benjamin, Walter. (1939) 1969. What Is Epic Theater? In *Illuminations*, trans. Harry Zohn, 147–154. New York: Schocken.

Berger, Sheila. 1990. *Thomas Hardy and Visual Structures: Framing, Disruption, Process*. New York: New York University Press.

Boylen, Rebecca. 2006. Phantom Photographs: The Camera's Pursuit and Disruption of Consciousness in *Jude the Obscure*. *Thomas Hardy Journal* 22: 72–84.

Brecht, Bertolt. (1929) 1964. A Dialogue About Acting. In *Brecht on Theatre: The Development of an Aesthetic*, ed. and trans. John Willett, 26–29. New York: Hill & Wang.

Crosby, Christina. 1992. Reading the Gothic Revival: 'History' and Hints on Household Taste. In *Rewriting the Victorians: Theory, History and the Politics of Gender*, ed. Linda M. Shires, 101–115. New York: Routledge.

Debord, Guy. (1967) 1995. *The Society of the Spectacle*. Trans. Donald Nicholson-Smith. New York: Zone Books.

Garson, Marjorie. 2000. Jude the Obscure: What Does a Man Want? In *New Casebooks: Jude the Obscure, Thomas Hardy*, ed. Penny Boumelha, 179–208. New York: Palgrave Macmillan.

Green, Jennifer. 1991. Outside the Frame: The Photographer in Victorian Fiction. *Victorians Institute Journal* 19: 111–140.

Hardy, Thomas. (1888) 1997. The Profitable Reading of Fiction. In *Selected Poetry and Non-Fictional Prose*, ed. Peter Widdowson, 242–254. Houndmills/London: Macmillan Press.

———. (1890) 1997. Candour in English Fiction. In *Selected Poetry and Non-Fictional Prose*, ed. Peter Widdowson, 255–260. Houndmills/London: Macmillan Press.

———. (1891) 1997. The Science of Fiction. In *Selected Poetry and Non-Fictional Prose*, ed. Peter Widdowson, 261–264. Houndmills/London: Macmillan Press.

———. (1895) 1965. *Jude the Obscure*. Riverside Edition. Boston: Houghton Mifflin.

———. (1911) 1997. General Preface to the Novels and Poems. In *Selected Poetry and Non-Fictional Prose*, ed. Peter Widdowson, 232–236. Houndmills/London: Macmillan Press.

Hugo, Victor. (1831) 1978. *Notre Dame de Paris*. Trans. John Sturrock. Harmondsworth: Penguin.

Ingraham, Catherine. 1998. *Architecture and the Burdens of Linearity*. New Haven: Yale University Press.

Jameson, Fredric. 1975. Magical Narratives: Romance as Genre. *New Literary History* 7: 135–159.

———. 1981. *The Political Unconscious: Narrative as a Socially Symbolic Act*. Ithaca: Cornell University Press.

Katz, Alison. 2006. *Jude the Obscure*: The (En)Graven Image. *Thomas Hardy Journal* 22: 85–104.

Lukàcs, Georg. (1937) 1983. *The Historical Novel*. Trans. Hannah and Stanley Mitchell. Lincoln: University of Nebraska Press.

Macherey, Pierre. (1966) 1978. *A Theory of Literary Production*. Trans. Geoffrey Wall. London: Routledge.

Mallett, Philip. 1995. *Jude the Obscure*: A Farewell to Wessex. *Thomas Hardy Journal* 11 (3): 48–59.

Mari, Francesca. 2013. Maybe This Is Why Warhol Stuck to Soup Cans. *New York Times*, September 14. http://www.nytimes.com/2013/09/15/us/maybe-this-is-why-warhol-stuck-to-soup-cans.html?_r=4&. Accessed 10 Sept 2016.

Matz, Aaron. 2006. Terminal Satire and *Jude the Obscure*. *English Literary History* 73 (2): 519–547.

Mitchell, W.J.T. 1986. *Iconology: Image, Text, Ideology*. Chicacgo: University of Chicago Press.

Musselwhite, David. 2003. *Social Transformation in Hardy's Tragic Novels: Megamachines and Phantasms*. New York: Palgrave Macmillan.

Pater, Walter. (1893) 1980. *The Renaissance: Studies in Art and Poetry*. Ed. Donald Hill. Berkeley: University of California Press.

Pyle, Forest. 1995. Demands of History: Narrative Crisis in *Jude the Obscure*. *New Literary History* 26 (2): 359–378.

Rogers, Shannon. 1999. Medievalism in the Last Novels of Thomas Hardy: New Wine in Old Bottles. *English Literature in Transition (1880–1920)* 42 (3): 298–316.

Ruskin, John. 1851. *The Stones of Venice*. Philadelphia: Reuwee, Wattley & Walsh.

Sumner, Rosemary. 1995. Discoveries of Dissonance: Hardy's Late Fiction. *Thomas Hardy Journal* 11 (3): 79–88.

Timko, Michael. 1991. Edinburgh, Oxford, Christminster: Self & Society in Victorian England. *Victorian Institute Journal* 19: 25–40.

Widdowson, Peter. 2004. Thomas Hardy at the End of Two Centuries: From Page to Screen. In *Thomas Hardy and Contemporary Literary Studies*, ed. Tim Dolin and Peter Widdowson, 178–209. New York: Palgrave Macmillan.

Wilson, Keith. 1995. *Thomas Hardy on Stage*. New York: St. Martin's.

CHAPTER 3

"The true Italy is to be found by patient observation"—Tourism as Spectacle in E.M. Forster's *A Room with a View*

On two separate occasions during his celebrated series of lectures at Cambridge titled *Aspects of the Novel*, E.M. Forster disparages Thomas Hardy's fiction as failed realism. Characterizing Hardy as a "poet who conceives of his works from a great height," Forster discerns a spectatorial distance that separates Hardy from his characters—an aloofness that infects the very experience of reading Hardy's novels ([1927] 1954, 141). I have discussed how Hardy's affinity for classical form has, for many critics, obscured the modernity of his themes and style, and Forster's reaction is no exception. While Forster allows for the presence of a "metaphysical voice" in realist fiction, he finds this voice in Hardy's writing to be so overwhelmingly fatalistic and uniformly tragic that it lacks adequate nuance to trace the contours of modern life (198). In Forster's estimation, Hardy's fiction is sufficiently alienated from human experience that it cannot address the central concerns of literary realism. Citing Hardy's final novel as the epitome of his argument, Forster observes that "there is some vital problem that has not been answered, or even posed, in the misfortunes of Jude the Obscure" (141).

Forster's critique of Hardy, however harsh, is nevertheless an implicit acknowledgment of Hardy's attempt at a realist gesture. Even more significant is that Forster recognizes in this gesture—incomplete as he finds it to be—a "vital problem" in modern culture that realist fiction can and ought to address. I have argued that Hardy depicts the alienating effects of spectacle on his characters and that, in so doing, Hardy responds to

© The Author(s) 2018
E. Barnaby, *Realist Critiques of Visual Culture*,
https://doi.org/10.1007/978-3-319-77323-0_3

Pater's call for modern art to portray the "bewildering toils" of contemporary men and women struggling to free themselves from their "entanglement" in a "magic web woven through and through us" ([1893] 1980, 185). As such, I dispute Forster's claim that the vital problem of spectacle is "not even posed" in *Jude the Obscure*, although I must agree that the problem remains unanswered. Forster's lectures suggest that literary realism is too surgical an instrument for Hardy, whose universalizing tragic vision is best conveyed within the sweeping lyrical insights of his poems or the colossal scale of his epic drama *The Dynasts*. For all its consciousness of spectacle, *Jude the Obscure* concludes with the spectacle's tragic inevitability as a condition that recuperates any and all attempts to exist outside of its alienating logic. Hardy and Forster share the realist impulse to elevate the role of visual detail in the novel from providing a naturalistic backdrop to staging and advancing a critique of spectacle in modern culture. However, Forster's realism, unconstrained by tragic form, succeeds in posing an answer to the "vital problem" broached in *Jude the Obscure* by tracing a path beyond the spectacle for his characters and readers that Hardy did not envision.

During the same lecture in which he questions the realism of Hardy's fiction, Forster reflects on the character of a self-proclaimed realist author in André Gide's novel *Les Faux Monnayeurs* who struggles to narrate his perceptions without distorting the original experience ([1927] 1954, 149). Forster uses this particularly transparent moment in Gide's novel to illustrate how realist fiction makes the reader conscious of the "vital problem" of spectatorial distance. The trick is that a realist novel—itself an act of mediation—must avoid placing the reader in the role of spectator, as this would replicate the very spectatorial stance that literary realism sets out to critique. To this end, the realist author must disrupt the reader's consumption of the novel as an aesthetic object and establish instead an ethical relationship with the reader akin to the Situationist gesture's critique of everyday life. Gide produces consciousness of the act of representation by incorporating directly within the text the figure of a realist author who grapples with this problem. Not all realist gestures are so patently self-reflexive, of course, nor would one want them to be. Forster analyzes in each of his lectures a different feature of the modern novel that, if handled with a realist sensibility, maintains a clear distinction for the reader between a critical restatement of reality versus a false reproduction of reality.

Forster's distinction between "round" and "flat" literary characters, for example, is predicated upon the ethos that the novel ought to participate in the subjectivity of authentic consciousness and not reinforce the illusion of an objective reality. "Round" characters, according to Forster, are those that confront the reader with the "incalculability of daily life" and exhibit the "intermittent knowledge" that plagues our own "perception of life" ([1927] 1954, 118, 123). For Forster, the novelist who captures the reality that "we are stupider at some times than others" and "can enter into people's minds occasionally but not always" allows the reader to encounter the incompleteness of his own consciousness. As Rahv and Macherey would later argue, such fiction serves as a corrective to ideological oversimplifications of the real. "Flat" characters, on the other hand, exhibit a consistent perspective that withers in the realist context as an unsatisfying and artificial embodiment of ideology itself. This interplay between round and flat characters in realist fiction enables the novel to function as a Debordian *détournement*, which neutralizes the spontaneous power of ideology by placing it within a broader restatement of lived experience. Forster warns, however, that a novel which merely theorizes about social conditions inserts spectatorial distance between the reader and the text that flattens its characters. This distance leads the reader to engage with the characters as "art objects," critiquing their effectiveness as reproductions of the real instead of critiquing the reality that they struggle to inhabit ([1927] 1954, 123). Such fiction merely reinforces the aesthetic disposition toward reality that Debord associates with post-industrial culture in general.

Forster's analysis of the consciousness of time in realist fiction further informs the novel's function as meta-spectacle. He argues that literary realism models a balance of "life in time" and "life in value" that invokes the tension between materiality and interiority in one's experience of the real ([1927] 1954, 65–8). "Life in time" refers to moments that we experience collectively in the form of an objective, chronological and shared temporality, whereas "life in value" reflects the subjective heightening, perpetuation and sometimes non-sequential return of certain moments within the continuum of individual consciousness. A novel dominated by "life in time" falsifies its depiction of the real as a linear transcript in which the events and non-events of daily life occupy consciousness equally—a complaint, as I noted above in the introduction, that Orwell and Rushdie register concerning the amoral and aestheticized reproduction of reality in naturalistic fiction. A novel dominated by "life in value," on the other hand, retreats into the incommunicable solipsism of stream of consciousness, a criticism that Forster levies against Gertrude Stein's modernist fiction and that Woolf, as noted above, raises against James Joyce. Literary realism thus integrates the objective and subjective dimensions of consciousness or, in some cases, depicts the dysfunctional consequences of their imbalance.

The imbalance of "life in time" and "life in value" to which realist fiction responds is a fundamental aspect of the society of the spectacle. Debord attributes this imbalance to a shift away from the predominantly cyclical experience of time in agrarian society toward the predominantly linear experience of time in industrial society. He observes that industrialization has enabled unprecedented proportions of the population to transcend the agrarian cycles of rural peasant life and witness the dynastic and "irreversible" narrative of political and economic history that was previously reserved for the aristocracy. Debord's innovation in this regard is not the concept of class mobility itself, but the spectatorial turn that he associates with that mobility. He perceives modern society as collectively transformed from authentic participants in contemporary time to alienated spectators of historical time. This spectatorial logic of post-industrial society, once normalized, yields a "pseudo-cyclical" delusion that one can participate subjectively within objectified representations of time and, in effect, inhabit a mirage (Debord [1967] 1995, 153, 155, 157).

As opposed to the reconciliation of "life in time" and "life in value" that Forster attributes to realist fiction, materialism and interiority function within "pseudo-cyclical" consciousness as schizophrenic extremes that culminate in the ideological distortion of reality. These extremes parallel the excessive materialism of the naturalists and excessive interiority of the modernists that Forster critiques in his lectures and which Woolf also critiques in her essay "Modern Fiction." "Life in time" is reduced within pseudo-cyclical consciousness to an antiquarian fixation that objectifies the material traces of lived experience as cultural commodities. These "artificially distinct moments," as Debord describes them, are produced and sold as part of the alienated labor of "augmented survival" in the post-agrarian economy (Debord [1967] 1995, 149, 150). Under such conditions, consciousness becomes untethered from its own historical moment, and the experience of "life in value" becomes a mere stream of consciousness that resembles Debord's description of the spectacle as "generalized autism" and "authorized amnesia" (153, 196). Realist fiction reveals to the reader these counterfeit versions of "life in time" and "life in value" that replace lived experience with an "illusion of encounter" (217).

Hardy's depiction in *Jude the Obscure* of the revival of Hellenism and medievalism in nineteenth-century England portrays the role of pseudo-cyclical consciousness in creating this illusion of encounter. Alienated from rural agrarian society by their indoctrination into an intellectualized and dynastic experience of time, Jude and Sue come to believe that they participate in classical and feudal cultures through their knowledge of art and architecture from those periods. The realist "roundness" of Hardy's characters derives from their misconstrued restatements of contemporary discourses that they have only partially internalized, thus making visible the chronic incompleteness of their consciousness. Anticipating Forster's distinction between literary realism and social commentary, Hardy notes that his fiction is not a "tract in disguise," but voices philosophies through his characters that are "as full of holes as a sieve" in order to portray the "reality of humanity" ([1888] 1997, 246). As such, Jude and Sue are not "flat" characters, but undergo "flattening" throughout the course of the novel by virtue of their subjection to the spectacle. As I argued in Chap. 2, Hardy portrays how they are reduced to a polarized vacillation between the extremes of materialism and idealism that Debord associates with pseudo-cyclical consciousness. Jude fetishizes his restoration of Gothic stonework as participating in the Gothic spirit of the original designers, which he understands only in summary through art critics like John Ruskin. In parallel with this materialist excess, Jude abstracts himself from lived experience to engage in a solipsistic dialog with scholarly treatises that have become separated from their historical context as objective truths. Exhibiting similar extremes, Sue's purchase of Greek idols and her other fleeting moments of liberated sensualism assert a skin-deep Hellenism that is belied throughout the novel by her nervous retreats into asceticism.

Like Hardy, Forster explores in his fiction the physical and psychological displacements wrought by industrialization and the emerging dominance of a visual culture of spectatorship in post-industrial society. Forster exhibits a similar concern that modern revivals of Hellenism and medievalism are "de-coupled," as Ann Ardis observes, "from sensual and emotional experience" and characterized by an "arid, deadening intellectualism." Notwithstanding rare cases like that of Johann Winckelmann—the eighteenth-century classicist whom Pater praises for genuinely inhabiting a Hellenic perspective—modern antiquarians typically fail to participate in the "Platonic [...] continuum between physical and intellectual stimulation" (Ardis 2007, 65). Forster anticipates Debord's concepts of spectatorial distance and the illusion of encounter in his depiction of the British tourist's ritualized cultivation of European cultural literacy and elite social networks through the tradition known as the Grand Tour. The concept of the Grand Tour originated in the seventeenth century as a launching point into social influence for young male aristocrats, who would undertake an extended sojourn on the Continent with a tutor to study antiquity and its revival during the Renaissance. The Tour later became a purchased point of access into the upper class for those who had obtained industrial wealth, and it was ultimately democratized even further by the mass production of guidebooks.[1]

While *A Room with a View* is disarmingly humorous in describing the foibles of tourists, the novel is not simply—as many have read it—a light satire of the legacy of the Grand Tour and its infiltration by the merchant class. Forster's characters are at grave risk of internalizing a "sense of cultural and historical belatedness" that, according to Ardis, typically accompanied the experience of the Grand Tour by the late nineteenth century and which served to "expose rather than resolve a sense of emotional and sensual alienation" (2007, 62). Spectatorial distance from reality is a form of dispossession that can go largely unnoticed amidst the familiar trappings and routines of the quotidian; hence the Situationists' call for a critique of everyday life. The experience of spectatorial distance is heightened for tourists, however, who often recognize that they are held at arm's length from the perspective of the inhabitant and confined instead to sites of visual legibility that have been packaged for their consumption. James Buzard has argued that "the special project of Forster's early work [...] is to investigate existence within the discourse and the 'state' of tourism and the possibilities of circumventing or transcending the obstacles tourism places between 'travellers' and the understanding they seek, both of themselves and of the places they visit" (1993, 15). Citing additional examples from Forster's short stories "Story of a Panic" and "The Eternal Moment" and his debut novel *Where Angels Fear to Tread*, Buzard argues in Debordian language that the characters in *A Room with a View* "repeatedly enact a failed encounter with the 'real' which they believe themselves to have met" (26). The frustration experienced by certain of Forster's tourists as they chafe in their role as spectators becomes the foundation for their consciousness of more insidious dynamics of spectatorship that alienate their domestic life. Alluding to Louis Althusser's account of "art that generates an 'an *internal distance* ... from the very ideology from which [it] emerged,'" Buzard suggests that Forster's fiction makes visible to his readers their separation from the real (14). *A Room with a View* differs, however, from *Jude the Obscure* as an instance of meta-spectacle in that Forster generates this "internal distance" not only for the reader, but for the characters themselves. Forster traces his characters' increasing awareness of the spectacle and invites the reader to participate in that liberation.

The first half of *A Room with a View* takes place in Florence, where Lucy Honeychurch and her chaperone, Charlotte Bartlett, have come to stay at the Pension Bertolini, a small hotel frequented by English travelers. There they meet the George Emersons, Senior and Junior. Emerson, Sr., is a progressive and boisterous businessman, and Emerson, Jr., is a sullen and world-weary clerk educated in nineteenth-century Romantic literature and philosophy—one of those "boys of a sort unknown in the last generation" whom Hardy describes in *Jude the Obscure* as "the outcome of new views of life" ([1895] 1965, 266). The Emersons represent a threat on many levels to Charlotte's attempts to introduce Lucy to polite society and guard her innocence. They offer to exchange rooms with Lucy and Charlotte when they overhear Lucy's complaint that her room lacks a view. George and Lucy meet again when he rescues her from a fainting spell after she witnesses an altercation in a public square that ends in murder. Shortly thereafter, during an excursion to the countryside organized by a local clergyman for the travelers staying at the Bertolini, George kisses Lucy. Confused by her feelings for George and afraid of the social repercussions of her momentary lapse in judgment, Lucy leaves immediately for Rome, where she runs into a long-time suitor, an urbane fop named Cecil Vyse, and accedes to Cecil's proposal of marriage in order to restore her respectability.

The second half of the novel takes place at Windy Corners, a rural village off of one of London's rail lines. Cecil has come to the Honeychurch home to deliver his proposal formally. Lucy's mother and her brother Freddy are not quite sure what to make of Cecil or of Lucy's decision to marry him. Cecil condescends to the local inhabitants and their customs, looking to groom Lucy instead for an introduction to London society. Meanwhile, the Emersons rent a house in Windy Corners, and George, Jr., becomes friends with Freddy, which leads to his visiting Windy Corners and spending time with the newly engaged couple. Recognizing that Lucy's relationship to Cecil is a contrivance, he confronts Lucy with his love for her and kisses her again. Lucy realizes that she has no genuine feelings for Cecil and breaks off the engagement, but her own sense of propriety and his parting remarks praising her liberated womanhood make it intolerable for her to reveal that she is leaving Cecil for another man. She resolves to flee Windy Corners and undertake another leg of the Grand Tour—this time accompanying a pair of spinsters to Greece—in order to bury her feelings for George once and for all. Just before she leaves, she meets Emerson, Sr., who convinces her to allow neither chauvinism nor reverse chauvinism to trump authentic emotion. Lucy and George elope, spending their honeymoon at the Bertolini in Florence where they first met.

Critics have struggled to understand how the Italian and English halves of *A Room with a View* cohere. What is the character development that Lucy Honeychurch and George Emerson undergo from their controversial encounters in Florence to their reunion in Windy Corners and ultimate return to Florence as a married couple? Two of the most-discussed scenes in the novel—the murder that Lucy witnesses in the piazza in Florence and the occasion on which George, Freddy and the Reverend Beebe bathe in a pond in Windy Corners—have often been invoked to answer this question. The murder scene has been interpreted as Lucy's sexual awakening, a moment that is punctuated by the Freudian image of a solitary tower throbbing in the sunset (Cosslett 2009; Buzard 1993). The bathing scene has been read as a momentary lapse into an authentic classical spirit that has been brought back to England by the tourists as part of their secular pilgrimage (Peat 2003). These scenes are, indeed, transformative, and such interpretations have prompted insightful reflections on Forster's attempt to locate opportunities for authentic encounter within the otherwise banal consumption of cultural commodities that constituted the Grand Tour. However, to reduce Lucy's experience in Florence to a sexual initiation or to suggest that the tourists imbibe an authentic Hellenic spirit while in Italy ignores the condition of spectatorial distance that Forster portrays systematically throughout the novel. A chauvinistic cosmopolitanism in which art, nature, native Italians and women are treated as mute icons to be narrated by English men alienates Lucy while she is abroad and threatens to maroon her in a celibate marriage to Cecil at home. There is exotic travel, a love interest, an engagement and a wedding, but not in the conventional progression which that sequence suggests. The real story lies in dispelling the illusion of encounter that informs Lucy's and George's role as spectators of dead culture—the aesthetic and philosophical residue of lived experience that they themselves have not lived.

Lucy's negotiation with spectacle involves a gradual awakening of her consciousness that is subject to numerous regressions. This process begins with her impatience to access the genuine Italy that lies beyond her guide-book and the circuit of galleries, museums and historical sites that map her movements through Florence. Lucy recognizes and resents the uniformity of the tourist's sphere, anticipating Debord's critique of tourism as "the chance to go and see what has been made trite" and of the "economic management of travel to different places" that results in their "inter-changeability" ([1967] 1995, 168). She laments that the occupants and décor of her hotel—right down to the furnishings of the drawing room—are so English that she might as well be in London (Forster [1908] 1986, 281). However, Lucy's affront at being deprived of the room with a view for which she paid suggests that she remains invested, at least for the moment, in the tourist's spectatorial stance. Overhearing Lucy's complaint, Emerson, Sr., immediately offers his room and his son's room to Lucy and Charlotte. Charlotte protests to the Emersons that it would be unsuitable for two women traveling alone to accept rooms from strangers. Emerson, Sr., responds that "women like looking at a view; men don't" and concludes that he possesses a commodity that he does not value and prefers to give it to someone who would. Although Lucy cannot articulate the amalgam of chauvinism and spectacle in which she is entangled, Forster plants the seed of nascent consciousness in the form of her "odd feeling" that the argument had "widened and deepened till it dealt [...] with something quite different, whose existence she had not realized before" (282).

Against Charlotte's wishes, she and Lucy switch rooms with the Emersons, but the view fails to bring Lucy any closer to the experience of Italy that she desires. On the first morning after her arrival, Lucy stands at a window overlooking the city and watches the inhabitants go about their morning routines. Men work along the riverbank as an electric tram makes its way through a crowd of people. The narrator notes the presence of a solitary tourist riding inside the windowed cabin of the tram, whereas the locals hang from its outer platforms hopping on and off (Forster [1908] 1986, 290). The tourist is isolated within a panoptical, disembodied experience of the city, observing life being enacted before him by the inhabitants. This figure reflects back to Lucy her own voyeuristic perspective from the balcony of her hotel room such that she begins to sense the spectatorial distance that separates her from the surrounding indigenous life.

Lucy's visit to the Santa Croce later that day exhibits similar glimmers of consciousness that are otherwise entrenched in spectatorship. She is accompanied by Miss Lavish, a fellow guest at the Bertolini, who fancies herself above the vulgar consumerism of tourists. Lavish declares to Lucy that the guidebook "does but touch the surface of things" and that Lucy must be "emancipated" from it (Forster [1908] 1986, 291). She takes Lucy's guidebook and commands her to "merely drift" through Florence until she is lost—in other words, to undertake a Situationist *dérive* and establish her own psychogeography of Florence. Lucy manages to locate the Santa Croce without her guidebook and, deprived of its commentary and footnotes, turns her attention from architecture and art to observe the native Italian Catholics who have come to the church for its cult value, as Benjamin would say, as opposed to its exhibition value. She takes pleasure in the fact that a group of children mistakenly venerate a statue of Machiavelli that they took to be a saint (295), a playful instance of *détour-nement* that momentarily destabilizes the theological and historical legibility of the icon.

On the whole, however, Lucy remains in thrall to the tourist's duty of visual consumption. Unlike the children, she is "unwilling to be enthusiastic over monuments of uncertain authorship or date" until she is able to confirm which ones "had been most praised by Mr. Ruskin" (Forster [1908] 1986, 295). To this end, she joins up with a lecture for English tourists delivered by the Reverend Eager, an English clergyman who is parson of an Anglican parish in Florence. Eager's talk is drawn directly from Ruskin's *Stones of Venice*. Eager observes how the church had been "built by faith in the full fervor of medievalism, before any taint of the Renaissance had appeared" and praises Giotto's liberation from slavish adherence to the rationalist "snares of anatomy and perspective" (297). As Buzard has noted, Ruskin published guides such as *Mornings in Florence* in order to dismantle the "the obstructing wall of distorting language" that separates the tourist from an authentic encounter with Florence, especially "the discourse of Murray and Baedeker, that textual beaten track running past starred attractions" (1993, 289). Buzard observes, however, that "far from being in a renewed and intimate contact with the real," Ruskin's "anti-touristic text" merely finds the tourist "reading Ruskin's reading of Murray's reading (itself the product of others' readings) of Italy." Forster's portrayal of this dynamic in *A Room with a View* transforms this novel from a mere satire of tourist guidebooks into the more fundamental critique of the "discursive and material structures surrounding 'the real'" (Buzard 1993, 291; Byerly 2013). Among Reverend Eager's audience is the skeptical Emerson, Sr., who calls Eager out for idealizing the exploitation of feudal laborers and Giotto's lack of realism. Lucy is at first exhilarated by Emerson's ethical challenge to the bubble of aesthetic pronouncements in which she and her fellow tourists are insulated. She is made uncomfortable, however, by the contentious scene between Emerson and Eager, and when Charlotte appears, she leaves Emerson to join her chaperon in reaffirmation of polite society.

Restless after her perturbing visit to the Santa Croce, and dissatisfied with the pronouncement of a fellow traveler that there was no point in leaving the hotel again that day since the galleries had all closed, Lucy escapes unchaperoned from the Bertolini to buy souvenir postcards in the square. Once again, Lucy's desire to penetrate the insulated province of the tourist is thwarted by her conflation of purchased views with lived experience. The narrator pauses at this moment in the text to meditate on the persistence of medievalism in the industrial age, not merely through the revival of its art and architecture, but in the perpetuation of a chivalric order in which women are insulated from the sphere of action and function instead as aesthetic objects that inspire the experiences of men. Lucy exhibits no clear discernment of these dynamics. She alternates between tolerating the dual role of icon and spectator assigned to women and, at other moments, rigorously seeking to transcend it. Committed to neither a medieval nor Hellenic ideology, Lucy enacts a series of superficial and impulsive transgressions that she quickly regrets, just as Sue Bridehead immediately regrets her impulsive purchase of the nude pagan idols from a street vendor (who has an Italian accent, coincidentally) on the outskirts of Christminster. Lucy similarly seeks out a postcard vendor and purchases images of classical and neo-classical art, extending "uncritical approval to every well-known name" that has been sanctioned as a commodity by cultural authorities (Forster [1908] 1986, 311). Like Sue, Lucy asserts her liberation through the purchase of images, but this fleeting gesture against the spectacle fails to stand outside the logic of consumption.

Soon after her unsatisfying purchase, Lucy undergoes a moment of heightened awareness. The setting sun evokes "the hour of unreality—the hour," the narrator explains, "when unfamiliar things are real." She becomes transfixed by the appearance of a tower blazing in the sunset, the very same circumstances in which Jude is first hypnotized by the Gothic towers of Christminster and Sue catches sight of the idols. The erotic language with which Forster describes the tower is not necessarily, as some have suggested, that of a young woman's Freudian epiphany, but echoes the voyeuristic parlance of Mediterranean guidebooks that is featured in

Forster's other so-called "Italian novel," *Where Angels Fear to Tread*. Whereas Jude and Sue never fully grasp their role as spectators and consumers of images, Lucy grows "conscious of her discomfort" at this moment, and we are told that "it was new to her to be conscious of it" (Forster [1908] 1986, 311). The romanticized still-life of Florence that has been packaged for tourists is disrupted when a fight breaks out among two men in the square and one stabs the other. As the dying man staggers toward Lucy and opens his mouth, his blood pours out onto the prints she has just purchased, its tactile presence overwhelming Lucy's spectatorial distance. George happens upon Lucy in the square at this moment and catches her as she faints. Once revived, Lucy attempts to trivialize the matter out of chivalry, observing that "these accidents do happen, and then one returns to the old life," but George insists, "I don't; I shall want to live" (315). Lucy's impulse is to hold the experience at arm's length as something seen and not internalized, but George refuses to insulate himself from this visceral encounter with life and death and allows it to work upon his consciousness.

Although Lucy cannot yet articulate her insights, she does not simply "return to the old life" after witnessing the murder in the piazza. Lucy's changed feelings toward Lavish and Eager, for example, serve as an index of her increasing consciousness of the spectacle. Following this incident, the narrator notes that Lucy had "tried" Lavish and Eager by "some new test" and "found them wanting" (Forster [1908] 1986, 311). There is a common trait in these two characters that reflects Lucy's own alienation and makes visible to her what they cannot see, namely, that in their role as consumers of culture they have falsely equated possessing knowledge about a place and its cultural products with inhabiting it. Lavish and Eager consider themselves to have transcended the role of tourist, but in reality they remain chauvinistic and condescending occupiers of Italy rather than inhabitants. Their imperialistic relationship to Italy is enacted by their acquisition of images, a dynamic that Susan Sontag has noted in tourists' impulse to take photographs so as to domesticate unfamiliar territory and overcome their own sense of dispossession (1977, 9–10).

Lavish embraces spectatorial distance as one who is involved in a scientific inquiry, instructing Lucy that "the true Italy is to be found by patient observation" (Forster [1908] 1986, 291). Although Lavish's advice that Lucy part with her guidebook seems at first to exhibit a Situationist spirit, we learn that Lavish's true purpose in deliberately straying from the tourist's beaten path is to collect details for a sensationalist novel that she is writing. The narrator describes Lavish's constant note-taking as "calculations in realism" that add "local colouring" to her otherwise conventional story (317). Lavish exemplifies Hardy's criticism of naturalistic writers who traffic in "scientific data" to achieve realistic visual descriptions at the expense of breathing consciousness of the real into their characters. She deploys Italians in her novel like the incidental staffage of a pastoral landscape painting, and her novel is an agent of spectacle that serves as a metafictional foil against which Forster's own authentic realism stands in stark relief.

As parson of an Anglican parish for expatriates in Florence, Eager fancies himself to have achieved the status of an inhabitant, whereas his experience of Italy is actually limited to its art and architectural history. When Eager meets Lucy and Charlotte in the square, he advises them on their purchase of souvenir postcards and invites them to participate on a sightseeing excursion. During the course of their conversation, a persistent street vendor foists so many postcards upon them that Eager becomes handcuffed to Charlotte by a "glossy ribbon of churches, pictures and views," one of Forster's more literal figurations of their imprisonment within the spectacle. Eager grows irate upon being solicited like an ordinary tourist, insisting that the vendor knows that Eager is "a resident" (Forster [1908] 1986, 320). Having extricated himself from the web of images and castigated the vendor, Eager continues to describe the tour he has arranged, entirely blind to his own role as an image-hawker. He promises the women the exotic experience of taking tea in a Renaissance villa, points out with antiquarian savor a private garden that may have been the setting of *The Decameron,* and outlines a connoisseurial quest to find the exact spot from which a Renaissance landscape artist painted a famous view of Florence. None of these activities will afford Lucy the authentic encounter with Italy that she seeks. Such diversions participate instead in what Debord would later describe as "the 'all-inclusive' purchase of spectacular forms of [...] collective pseudo-travel, of participation in cultural consumption and even of sociability itself, in the form of 'exciting conversation,' 'meetings with celebrities' and suchlike" ([1967] 1995, 152). During the outing itself, Eager's indignation is incited once again, this time by an opportunistic carriage-driver whose crime, like the vendor's, is mistaking Eager for a typical tourist (Forster [1908] 1986, 328).

In spite of yearning to break free from the alienating illusion of encounter that has taken hold of Lavish and Eager, Lucy is intimidated by the two moments with George during her time in Italy during which spectatorial distance collapses into tactile proximity, mediated as those moments might be by the exotic backdrop of Italy. When reality comes too close, Lucy clings to a protective bubble of spectatorship. She dutifully completes the remainder of her Grand Tour, sublimates her emotions into passionate drawing-room performances of Beethoven piano sonatas, and acquiesces to a socially advantageous proposal of marriage from Cecil.

A glimmer of hope for Lucy lies in the fact that her heightened experience of the spectacle as a tourist prompts her to inhabit her domestic sphere more consciously. The narrator explains that Lucy returns from Italy "with new eyes" and that the Windy Corners of her childhood is held up to her for critical inspection like so many "pictures in a gallery to which, after much experience, a traveler returns" (Forster [1908] 1986, 324). As opposed to the voyeuristic consumption of visual culture that preoccupied Lucy in Italy, Forster's visual metaphor in this instance speaks instead to the sort of consciousness that realist representation generates when it restates and estranges the familiar. Realism, in Macherey's words, "establishes myth and illusion as visible objects" ([1966] 1978, 133). Upon her return from Italy, Lucy is confronted with the mythology of Windy Corners in which she has participated since childhood. She realizes that she had been raised within "a circle of rich, pleasant people with identical interests and identical foes" and had "hitherto [...] accepted their ideals without questioning" (Forster [1908] 1986, 367). Lucy's experiences abroad do not alienate her from her home, but instead motivate her to negotiate relationships with the inhabitants of Windy Corners that are grounded in deeper "personal intercourse" (368).

Cecil, on the contrary, has internalized the cosmopolitan homelessness exhibited by Lavish and Eager such that even his emotional life is a form of tourism. Whereas Lucy is moved by her frustration as a tourist to seek a deeper domestic life, Cecil's response is to "substitute a society he called broad" when faced with the realization that "local society was narrow" (Forster [1908] 1986, 368). Travel renders Cecil restless, alienated and subject to insatiable cycles of consumption. The drawing room at Windy Corners and its occupants are as confining and irritating to him as the drawing room at the Bertolini was to Lucy. He has come to prefer the illusion of encounter to encounter itself. We see Cecil's future in the fate of his mother, for whom repeated illusions of encounter in the form of "too many seasons, too many cities and too many men" had abstracted her to the point of adopting a lifeless and "mechanical" manner, even toward her own son (377).

As with Eager's pretensions to be regarded as a resident of Florence, Cecil's self-proclaimed membership in the "cult of fresh air" during his visits to Windy Corners is nothing more than a false sense of inhabiting a pastoral fantasy. Cecil theorizes to Lucy about his ability to be equally at home in the city or in the country. He patronizes country-dwellers as having "a taut sympathy with the workings of Nature which is denied to us of the Town" only to recoil a moment later from the townswomen's vulgar procreational interest in their engagement (Forster [1908] 1986, 357). Vacillating once again, he grows impatient with Lucy's mother, herself a country-dweller, for failing to take interest in his intellectual abstractions about the rural natives. The countryside is, for Cecil, an image in need of constant captioning, either through discourses on architectural style or the conventions of picturesque landscape painting. This spectatorial relationship to Windy Corners extends to Cecil's relationship with Lucy herself. Cecil's engagement to Lucy is part of a larger plan to cultivate and then circulate her like a piece of fine art within London society. Their marriage is but an extension of the conquest of Italy by the Grand Tourists and an emblem for Forster of the infiltration of London's industrial culture into rural England. Cecil's trips to Windy Corners resemble those of the architects in *Jude the Obscure* who "run down from London and back in a day" to remodel Wessex in a fashion that is "unfamiliar to English eyes" (Hardy [1895] 1965, 12).

Cecil's nervous vacillations and statuesque lack of tactile physicality echo qualities that Hardy ascribes to Sue Bridehead in *Jude the Obscure*. Observing that "a Gothic statue implies celibacy," the narrator compares Cecil to one of those "fastidious saints who guard the portals of a French cathedral" (Forster [1908] 1986, 349). Cecil routinely declines to play tennis in public and is "the kind of fellow," as Lucy's brother Freddy notes in disgust, "who would refuse to wear another man's cap" (348). Cecil explains to Lucy that he associates her with "a certain type of view" but is dismayed to learn that she associates him with "a drawing room [...] with no view" (364–5). Lucy intuitively associates Cecil with the stuffy interior drawing room of the Pension Bertolini, a portable simulacrum of London that is insulated from its locale and circulates with dull uniformity among European cultural capitals. Cecil reproaches her for failing to connect him instead with "the open air" (365). In deference to Cecil's moody reaction, Lucy assents to a walk in the woods, during which they come to the Sacred Lake—a vernal pond, Lucy explains, in which she was once caught bathing when she was younger. The story of Lucy's bawdy exploit stirs in Cecil a desire to kiss her, but the result is unspontaneous and rigid. Although perhaps not quite as esoteric as the exchanges between Jude Fawley and Sue Bridehead, Cecil asks formal permission, to which Lucy awkwardly submits. Spectatorial distance achieves literality when Cecil's gold pince-nez becomes dislodged and flattened between their faces. He critiques the kiss as one would a piece of failed theater or an outtake that needs to be reshot, replaying in his mind an idealized version of the scene as it should have occurred. An alienated spectator of his own experiences, Cecil "found time to wish that he could recoil" just before the kiss occurs, and their relationship remains abstract (366).

Meanwhile, George has resumed his existential sullenness upon learning of Lucy's engagement to Cecil. Through an unwitting intervention by Cecil, George and his father relocate from London to Windy Corners. As a gesture of welcome and with no knowledge of George's feelings for Lucy, her brother Freddy invites George and the Reverend Beebe to bathe in the Sacred Lake during its temporary spring appearance. The scene opens in a sitting room in the Emersons' house, which is entirely "blocked with books" that form both a literal and speculative barrier between George and lived experience (Forster [1908] 1986, 379). The narrator notes among these volumes the prevalence of German philosophy (in particular, the atheistic pessimism of Schopenhauer and Nietzsche), morbid romantic poetry (especially Byron's melancholy heroes and Housman's nostalgic descriptions of rural England and premature mortality in *A Shropshire Lad*), and critiques of Christian hypocrisy (Butler's *Way of All Flesh* and Gibbon's treatise on the fall of Rome). Among these are the very books Sue Fawley reads during her secular liturgy in *Jude the Obscure*.

They depart to the sound of Emerson, Sr., discoursing in neo-Hellenic fashion on the modern individual's need to come to terms with the body and rediscover the paradise of Eden, but it is the bathers who put these echoes of Pater into practice. After an awkward walk to the pond during which Beebe attempts to fill long silences with banal chatter, we are told that upon entering the water "they forgot Italy and Botany and Fate" and "began to play" (Forster [1908] 1986, 384). By the end of the scene, their clothes are strewn about the lake and surrounding woods, and Lucy, her mother and Cecil happen upon them. George appears before her "barefoot, barechested, radiant and personable against the shadowy woods"—a true denizen of the open air and the classical foil to Cecil's ascetic figure (385). The narrator notes that something sacramental occurred in this moment, an awakening of vitality similar to the murder in the piazza, "a passing benediction whose influence did not pass" (386).

Some critics have read the bathing scene as an authentic display of Hellenic spirit brought back to England by the travelers—a point of continuity between the Italian and domestic halves of the novel. Tess Cosslett speaks of Forster's attempt to access a more authentic version of Italy that exists outside the prepackaged Grand Tour, arguing that he places "a new stress on the pagan, the countryside and the people" to enable Italy to serve as "a space of spiritual transformation" (2009, 326). Amanda Peat has similarly suggested that Beebe—as both a "member of the church" and a "humanitarian"—is a "linking point between Freddie and George, England and Italy" (2003, 8). One can hardly disagree that something decidedly Hellenic underlies this charismatic moment of play at the lake. Returning once again to Pater's description of Winckelmann, one could say that the bathers exhibit a unity with themselves, their physical nature and the outward world, which collapses their spectatorial distance from life. However, neither Italy, George nor the Reverend Beebe are responsible for this moment—it happens in spite of them. The venture to the Sacred Lake is initiated by Freddy, the one member of the party who has not traveled to Italy.

Italy functions in the novel as an agent of spectacle and exists for the characters merely as a collection of views and objects. When Cecil declares Lucy's trip to Italy a success, it is in terms of obtaining the cultural literacy that will advance her assimilation into London society. The narrator characterizes Mrs. Vyse's experience of Italy in terms of "the museum that represented Italy to her," and during a discussion in which Lucy confuses the names of two painters, Cecil accuses her of "forgetting her Italy" (Forster [1908] 1986, 377, 399). "Italy" is a metonym for art and culture in these formulations. Further, Peat's argument that the bathing scene reconciles Christian and humanist sensibilities is not borne out by Beebe's actions during the remainder of the novel. Even after his experience of Hellenic liberation at the Sacred Lake, Beebe judges Lucy harshly for breaking her engagement to Cecil and abets her plan to abandon George and flee to Greece. Our last glimpse of Beebe finds him lingering voyeuristically beyond the window of the Honeychurches' drawing room to observe a moment of family intimacy between Mrs. Honeychurch and her children. He labels the scene as an instance of "*santa conversazione*" (431), an artistic convention in paintings of the Madonna and Child. Beebe's impulse to inscribe this moment within his cultural literacy of the Italian Renaissance illustrates his impotent spectatorial relationship to domestic life.

74   E. BARNABY

Instead of looking to the Sacred Lake to yoke together the two halves of *A Room with a View*, I contend that the revival of Hellenic humanism in this scene is intended to contrast with the tourists' consumption of Italian culture and is not an extension of it. Unlike Sue Bridehead's juxtaposition of the pagan statues and crucifix in *Jude the Obscure* (a gesture that maroons her in relativism), Forster's narrator mingles pagan iconography and sacramental language from the Catholic Mass in a non-historicist, Pico-like moment of simultaneity such that neither perspective is vindicated over the other. In a pastiche akin to the Situationist *détournement*, baptismal immersion in a lake-turned-"chalice" conveys "benediction" on bathers who are also described as the "nymphs in Götterdämmerung" and "Michelangelesque" (Forster [1908] 1986, 383). This scene shuns continuity with the iconophilia and antiquarianism of the characters' experience of Italy. They "forgot Italy," we are told, and fully inhabit themselves and their surroundings in the present moment (384). The spontaneous pleasure of the bathers—who are not viewing objects, consuming culture, or philosophizing—coincides with the cyclical return of the vernal pool that momentarily suspends the spectacle of historicized, "irreversible" dynastic time by which Forster's characters are otherwise dominated.

The frivolity ends when Cecil, Lucy and Mrs. Honeychurch happen upon the bathers. After the pond has receded, on whom do the lasting effects of its "benediction" fall? Freddy needed no conversion, Cecil chauvinistically shields the ladies' eyes, and Beebe attempts to hide his nakedness until the contingent passes. George, however, is empowered to express his love to Lucy, and Lucy is empowered to end her inauthentic relationship with Cecil. Lucy's breakup with Cecil repudiates all false relationships predicated exclusively on the consumption of culture and the conflation of images with living objects. She accuses Cecil of insulating himself from the world with "art and books and music" when "people are more glorious" (Forster [1908] 1986, 418). The narrator characterizes Lucy's self-assertion as a movement from the visual to the tactile and describes her transformation from "a Leonardo" to "a living woman [...] with qualities that even eluded art" (417). In asserting her freedom from Cecil's chauvinism, however, Lucy feels compelled to reject George, as well, in order to transform herself into the image of liberated womanhood that she has articulated. Her consciousness of spectacle undergoes one final act of recuperation from which she nearly fails to escape. For the moment, ideology continues to trump authentic freedom, and the narrator explains how Lucy "joined the vast armies of the benighted, who follow neither the heart nor the brain, and march to their destiny by catch words" (419).

Indicting Lucy for having "sinned against Eros and against Pallas Athene," Forster couches this final setback in Lucy's bout with spectacle as an anti-Hellenic retreat into asceticism that recalls Sue's retreat from Jude after Father Time's suicide (Forster [1908] 1986, 420). Abetted by Reverend Beebe, Lucy hatches a plan to suppress her love for George by accompanying a pair of spinsters whom she met in Florence on a trip to Greece. She purchases a new guidebook and deliberately resumes the role of tourist in which she began the novel (434). Lucy actively cultivates a spectatorial relationship to Hellenic culture, frequenting galleries of Greek sculpture in the British Museum and borrowing a dictionary of mythology to memorize the names of gods and goddesses in preparation for this next leg of her Grand Tour. She uses the spectacle to numb herself, deliberately "disordering the very instrument of life" by enveloping herself in art and books just as she had accused Cecil of doing (435). Lucy even begins to exhibit Cecil's ennui, growing impatient with her mother and suddenly criticizing Windy Corners as stiflingly provincial.

Lucy's encounter with Emerson, Sr., at the end of the novel constitutes a showdown with the spectacle. They meet in Beebe's library at the rectory just before she is to leave for Greece. Much like the Emersons' drawing room, the library is lined from floor to ceiling on all sides with books that crowd out lived experience with theorized life, except that Beebe's books are bound uniformly in "acrid theological blue" (Forster [1908] 1986, 440). Emerson acknowledges to Lucy his error in attempting to liberate his son from the asceticism of medieval Christianity by steeping him instead in Romantic philosophy and poetry (440). Like Ruskin's attempt to steer the tourist away from Murray and Baedecker, Emerson, Sr., had simply added to the "wall of text" separating George from the real. Emerson confesses to Lucy that "I used to think I could teach young people the whole of life, but I know better now" (442). Lucy later credits him, however, with enabling her to "see the whole of everything at once" (445), a phrase which aptly describes literary realism's recalibration of "life in value" and "life in time" that Forster describes in *Aspects of the Novel* and anticipates Debord's concept of *détournement* through which ideological statements about the real are restored to a holistic context.

Lucy elopes with George and they end up back in the very room at the Pension Bertolini from which Lucy first gazed out upon Florence. This time, however, the scene focuses on the discussion taking place inside the room, as she and George ponder the fragile consciousness of the spectacle that they have achieved. All that enters the window is sound—not the view—as the cries of street peddlers, the rush of local life and the roar of the river Arno punctuate their conversation. This shift from views to sounds parallels Forster's rhetorical move in his final lecture at Cambridge to reframe the realist perspective within a musical trope instead of a visual one. Forster criticizes Henry James for sacrificing realism in order to achieve a well-wrought "beauty" that is, in Forster's words, "not worth attaining" ([1927] 1954, 233). He compares reading James' fiction to viewing a painting or sculpture—an experience that he characterizes as one of "completion" and "rounding off." In contrast, Forster identifies a sense of continuity between realist fiction and lived experience that he describes as the sensation of "opening out" and "expansion" which accompanies the silence that follows an orchestral performance. He likens the characters and plot of realist fiction to the notes and passages of a musical composition in that they retain their "individual freedom" while contributing to the "rhythm of the whole" (242).[2]

Forster's decision to conclude the novel with Lucy and George honeymooning in Florence has understandably led some critics to fixate on the novel's portrayal of Lucy's sexual initiation. Mature visuality rivals mature sexuality, however, as the primary concern of Lucy's coming of age—the dismantling of an isolating wall of images that separates Lucy from an authentic encounter with the real. In this manner, *A Room with a View* reinterprets the *bildungsroman* and the trope of the *ingénue* for the post-industrial age. The debate over who should have the room with a view and the moment when George throws Lucy's bloodied postcards into the river prove to be more dynamic and pivotal than their first kiss. I take issue with John Colmer's complaint that it is both "paradoxical" and "illogical" that Forster "retains marriage as the happy climax" to the novel, with the result being "a certain falsity of tone that impairs its ending" (1982, 118). Theirs is not the order-restoring marriage of a Jacobean comedy, nor is *A Room with a View*—despite its Italian themes—a latter-day *opera buffa*. The marriage at the conclusion of a comic work typically mends a trivial rift in the social fabric or celebrates the momentary triumph of love over local obstacles. In this case, Lucy and George have alienated the Honeychurches and the community at Windy Corners through their secret courtship, various deceptions, her broken engagement and their elopement. Furthermore, the specter of Lucy's cousin Charlotte looms over the couple's final conversation. While Charlotte may have sided momentarily with Eros in facilitating Lucy's encounter with Emerson, Sr., in the rectory, Charlotte is otherwise abandoned along with Cecil and Beebe as the spectacle's collateral damage. The novel is more realist than comic in the sense that it responds constructively to the problem of spectacle without claiming to provide any permanent or generalized solution to the experience of alienation in modern society. One should expect Lucy and George to continue to struggle with spectacle in their married life that follows, as Forster (1958) describes in an essay titled "A View without a Room" published on the fiftieth anniversary of the novel's publication.

Forster himself acknowledged that the consciousness of the real advanced by literary realism is prone to recuperation by the culture industry. Anticipating Debord's concept of "pseudo-cyclical consciousness," Forster criticizes literary "pseudo-scholarship" that reinforces the very imbalance of "life in time" and "life in value" that realist fiction attempts to correct.[3] Forster argues that excess historicism—an overemphasis on literary chronology and the novel "in time"—reduces the text's horizon of meaning to its moment of production and proliferates artificial boundaries between authors and works that resonate across time. Conversely, he further argues that excess structuralism—an overemphasis on literary form and the novel "in value"—abstracts fiction from the ethical sphere that informs it, fragmenting its performance into a collection of aesthetically isolated readings. Instead, Forster urges the scholar to "visualize the English novelists not as floating down the stream" in linear succession, "but as seated together in a room, a circular room, a sort of British museum reading room, all writing their novels simultaneously" ([1927] 1954, 28). Like Pico's authentically humanist scholarship, Forster's concept of the writing circle recognizes the historicity of the text and its moment of production, but allows for both a linear and cyclical experience of literary tradition that is true to the manner in which the past and present mutually inform one another. Forster's model for criticism is neither predominantly historicist nor structuralist, but—as Emerson, Sr., does for Lucy—allows us to "see the whole of everything at once."

Forster concludes his Eton lectures with the proposition that realist fiction affords the reader an authentic encounter with lived experience and the formation of consciousness. Literary realism signifies for Forster a distinctly modern technology—a refined "instrument of contemplation" that updates Shakespeare's mirror-held-up-to-nature with a "new coat of quicksilver" ([1927] 1954, 246). Forster suggests that it is even possible for this "instrument of contemplation to contemplate itself," observing that realism pushes fiction to the limits of representation and warning that its full realization would bring about "the end of imaginative literature" itself (244, 245). There is a flourish at the conclusion of the lecture that stakes out a manifesto for art such as one might expect to hear from the Situationists. Forster calls upon the writers of modern fiction to expose the dynamics of spectacle through their realism, while chastising critics of modern fiction for inserting a spectatorial distance between the reader and the text by affixing realism to its place in cultural history as a nineteenth-century aesthetic form.

NOTES

1. See Buzard (1993) regarding the legacy of the Grand Tour in late-nineteenth-century England.
2. Hutcheon (1982) questions the philosophical precision with which Forster employs musical tropes. Building upon Stephen Spender's analysis of the tension between classical aesthetic categories and an impressionist subjectivity in the criticism of Eliot, Joyce and Pound, Hutcheon points to a similar ambivalence between "objective form" and "subjective responses" in Forster's "application of musical motifs to criticism of the literature" (96–7). However, Forster's recurring argument in *Aspects of the Novel* that literary realism critiques the spectatorial distance to which modern culture is prone suggests instead that the significance of the trope of realist "rhythms" lies not in the opposition between musicality as a structuralist or reception-oriented impulse, but in the moving beyond an opticentric or scopophilic model for understanding realism.
3. Heath's analysis of the concept of "pseudo-scholarship" reinforces this connection between Forster and Debord. Heath rigorously defines his own role as critic so as to avoid participating in the dynamics of spectacle, noting his intent to "describe the experience embodied in the novel and not counterfeit it with additional layers of critical interpretation" (1994, 393). For Heath, Forster's realist fiction is a place to observe "incomplete and segregated selves masquerade[ing] as the whole story"—a concept taken nearly verbatim from Debord's account of how ideology functions within the spectacle. Debord argues that the cyclical experience of time is displaced by a falsely linear experience of time within the spectacle, and Heath similarly describes Forster's characters as engaged in the struggle to achieve an authentic balance between "a consecutive life in time" and a "self that flows 'in common' with other deep, timeless selves" (1994, 407). However, Heath accounts for Forster's engagement with spectacle almost entirely on the level of language, focusing on narratorial intrusion instead of the novel's depiction of industrialized visual culture.

REFERENCES

Ardis, Ann. 2007. Hellenism and the Lure of Italy. In *The Cambridge Companion to E.M. Forster*, ed. David Bradshaw, 62–76. Cambridge: Cambridge University Press.

Buzard, James. 1993. *The Beaten Track; European Tourism, Literature, and the Ways to Culture, 1800–1918*. Oxford: Oxford University Press.

Byerly, Alison. 2013. *Are We There Yet?: Virtual Travel and Victorian Realism*. Ann Arbor: University of Michigan.

Colmer, John. 1982. Marriage and Personal Relations in Forster's Fiction. In *E.M. Forster: Centenary Revaluations*, ed. Judith Scherer and Robert K. Martin, 113–123. London/Basingstoke: Macmillan Press.

Cosslett, Tess. 2009. Revisiting Fictional Italy, 1887–1908: Vernon Lee, Mary Ward, and E.M. Forster. *English Literature in Transition (1880–1920)* 52 (3): 312–328.

Debord, Guy. (1967) 1995. *The Society of the Spectacle*. Trans. Donald Nicholson-Smith. New York: Zone Books.

Forster, E.M. (1908) 1986. *A Room with a View*. New York: Signet.

———. (1927) 1954. *Aspects of the Novel*. New York: Harcourt, Brace & Company.

———. 1958. *A View Without a Room*. New York: Albondocani Press.

Hardy, Thomas. (1888) 1997. The Profitable Reading of Fiction. In *Selected Poetry and Non-Fictional Prose*, ed. Peter Widdowson, 242–254. Houndmills/London: Macmillan Press.

———. 1895. *Jude the Obscure*. Riverside Edition, 1965. Boston: Houghton Mifflin.

Heath, Jeff. 1994. Kissing and Telling: Turning Round in *A Room with a View*. *Twentieth Century Literature* 40 (4): 393–433.

Hutcheon, Linda. 1982. 'Sublime Noise' for Three Friends: Music in the Critical Writings of E.M. Forster, Roger Fry and Charles Mauron. In *E.M. Forster: Centenary Revaluations*, ed. Judith Scherer and Robert K. Martin, 84–98. London/Basingstoke: Macmillan Press.

Macherey, Pierre. (1966) 1978. *A Theory of Literary Production*. Trans. Geoffrey Wall. London: Routledge.

Pater, Walter. (1893) 1980. *The Renaissance: Studies in Art and Poetry*, ed. Donald Hill. Berkeley: University of California Press.

Peat, Alexandra. 2003. Modern Pilgrimage and the Authority of Space in Forster's *A Room with a View* and Woolf's *The Voyage Out*. *Mosaic* 36 (4): 139–153.

Sontag, Susan. 1977. *On Photography*. New York: Farrar, Strauss & Giroux.

CHAPTER 4

"You've stirred in me my unacted part"— Historical Pageantry as Spectacle in Virginia Woolf's *Between the Acts*

Virginia Woolf positions literary realism as a middle way between pure exteriority and pure interiority, outlining in "The Narrow Bridge of Art" a new literary form that portrays not only "people's relations to each other [...] as the novel has hitherto done," but also "the relation of the mind to general ideas and its soliloquy in solitude" ([1927] 1966, 224, 225). Locating realism at the intersection of individual consciousness and collective understandings of the world, Woolf uses fiction to "take the mould of that queer conglomeration of incongruous things – the modern mind" (226). Just as Hardy describes *Jude the Obscure* as an attempt to give "shape and coherence to a series of seemings, or personal impressions," Woolf explains in her essay "Modern Fiction" that the novel "traces the pattern, however disconnected and incoherent in appearance, which each sight or incident scores upon the consciousness" ([1925] 1984, 150). Like Forster, Woolf recognized that certain fiction falsifies the reader's understanding of the real. She criticizes naturalistic literature because it objectifies the real as the material environment. At the same time, she criticizes experimental modernist literature for subjectifying the real as an incommunicable mental abstraction. In doing so, she parallels Forster's distinction between fiction that suffers from an overly objective portrayal of "life in time" and an overly subjective portrayal of "life in value," categories which inform Woolf's critique of pageantized historical consciousness that I will explore in this chapter.

© The Author(s) 2018
E. Barnaby, *Realist Critiques of Visual Culture*,
https://doi.org/10.1007/978-3-319-77323-0_4

Despite cultivating a distinct literary style from that of Hardy and Forster, Woolf practices and theorizes literary realism in concert with their ethical concern for the "vital problem" of spectacle in modern industrial society. The characters in Virginia Woolf's fiction often struggle to achieve an authentically shared consciousness that can bridge the chasms of interiority separating their everyday lives. Her exploration of the modern mind addresses head-on the internalized "entanglement" that Pater regards as the greatest threat to authentic consciousness and which Debord describes as the spectacle. Woolf's critical essays suggest that she is less concerned with the novel's aesthetic form than with its ethics of representation. She engages in a decades-long dialog with Forster over how to represent lived experience in fiction most authentically (Henley 1989). She chides "modern poetic playwrights" who set their works in the past and refuse to "express the thoughts, the visions, the sympathies and antipathies which are actually turning and tumbling their brains" because "poetic decencies would be violated" ([1927] 1966, 221). Woolf contends that there is no single method for achieving realism, as long as a novel enables the author to "come closer to life" and the reader to come "closer to the novelist's intention" ([1925] 1984, 150, 152).

Between the Acts, set on the day of a history pageant at an English country manor, provides a particularly lucid context through which to explore the phenomenon of spectatorship. The literal presence of pageantry in *Between the Acts* illuminates a more general pageantized orientation toward the real in other parts of the novel, as well as in Woolf's earlier novels such as *Orlando* and *The Years*. In addition, the intersection of dynastic history, lived experience and spectatorial distance that Woolf stages in *Between the Acts* places Woolf's novel into dialog with T.S. Eliot's *The Family Reunion* and Hardy's *The Dynasts*. These connections, which I will explore later in this chapter, reinforce Woolf's place in this study as an author who uses literary realism to depict the spectacle's flattening of consciousness.

Certain critical treatments of *Between the Acts* have reduced it to a satire of the so-called "pageant craze" instigated by Louis Napoleon Parker in England at the turn of the twentieth century,[1] or to a polemic against fascism on the eve of the Second World War.[2] Parker's celebrated productions no doubt inform Woolf's fictional pageant, and fighter planes passing overhead at the end of the pageant indeed invoke the specter of war. However, *Between the Acts* is concerned more broadly with a pageantizing mindset rooted in the same false consciousness of revived culture that

Hardy identifies with the Gothic Revival and Forster identifies with the Grand Tour. To demonstrate this point, I will turn outward from the pageant portrayed in the novel to examine other more spontaneous acts of spectatorship that the characters undertake. I will then analyze the production itself in order to articulate a more nuanced role for the pageant-master Miss La Trobe that recognizes the artist's unique struggle with the spectacle she attempts to critique—a knotty dynamic that Debord is particularly suited to unravel.

Between the Acts stands apart from previous satires of Parker's pageants as an instance of meta-spectacle. Two earlier treatments of the modern historical pageant—*Brother Copas* by Sir Arthur Thomas ("Q") Quiller-Couch in 1911 and *A Glastonbury Romance* by John Cowper Powys in 1932—lay bare the reductive historical narratives, facades of class unity and megalomaniacal directors of Parker's productions. Woolf, however, does not merely satirize components of La Trobe's pageant in this manner, but uses the pageant production to foreground the experience of spectatorial distance that afflicts her characters, including the pageant-master La Trobe herself. The incongruity between their lived experience and the various discourses and visibilities spliced together by the pageant epitomizes the alienated reality of the spectacle. Like Lucy Honeychurch's experiences as a tourist, the pageant temporarily heightens their consciousness of this alienated reality. They begin to recognize two key insights about historical consciousness that Debord would later articulate in *Society of the Spectacle*, namely, that "the pseudo-events that vie for attention in the spectacle's dramatizations have not been lived by those who are thus informed about them," whereas "everything really lived has no relation to society's official version of irreversible time" ([1967] 1995, 157).

The spectacle maroons Woolf's characters between two inauthentic relationships to the real. On the one hand, certain characters pageantize their own lived experience as a form of illusory participation in the spectacle's mirage of "paralyzed history" and "paralyzed memory" (Debord [1967] 1995, 158). Engaging in what Debord describes as the "abandonment of any history founded in historical time," these characters distort their consciousness in order to participate in the spectacle's version of the real. Other characters recognize and resent their alienated condition as spectators of a false reality. However, they acquiesce to the spectacle as a universal condition instead of an historical phenomenon specific to industrial society. Debord attributes the spectacle's immunity from critique to the fact that "individual lived experience of a cut-off-everyday life remains

84 E. BARNABY

bereft of language or concept" and "lacks any critical access to its own antecedents, which are nowhere recorded" (157). While La Trobe's pageant itself fails to provide the "language or concept" to elevate the fictional audience to critical consciousness, Woolf's realist restatement of La Trobe's pageant does make visible to the reader the "cut-off-everyday life" of her characters and thus disrupts the reader's own spontaneous experience of spectacle. As with *Jude the Obscure* and *A Room with a View*, *Between the Acts* participates in the "progressive or critical realism" that Jameson seeks from modern fiction, as opposed to realistic novels that merely "reflect or express the phenomenology of life under capitalism" with a sense of inevitability (1981, 134).

The novel opens the evening before an annual folk pageant hosted by the Oliver family at their estate, Pointz Hall. Patriarch Bartholomew Oliver describes to a local gentleman farmer and his wife the planned location of a cesspool that will bring modern sanitation to their village. The pageant mindset manifests immediately as Bartholomew incorporates the cesspool project into an historical survey of the English countryside based on the site's proximity to a Roman road. He describes the cesspool as the latest in a series of "scars" on the landscape "made by the Britons; by the Romans; by the Elizabethan manor house; and by the plough, when they ploughed the hill to grow wheat in the Napoleonic wars" (Woolf [1941] 1970, 4). Bartholomew unifies these developments within a pageant of interventions in the landscape. He exemplifies Debord's concept of pseudo-cyclical consciousness by concealing the industrial displacement of agrarian culture that concludes this sequence and collapsing historical difference across two millennia of society's relationship to the land. The narrator subsequently engages in a similar act of pseudo-cyclical consciousness when quoting a description of the grounds at Pointz Hall from a guidebook published in 1833. Concluding that what was true in "1833 was true in 1939," the narrator asserts that the land "had changed only in this – the tractor had to some extent superseded the plough" (52). The observer's relationship to the land had most certainly been transformed in radical ways by industrialization during this hundred years, a reality that is suppressed by the seeming insignificance with which the narrator characterizes the substitution of the tractor for the plough.

In his 1927 essay titled "The Pageantry of Civilization," Leonard Woolf criticizes modern historical practice for concealing social transformations in this very manner. Describing the transfer of ownership of history from the nobility to the common man after the French Revolution, Leonard laments that this shift yielded no authentic historical consciousness of the reconfiguration of society that had occurred, but merely a change in subject matter from the "cavalcade of kings and great men" to a "panorama of ordinary life" (Woolf 1927, 134, 127). His observation anticipates Debord's argument in *Society of the Spectacle* that an ideological "irreversible" time had replaced the authentic dimensions of cyclical and dynastic time within the industrialized social psyche. According to Leonard, the democratized pageant of history suppresses popular consciousness of social transformation beneath an "infinite series of small changes" on the level of material culture. Antiquarian detail and universalizing sentiment conspire to falsify history as being "almost changeless" in appearance (Woolf 1927, 131); hence Debord's use of the term "pseudo-cyclical." Debord similarly points to the desire of the bourgeois class to arrest the process of historical change after its own ascendency, which it achieves by depicting the industrial revolution that brought it to prominence as the teleological end of history ([1967] 1995, 143–4). Jameson's critique of literary realism is another version of this argument that indicts the modern novel for functioning as a "containment strategy" that objectifies post-industrial bourgeois society as a timeless, stable reality.

Bartholomew's insinuation of the cesspool and the narrator's insinuation of the tractor into a timeless landscape untouched by industrialization are examples of this pageantizing mindset that Leonard Woolf critiques. These moments in *Between the Acts* are echoed by numerous advertisements in souvenir brochures for actual pageant productions of the era. These advertisements invoke the pageantizing mindset to assimilate industrialization within the continuum of feudal dynastic history. In the program for the Colchester Pageant of 1909, for example, full-page advertisements sponsored by the Colchester Fishery Board and Essex & Suffolk Fire & Accident provide aristocratic genealogies of the town's local oyster trade and mutual insurers (*Colchester* 1909). An ad in the program for the Chester Historical Pageant of 1910 sponsored by Welsbach incandescent gas burners presents the reader with a series of illustrations titled "Ancient Light in Modern Form, An Incident in the Pageantry of Light." Drawn in the style of medieval stained glass windows, one panel depicts "the good Knight Welsbach presenting the king with a globe of brilliant light" produced by modern science. Another ad in the Chester program hails the role of the United Gas Company in the evolution of domestic life (Hawtrey 1910). Juxtaposing images of a bedraggled Maori woman struggling to cook over a hot spring and an urbane contemporary woman presiding over a gas stove, the ad suggests that more efficient technologies of cooking is all that separates these two figures across time.

Leonard Woolf's critique of historical materialism is paralleled by Virginia Woolf's critique of Arnold Bennett and the literary naturalists. Leonard seeks history not in ledgers of what people bought and sold to each other, but in social relationships—a "pageant of what went on in the heads of ordinary men and women whether they were the Lords of Lyme and Moncoffer or village grocers or middle-class young ladies" (Woolf 1927, 134). In other words, he—like the Situationists—seeks a critical perspective on the experience of everyday life. Virginia performs just such a "pageant of consciousness" alongside the historical pageant in *Between the Acts*. That is to say, the true pageant at Pointz Hall is not La Trobe's production itself, but the parade of characters brought into relationship by the occasion of La Trobe's production. Bartholomew Oliver, recently retired from the Indian Civil Service, exhibits a stoic discomfort in his new role as steward of the family estate. To cope with his transition from empire-builder to spectator of dynastic history, he takes up landscape painting, a genre that has itself been identified as an extension of the imperialist gaze.[3] Bartholomew's widowed sister, Lucy Swithin, seeks out vicarious connections to history as she struggles to reconcile her creationist worldview with the decentering timescale of geological history and the threat of annihilation posed by modern warfare.[4] Bartholomew's son, Giles, resents his career as a London stockbroker, which he feels compelled to pursue in order to support the family estate. A self-conscious slave to the "ghost of convention," Giles maintains a façade of propriety while seething impotently against his role in the family tableau and "the conglomeration of things" that "pressed you flat; held you fast" (Woolf [1941] 1970, 47). Giles' wife, Isabella, is torn between her domestic identity and artistic sensibility. She conceals her poetry in a journal bound like a household account ledger and is portrayed throughout the novel as an abstracted spectator of her own life.

Much of the novel focuses outside the actual performance of La Trobe's pageant, and it is during those moments that Woolf is able to explore her characters' spontaneous and unconscious experience of spectatorship. The day of the pageant, unexpected visitors—Mrs. Manresa and her younger friend William Dodge—stop at Pointz Hall while looking for a place to picnic and are invited to lunch with the family. Bartholomew and his sister Lucy Swithin promptly begin to pageantize Pointz Hall for their guests, rehearsing family lore, formally presenting the view of the grounds cited in local guidebooks, and offering a tour of the house.

During the luncheon, Bartholomew takes on the role of a docent as he describes two antique portraits that hang on the dining room wall. One is a painting of a male ancestor that has accrued a paratext of humorous anecdotes. The image is afforded a logo-centric masculinity by the narrator, who notes of the figure that "He had a name ... He was a talk producer" (Woolf [1941] 1970, 36). The other portrait is of a woman who holds no historical connection to the family, but had been purchased by Bartholomew for purely aesthetic reasons. Like another antique portrait that hangs atop the grand stair and a glass case containing a watch that had stopped a bullet at Waterloo, this portrait is an imposter in the family pageant, a simulacrum of aristocratic history that has been acquired and displayed by the Olivers rather than lived by them. Described mainly in terms of her shape and color, the female figure resists incorporation within the dynastic narrative and paralyzes the conversation. Bartholomew's ability to caption the male portrait provides a temporary illusion of participation in history, but the female portrait cannot be captioned and confronts the luncheon party with a moment of pure spectatorship that borders on voyeurism. Dodge's propensity to gaze at the image is called out by the narrator as a feminizing trait, recalling Emerson's chauvinistic assertion in *A Room with a View* that "women like looking at a view; men don't" (Forster [1908] 1986, 282).

Having thus been "led down paths of silence" by the portrait, the party attempts to rejoin the sphere of action by moving outside, where they are immediately recuperated as spectators by the view of the landscape. Giles dutifully assembles chairs in a semi-circle "so that the view might be shared" as in a gallery or amphitheater (Woolf [1941] 1970, 52). Placed before the landscape in this manner, the characters are once again threatened by a lapse in conversation and attempt to remedy this by labeling the view. Bartholomew sublimates this tension between word and image into an aesthetic question for discussion, asking the group to consider why poetry is typically privileged over the visual arts in common cultural literacy. Several of them quote lines from Shakespeare and Keats in the attempt to prove his point, but the discussion fails to take root, reinforcing Debord's observation that "culture is the locus of the search for lost unity" and that cultural literacy merely attests to "the fact that the real language of communication has been lost" ([1967] 1995, 180, 187). The narrator observes, "How tempting, how very tempting, to let the view triumph," as the group is once again confronted with the pure immediacy of the present moment (Woolf [1941] 1970, 66). Manresa suddenly blurts out

"What a view!" as if to reassert discursive control, but no one answers her. As with the portrait in the dining room, their impotence before the mute image of the landscape occasions great "irritation" and "rage" for Giles, who resents being forced to entertain "old fogies who sit and looked at views after coffee and cream when the whole of Europe – over there – was bristling on the brink of destruction" (53).

Finally, Swithin announces ("as if," we are told, "the exact moment for speech had come") that it is time for a tour of the house (Woolf [1941] 1970, 67). She reasserts the spectacle of irreversible progress through narrative and procession as she wends her way upward from one floor to the next. Swithin confides in Dodge her vicarious existence within the spectacle, explaining that "we have other lives ... we live in others ... we live in things" (70). "Words raised themselves and became symbolical," as she captions each room and its furnishings with quotidian details of aristocratic life, all of which she elevates to sacred, ritualistic significance. Straining to assert Pointz Hall's lineage within the dynastic record, Swithin recalls the reception of notable guests whose names she has forgotten. Passing by a bookcase, she alludes to "the poets from whom we descend by way of the mind." She points out the bed in which she was born and presents the nursery to Dodge with such solemnity that she "seemed to say" it was the "cradle of our race." Breathless from climbing flights of stairs, Swithin ceases to narrate. Their illusion of participation in a communal "life in time" dissipates, and she and Dodge become conscious once again of their identity as spectators. They catch sight of each other's eyes in a high mirror and are temporarily reduced to disembodied agents of seeing: "cut off from their bodies, their eyes smiled, their bodiless eyes, at their eyes in the glass" (71).

Hearing noises outside, Swithin and Dodge move to a window and observe the throng of pageant-goers assembling on the patio and lawn. The audience members themselves take on the aspect of an historical pageant, appearing to Swithin as parading proxies of the village's oldest families from the aristocracy and peasantry alike. The narrator remarks upon various newcomers and absentees within this historical "roll call" and attributes both phenomena to industrial transformation. Woolf is careful to note that many of the newcomers have bought their way into the village with industrial wealth, "bringing the old houses up to date" and "adding bathrooms" (Woolf [1941] 1970, 74). The narrator also notes the "unattached floating residents" who are introduced by "the building of a car factory and of an aerodrome in the neighbourhood" (74–5).[5] On the other hand, certain long-time residents are notably unrepresented at the folk ritual, having been drawn off by industrial-age diversions such as "the motor bike, the motor bus, and the movies" (75). Woolf momentarily reframes the spectators of La Trobe's production as actors in the broader "pageant of civilization" playing out that day at Pointz Hall. Swithin's act of watching the audience of La Trobe's pageant as they congregate makes the condition of spectatorship visible to the reader. It is similar to a scene in *A Room with a View* cited in the previous chapter, in which Lucy Honeychurch watches from her balcony as a tourist in a glass-enclosed tram takes in sights of Florence.

With the audience seated and Woolf's fictional pageant set to begin, I turn now to the pageant-master La Trobe's relationship to fascism. La Trobe has been identified by critics as a stand-in for Parker and even Hitler, but there is much evidence in the text to contradict the notion that she is a propagandist. She is not a satirical effigy of Parker, as her production subverts his principles in several fundamental ways. La Trobe aspires to alert her audience to its passive reception of a mediated reality, but she fails to recognize that the pageant through which she conveys this message is itself an alienated medium that further mires her audience in spectatorship instead of liberating them from it. Indeed, La Trobe's work suffers immediate recuperation as spectacle in the same manner that Debord attributes to Dada and other iconoclastic gestures which fail to step outside the logic of consumption that they critique.

To appreciate La Trobe's true role in Woolf's critique of spectacle, one must understand folk pageantry's evolution from a pre-modern festival into Parker's modern didactic exhibition. Traditional folk pageantry consisted of carnivalesque parades in which mythological and allegorical figures from legend and lore mingled anachronistically with historical figures.[6] State-sponsored city pageants and Lord Mayor's Shows of the seventeenth and eighteenth centuries gradually introduced themes of industrial progress and imperial triumph that ushered in the pageant's modern ideological function.[7] By the time of the Lord Mayor's Show of 1884, pamphlets supplemented the visual display to make clear that its didactic "purpose" was to "bring before the minds of the public some of the glorious traditions of our ancient city – to show how, from time almost immemorial, the Corporation has been both loyal to the Crown and true to the People" (Withington 1963, vol. 2, 122–3). Seeking to disentangle pageantry from these overtly political and commercial uses, Parker emphasized the pageant's antiquarian role as a means of preserving England's pre-industrial past. He revived a superficial folk element in his productions by soliciting large-scale involvement from the local population. In every other way, however, Parker reinforced the experience of pageantry as spectacle in Debord's sense of the term by exchanging its original cult value as an anarchical populist gesture for its exhibition value as a heritage museum.[8]

Combining the nationalistic didacticism of state-sponsored pageantry with the populist trappings of a festival, Parker's folk pageants exhibit a fascist air of engineered cultural unity. Alongside assertions that his pageants invoke a democratic spirit, Parker describes the ideal pageant-master as an autocrat "tempered by common sense" in the fashion of Benito Mussolini (Parker 1928, 284). Gilbert Hudson, the pageant-master of Parker's Yorkshire production, praises Parker's pageants for uniting "all classes and all sorts of people" and putting aside all "artificial restraints and enmities among them." This unity, however, bears no resemblance to Bakhtin's account of the medieval carnivalesque in which the classes participate mutually in a subversive moment of liberality. On the contrary, Parker's pageants are characterized by a "rational artistic manner" that Hudson credits with "the instructing of people how to entertain themselves [...] as communities" and "the awakening or creation of a communal historical sense" (Withington 1963, vol. 2, 203). In other words, the neo-folk pageant unites the classes as spectators of the performance of a shared past that they had never actually lived, but which they were now expected to embrace with nostalgia.

The aura of authentic folk pageantry is central to this illusion, and Parker describes the effort required to achieve a simulacrum of the festival's spontaneity. Noting that "the whole pageant must seem [...] to be extemporized; must, indeed, seem accidental," Parker warns that "the moment the audience becomes aware of stage management, you may be sure there is something wrong" (1928, 283). His success further depends upon an audience that is susceptible to his ahistorical folk-product. As with the neo-Gothic and neo-Hellenic impulses that Hardy and Forster critique in their fiction, Parker's neo-folk pageant cannot authentically revive a pre-industrial ethos, but instead feeds vampirically off of its remains. Hudson highlights this aspect of Parker's pageants when he observes that they are better received "in a small old-fashioned town [...] than in a larger and more commercialized place" because of the "better preservation of the old social traditions [and] feudal conditions." Hudson regards modern urban culture as hostile to pageantry because it has "not yet produced any unifying idea" to compensate for the feudal social structures that it displaced (Withington 1963, vol. 2, 204). This affirms, however, that pageantry is incapable of reviving such unity, but merely erects an illusory Maypole around which the likes of Bartholomew Oliver and Lucy Swithin, clinging to a mostly vanished way of life, can gather.

The unwilling members of the audience—particularly Giles, Isa and Dodge—writhe under the yoke of spectatorship. The neo-folk pageant does not merely fail to evoke for them an experience of social unity, but taunts them with idealized re-enactments of festival culture from Merrie Olde England that merely heighten their own sense of belatedness and spectatorial distance. Although Giles recognizes this pseudo-cyclical sham perpetrated by the pageant, he is tragically powerless to act upon it, prompting the narrator to describe him in Promethean terms as "manacled to a rock" and "forced passively to behold indescribable horror" (Woolf [1941] 1970, 60). At one point he recalls lines from a poem about a stricken deer that is "exiled from its festival, the music turned ironical" (85). One is reminded of young Jude Fawley's sentimental meditations on the more genuine life of the pre-industrial peasantry while he stands alone in a machine-ploughed field working as a human scarecrow. In spite of their shared alienation, Giles, Isa and Dodge remain separated and silenced within the audience. They exemplify the spectacle's atomized community that is "linked only by a one-way relationship to the very center that maintains their isolation from one another" (Debord [1967] 1995, 28, 29).

Even the willing participants, however, exhibit the automatism of those who have perpetuated a custom far beyond the point at which its cult value, to use Benjamin's term, has been exhausted. Woolf compares the unfolding events of the day to the inevitability of sequentially tolling bells, such that "as the first peals, you hear the second; as the second peals, you hear the third" (Woolf [1941] 1970, 21). Isa overhears the first line of a conversation between Swithin and Bartholomew on the morning of the pageant and is able to predict the remainder verbatim. "Every summer, for seven summers now," the narrator explains, "Isa had heard the same words; about the hammer and the nails; the pageant and the weather. [...] The same chime followed the same chime" (22). Woolf literalizes this repetition to highlight the pseudo-cyclical experience of clinging to a discourse because a form of expression more appropriate to the age has not yet emerged. Such conditions render the public particularly susceptible to the spectacle of folk culture, and Hudson's comments indicate that Parker preys upon this very scenario.

It is too simplistic, however, to equate the fascist dimensions of Parker's pageantry with La Trobe's intentions. La Trobe is more aptly described as a frustrated Brechtian dramaturge than a peddler of sentimental nationalism.[9] Unlike Parker, she seeks to impart to her audience an awareness of the constructed nature of historical reality and identity. In sympathy with Brecht's concept of "theater for the scientific age," La Trobe wants her audience to critique the situations depicted on stage instead of succumbing to a vicarious illusion of participation in the grand narrative of dynastic history. Consider La Trobe's reaction to Swithin's praise for the pageant during the first intermission. Swithin expresses her gratitude to La Trobe for the opportunity to transcend the narrowness of her life by making her feel like she "could have played Cleopatra." Loathe to have enabled such an escapist fantasy, LaTrobe reinterprets Swithin's remarks to reassure herself that she had moved Swithin beyond spectatorship: "'I might have been – Cleopatra,' Miss LaTrobe repeated. 'You've stirred in me my unacted part,' [Swithin] meant" (Woolf [1941] 1970, 153). In similar fashion, when a member of the audience grumbles "all that fuss about nothing" after an ironically histrionic scene from the "Age of Reason," La Trobe "glowed with glory" that "the voice had seen; the voice had heard," as if she had brought the audience to a moment of ethical insight and not simply aesthetic disappointment (138–9). These instances of self-delusion stem from La Trobe's simultaneous recognition of the spectacle and her isolation within it. She is desperate to share her consciousness of spectacle with the audience by inciting them to intervene critically in the process of pageant-making. The goal of her performance is to produce what Brecht describes as a "non-Aristotelian" catharsis. For Brecht, the catharsis of classical tragedy is an aesthetic illusion of unity that temporarily conceals the audience's alienation beneath a collective emotional purge, but leaves their spectatorial distance intact. Brecht's ethical catharsis seeks to transform the audience from alienated spectators of a mirage into active participants in the real ([1929] 1964; Benjamin [1939] 1969).

La Trobe's Brechtian principles are ineffectual, however. Instead of conditioning the audience as Brecht does to participate in his dismantling of the spectacle, she attempts in vain to transform them into even more perfect spectators so that, paradoxically, they can receive her critique of spectacle. Recognizing that long-engrained habits of spectatorship will require sustained effort to break, Brecht embeds his plays with alienation effects that disrupt the spectator's reverence for the production as a unified aesthetic object and intrude upon the actors' emotional hold over the spectator. La Trobe, on the other hand, obsessively engineers a moment of collective consciousness through supreme aesthetic unity, fretting constantly over any ripples in the production that might break the audience's concentration. Instead of disrupting the production in order to disrupt the act of spectatorship, La Trobe attempts to communicate her critique of spectatorship to an audience held in thrall by the performance itself. As the first intermission begins, La Trobe triumphs that "for one moment she held them together [...] for twenty-five minutes had made them see – a vision imparted was relief from agony" (Woolf [1941] 1970, 98). For the most part, however, LaTrobe panics constantly that her audience is "slipping the noose" and that her "illusion had failed," muttering "death, death, death" when awkward scene transitions and the eccentricities of the outdoor venue threaten to distract them (140, 180). Instead of engaging the audience from a critical perspective, she comes to despise it as an unpredictable variable within her theatrical calculus. At one point she indulges a rationalist fantasy about writing "the play"—a total and objective representation of the real—that dispenses with the audience entirely (180).

La Trobe's approach during these first three acts of the pageant backfires insofar as it merely reinforces the audience's passive role as spectators and evokes the very same fascist sensibility of Parker's pageants that she seeks to expose. Her amateur production's half-garbled lines, awkward silences, miscued soundtracks and outbursts from the gallery could all have functioned as Brechtian alienation effects if she provided the context for them to do so. However, the first half of La Trobe's performance is highly conventional and affords the audience neither the "language" nor "concept" (recalling Debord's words) to step back and critique the genre. She excerpts plays from successive literary periods to dramatize the passing eras, a common trope among pageants at the turn of the twentieth century.[10] In doing so, La Trobe replays the verbal and visual discourses of Merrie Olde England and the Elizabethan and Augustan ages with a literality that facilitates rather than disrupts the audience's antiquarian consumption of period diction and costume. Bartholomew and Lucy commit themselves to this occupation of the pageant-goer as part of their illusion of participating in the spectacle. "Our part [...] is to be the audience," Bartholomew solemnly explains—"a very important part too" (Woolf [1941] 1970, 59). Although Giles, Isa and Dodge resent this role, the rest of the audience bears witness to the pageant with cultish devotion, looking on "gently and approvingly without interrogation, for it seemed inevitable" (134).

The careful observer will note La Trobe's subversive gesture of representing each age with scenes from romances instead of the usual dynastic fare of military battles and political events. Her repetition of marriage plots in each act introduces a cyclical countercurrent of love and desire alongside the pageant's reductively linear portrayal of historical periods.[11] Nevertheless, other than a retired colonel in the audience who questions "what's history without the Army," La Trobe's initial experimentation with the content of the pageant fails to register with the audience. She further punctuates each act with a recurring (Greek) chorus of peasants who catalog the rise and fall of various empires and chant "all passes but we, all changes ... but we remain forever the same" (Woolf [1941] 1970, 139). Through this peasant chorus La Trobe reasserts another experience of cyclical time—that of agrarian culture—which is marginalized by pageantry's typical preoccupation with dynastic progress. However, the peasants' song is partially drowned out by a series of loud breezes so that instead of their commentary on the passing influence of empires, the audience hears "only a few great names – Babylon, Ninevah, Clytemnestra, Agamemnon, Troy" (139–40). Instead, this litany of monarchs and imperial seats reinforces the spectacle's "irreversible" experience of time that La Trobe sought to critique.

La Trobe's peasant chorus is a prime example of how Woolf's critique of spectacle differs from other satires of pageantry. The pageant-master in Q's *Brother Copas* makes use of a recurring chorus of monks whose "antique garb" is intended to invoke an experience of cyclical time for the audience. Brother Copas calls this out, noting that the continued presence of the mendicant order merely demonstrates the persistence of poverty, while the pageant otherwise reinforces a fundamentally linear experience of time. Q's narrator observes wryly that "for an hour Saxon followed Roman, Dane followed Saxon, Norman followed both" with the inevitability of "a tapestry swiftly, continuously unrolled" (1911, 289–90). Instead of mere satire, however, Woolf presents her readers with La Trobe's sincere attempt to convey a critique of linear time to the audience, but then also presents the manner in which the alienated medium of the pageant recuperates La Trobe's critique as an instance of spectacle itself.

Even in the absence of conspiratorial breezes that drown out crucial lines from the peasants' song, La Trobe's audience has been conditioned to tune out dissonance (both intentional and accidental) or reincorporate it into the pageant's false consciousness. Several intrusions of nature during La Trobe's production illustrate the power of the audience's impulse to participate in the pageant's spectacle of aesthetic unity. There are two moments when the stage sits empty for an extended period. As the crowd strains to hold its composure and La Trobe feels that she has lost the moment for good, a *deus ex machina* suddenly reconnects the audience with the universalizing sentiment of the pageant. The first instance is the result of a botched scene-change that inserts a significant pause in the action. In the interim, the "dumb yearning" of cows in a nearby field lowing over a misplaced calf is perceived by the audience as a "primeval voice" that "sounded loud in the ear of the present moment." The narrator explains that "the cows annihilated the gap; bridged the distance; filled in emptiness and continued the emotion" (Woolf [1941] 1970, 140–1). The second instance is an experimental "dose of pure realism" that La Trobe ham-handedly inflicts upon the audience. Having noted in the marginalia of her script to "try ten mins. of present time," La Trobe reproduces the material surface of the present moment with literality by simply abandoning the audience to contemplate the empty stage and the landscape beyond (179). This, however, conflates naturalism with realism in the same manner for which Woolf criticizes Arnold Bennett and merely reproduces *en masse* the awkward silence that overtakes the Olivers and their guests earlier that day on the patio after luncheon. This time a passing rain shower reunites the audience within a spontaneous homage to universal suffering. Embodying the falseness of this moment, drops of rain roll down Isa's cheeks like surrogate tears. Although she feels them "as if they were her own tears," they are the abstract tears of the spectacle, the artificiality of catharsis laid bare, a response to something she has not directly experienced: they were "all people's tears, weeping for all people" (180).

This participation of the natural environment in the unifying function of pageantry is noted in a variety of contexts beyond Woolf's novel. While Parker exerted strict control over all aspects of his productions, he recollects that their outdoor setting sometimes yielded serendipitous features that reinforced aesthetic unity, such as a timely clap of thunder during his pageant at Sherborne (1928, 298). In the preface to E.M. Forster's pageant "England's Pleasant Land"—which he staged in 1938 while Woolf was writing *Between the Acts* and which was published by the Woolfs' Hogarth Press in 1940—Forster describes similar "unrehearsed blessings" of the outdoor venue that complemented the action on stage. He recalls a "lovely flock of white pigeons, which descended on one occasion among the ghosts," as well as airplanes that "messed about overhead and anticipated the final desolation" (Forster 1940, 8). Even the satirical narrator of *Brother Copas* cannot resist romanticizing a flock of swallows that fly low over the audience as part of the pageant's unified consciousness, noting that they had "skimmed every summer's evening since English history began" (Quiller-Couch 1911, 298). Menacing aircraft and skimming swallows each make an appearance at the end of *Between the Acts*, as well.

I have focused to this point on the conventionality of La Trobe's pageant that renders her audience immune to her critique of spectatorship. As the production approaches the present day, however, its essentialized representations begin to chafe at the audience. Lucy Swithin initially embraces the pageant as a form of collective and externalized memory that enables her to stand alongside "the Elizabethans" and "the Augustans." She cannot, however, recognize herself among "the Victorians" and instead experiences an alienating disjunction between the pageant's representation and her own lived experience of that era. Unwilling to confront the implications of this discrepancy, Swithin recommits to the spectator's task of discerning the unity among all living things. She derives tenuous comfort from the idea that all is in harmony when "seen from a distance" by the eye of God—the same spectatorial distance that enabled her to appreciate the earlier scenes in the pageant (Woolf [1941] 1970, 175). Swithin clings to the pageant's illusion of unity, although her faith in that unity is shaken.

Parker was careful not to depict events in his pageants any closer to the present time than the Reformation in order to maintain the spectator's aesthetic disinterest (Withington 1963, vol. 2, 221–2). Q satirizes this characteristic of Parker's productions when the Merchester pageant-master informs Brother Copas that the Reformation has been omitted from the program in order to preserve the production's "unifying civic sense" (Quiller-Couch 1911, 204). Q's pageant proceeds instead with a musical interlude titled the "Ballet of Imperialist Expansion" that literally dances around any discursive examination of the empire question. Parker's avoidance of the present day exemplifies Debord's accusation that the bourgeoisie, having come to participate in the level of dynastic history once monopolized by the nobility, sought to freeze historical progress at the moment of its ascendency and immobilize the working class within the same cyclical experience of time as the agrarian peasantry. While the agrarian peasantry was authentically insulated from the experience of dynastic time, the aspirations of the working class, however, would need to be stunted through an engineered ignorance of historical change, or what

Debord describes as the "organized spectacle of error" ([1967] 1995, 177). Parker's didactic revival of the folk pageant participates in this engineered ignorance by truncating history in order to preserve an illusion of shared experience among the classes. Debord's concept of "immobilized history" achieves literality in the conventional *tableau vivant*—or living still-life—with which Parker concluded each of his productions. The tableau was typically followed by a recessional "march past" that buttressed the pageant's illusion of totality by parading the cast from each period before the audience in chronological order.[12] These gestures are ripe for Debord's critique of the spectacle's objectification of "irreversible time" that conflates the "progression through which history has unfolded" with "the object of that history" itself (74).

La Trobe's depiction of the Victorians begins to deviate sharply enough from Parker's conventions to allow for a truly Brechtian disruption of her pageant. Furthermore, La Trobe's subversion of the *tableau vivant* and march past at the end of her pageant collapses the aesthetic distance that had insulated the audience from her critique of spectacle during the first several acts. She engages in Brecht's technique of the "quotable gesture" and Debord's practice of *détournement,* each of which involves the repetition or restatement of a phrase, image or action so as to estrange it from conventional encounter and elevate it to critical sensibility. Instead of congealing into a statuesque pose that brings history to an artificial denouement, the actors in La Trobe's final tableau continue to move as they engage in a pantomime of building a wall. Her tableau aspires to Brecht's non-Aristotelian catharsis by reminding the audience that history is forever incomplete and entreating them to rise from their seats and join the world of action. La Trobe then replaces Parker's chronological recession with one in which the entire cast converges upon the audience while repeating lines at random from all parts of the pageant. This paradigm of convergence counters the pageantizing mindset with a syncretizing one and recalls Pico's unmodern humanist impulse to recognize the simultaneous claim of competing historical discourses on the present moment. La Trobe concludes the pageant with the actors holding up mirrors to the audience and reflecting back to them a cubist deconstruction of their own collective act of spectatorship, capturing them "not whole by any means, but at any rate sitting still" (Woolf [1941] 1970, 185). La Trobe's depiction of the production and consumption of history in her finale participates in the process that Debord describes as humanity achieving "consciousness of its own activity" ([1967] 1995, 74).

Forster's analysis of realism in *Aspects of the Novel* allows us to comprehend La Trobe's gesture as a reassertion of the subjective experience of "life in value" and as an antidote to the pageant's objectification of "life in time." La Trobe's versions of the *tableau vivant* and march past avoid the false sense of "completion" or "rounding off" that Forster associates with viewing painting and sculpture and for which he criticizes the novels of Henry James. Her pageant ends instead with a tableau that gestures toward the unceasing production of history beyond the present moment. The chaotic curtain call acknowledges the endless permutations through which historical experience can resonate and resurface within our individual and collective consciousness—much like Forster's image of the great authors of English literature sitting together in the round Reading Room of the British Museum. She achieves a continuity between representation and lived experience that Forster describes as the sensation of "opening out" and "expansion" and which he compares to the silence that follows an orchestral performance ([1927] 1954, 242). Indeed, so self-effacing is the denouement of La Trobe's pageant as it arrives at "The Present Time – Ourselves" that the audience cannot tell exactly when the pageant has ended and real life has resumed (Woolf [1941] 1970, 186).

The remainder of the novel traces the expansion of this moment of consciousness during the finale of La Trobe's pageant beyond the context of that performance to its reception and reformulation by the audience. Woolf is not the only novelist to depict the audience of a pageant within a novel, but her nuanced depiction of the process whereby individual audience members internalize or resist the pageant's aesthetic unity distinguishes *Between the Acts* from other fictional treatments of pageantry. In Powys' ([1932] 1987) *A Glastonbury Romance,* the audience is a mute visual component within a pastoral description of the landscape that is described by the narrator from the vantage point of a remote hilltop. In *Brother Copas,* Q portrays the audience's reaction to the finale of the Merchester pageant with complete uniformity, abstracting even the skeptical Brother Copas himself into its mass experience. The narrator describes how "the rite took possession of them, seizing on them, surprising them with a sudden glow around the heart, sudden tears in the eyes." Surrendering to the notion that the pageant "*was* history of a sort," Copas falls prey to Swithin's Cleopatra effect: a sudden "infection of nobility – this feeling that we are indeed greater than we know" (Quiller-Couch 1911, 296). The audience is a homogenous pawn in Q's satire of Parker's manipulative productions, whereas Woolf's audience retains the aspect of individuals struggling to create meaning from the representations and images in circulation around them.

Woolf's characters, including unnamed audience members, exhibit an authentically spontaneous ebb and flow of consciousness, recalling Forster's observation that realist fiction ought to account for the fact that "we are stupider at some times more than others" ([1927] 1954, 123). It would be as unrealistic for La Trobe's audience to move steadily along a linear trajectory of increasing consciousness of the spectacle as it is for Q's audience to swoon in unison at the Merchester pageant. Instead, Woolf traces the engagement of individual members of the audience in real time as they become piqued at various moments by one aspect of the pageant or another, dismiss their own concerns and attempt to follow the pageant's lead, or puzzle mildly over La Trobe intentions. Woolf also depicts the pressures placed on their moments of consciousness by the impulse to caption the performance with "official" meanings. She notes, for example, the presence of a reporter taking notes for an article. Observing that the final tableau involves people of both sexes and various races, he describes it definitively as a tribute to the work of the League of Nations, and this is the objective reality that will be circulated to the paper's readership who were not present at the event themselves. The Reverend Streatfield interprets the act of wall-building through the tropes of Christian unity and humility, validating the spectatorial role of the audience and flattening historical difference through a series of platitudes concerning how we "play different parts, but are the same," how "nature takes her part," how "there is a sprit that inspires, pervades" (Woolf [1941] 1970, 192). The audience recoils in embarrassment from the clergyman's "servitude to the summing up," recognizing it as "an intolerable constriction, contraction and reduction to simplified absurdity" of their experience of the pageant (190). Nevertheless, as soon as he begins to speak, "they folded their hands in the traditional manner as if they were seated in church" (191).

Regardless of what La Trobe intends to convey through her final tableau of wall-building, the audience seems intent on rebuilding the aesthetic "fourth wall" that insulates them as spectators. Woolf replays for the reader an extended pastiche of the audience's parting chatter that echoes La Trobe's chaotic version of the march past itself. Profundity mixes with the banal as they struggle to discern the meaning of the pageant and sense the inadequacy of conventional aesthetic standards to explain it. There are some who believe that the play was a failure because it left questions unanswered, while others intuit that its lack of a clear moral could be "part of the point" (Woolf [1941] 1970, 200). Their moments of insight, however, are continuously interrupted by gossip and allusions to the deteriorating political situation on the Continent. As car engines start and the audience breaks into farewells, the reader is shown that any remaining consciousness advanced by La Trobe's Brechtian gestures is engulfed by the audience members' return to the spontaneous and uncritical experience of the quotidian.

Although collective consciousness of the spectacle proves to be ephemeral, Woolf—like Forster—portrays the possibility for individuals to address the influence of spectacle in their lives. To contain the spectacle is not to transcend it definitively, but to engage in an ongoing and conscious negotiation with the real. Forster argues in *Aspects of the Novel* that the constructive tension between "life in value" and "life in time" in realist fiction provides the reader with an authentic model for this negotiation. La Trobe's violent reassertions of "life in value" within the pageant disrupt its exclusive emphasis on "life in time" in order to establish provisional consciousness of the problem of spectacle, but are mere negations of the pageant form that do not model a livable balance between these modes of experience. At the end of the novel, however, Woolf affirms two instances of this constructive tension in the sibling relationship between Bartholomew and Lucy and the marital relationship between Giles and Isa. As I argued above in Chap. 2 with respect to the marriage of Lucy Honeychurch and George Emerson at the conclusion of *A Room with a View*, there is neither a tragic resolution whereby Woolf's characters are marooned within the spectacle nor a comic resolution in which the spectacle is eradicated, but a realist resolution in which the characters identify a provisional way forward.

The ongoing quarrel between Bartholomew's materialism and Lucy's spirituality evokes competing experiences of objective "life in time" and a subjective "life in value" within the novel. Bartholomew puzzles over his sister's piety, marveling that a "prayable being" could reside "within Lucy's skull, shaped so much like his own" (Woolf [1941] 1970, 25). He regards the village church as a deteriorating physical structure and the faith it embodies as an antique object—a "fern leaf in a lump of coal," as Hardy describes Jude's medievalism ([1895] 1965, 69). Lucy, however, regards the church not as an historic landmark, but as the locus of a living faith that she renews perpetually in the present moment by cultivating and exercising a distinct vision of the real. Bartholomew is a reader of newspapers and an actor in England's imperial dynasty. Lucy, on the other hand, is a reader of the geological "Outline of History," forsaking the dynastic narrative of European history to contemplate a timescale in which God's creation is unified, when there were "rhododendron forests where Picadilly now stands," the continents were one, and no channel divided England from the Continent (Woolf [1941] 1970, 8). Taken together, Lucy and Bartholomew exhibit a Pico-like simultaneity of Christian and secular cosmologies. The narrator explains that "what she saw he didn't; what he saw she didn't – and so on, *ad infinitum*" (26).

Prior to the pageant, however, there is a sense of imbalance in this relationship. Like the portrait that hangs in his dining room, Bartholomew is a "talk producer," and his logo-centric empiricism overwhelms the more abstract and private vision that Lucy finds difficult to articulate. As with the pageant itself, his objective "life in time" dominates and marginalizes her subjective "life in value." This dynamic shifts during the evening after the pageant when Lucy meditates on the fish swimming in a lily pond at Pointz Hall. "Retrieving a glint of faith from the grey waters," we are told, "she followed the fish; the speckled, streaked, and blotched; seeing in that vision beauty, power and glory in ourselves" (Woolf [1941] 1970, 205). Woolf's use of the term "pied" to describe the fish suggests a possible allusion to Gerard Manley Hopkins' poem "Pied Beauty," in which the speaker points to the "dappled" diversity of nature and human experience as an index of the unified genius of the Creator "whose beauty is past change" (Hopkins [1877] 1953, ll. 1, 10). Woolf's own 1928 essay "The Sun and the Fish," however, provides a materialist gloss on Swithin's epiphany which suggests that her spirituality has undergone an historicist correction. Woolf describes her own encounter with a display of fish and lizards at London's Zoological Gardens in which "time seems to have stopped and we are in the presence of immortality." Woolf takes comfort in the persistence of the Mesozoic Era into the present day, which promises "after destruction, calm; after ruin, steadfastness" ([1928] 1967, 182). Having struggled to identify an empirical manifestation of her own intimations of immortality and unity, Lucy Swithin is similarly empowered by the connection she draws between the fish and "ourselves."

A breeze blows past Swithin while she watches the fish swimming under the water, and the narrator observes that she "stood between two fluidities" (Woolf [1941] 1970, 204). Following La Trobe's pageant, Swithin is no longer marginalized within the spectacle of modern historicism, but discerns the transparent mediations that compete to objectify her reality. She will not be bullied by Bartholomew and resolves to protect her vision of the world from his "torch of reason" (204–5). She has come to understand her spiritual perspective on the beauty, goodness and cyclical persistence of creation as being authentically simultaneous with Bartholomew's materialist perspective on the linear evolution of nature's "battle in the mud" (203). She imagines the argument she would have with him regarding the fish, conceiving of the exchange as a whole and not simply as a partisan:

> Fish had faith, she reasoned. They trust us because we've never caught 'em. But her brother would reply: "That's greed." "Their beauty!" she protested. "Sex," he would say. "Who makes sex susceptible to beauty?" she would argue. He shrugged who? Why? (205)

Lucy's dialectic with Bartholomew holds their competing perspectives in productive tension without vindicating one over the other or synthesizing them in Hegelian fashion. Lucy's participation in this non-Hegelian dialectic delivers her from the ideological solipsism that Debord associates with the spectacle and exemplifies realist fiction's capability to model authentic consciousness.

The novel closes with Bartholomew, Lucy, Giles and Isa reading silently in the drawing room of Pointz Hall at dusk. The room's colors intensify in the setting sun, creating a surreal visual effect that I have noted in other moments of acute consciousness of the spectacle in realist fiction—as when Jude Fawley becomes transfixed by the glimmering spires of Christminster, Sue Bridehead eyes the blazing white pagan idols in relief against the Gothic towers, and Lucy Honeychurch grows faint before the throbbing tower in the Florentine piazza. As Lucy Swithin reads a passage from the *Outline of History* describing how "prehistoric man [...] roused himself from his semi-crouching position and raised great stones," the lengthening shadows of Bartholomew, Giles and Isa take on the "monumental" proportions of Easter Island *moai*. The view through the windows fades into darkness, and the narrator compares it to a "night that dwellers in caves had watched from some high place among rocks" (Woolf [1941] 1970, 218). The scene restates another passage from "The Sun and the Fish," in which Woolf describes the re-emergence of the "primeval world" within the present moment on the occasion of a solar eclipse. Like the figures in the drawing room at Pointz Hall, the party watching the eclipse is stripped of its "little badges and signs of individuality" and "strung out against the sky in outline" like "statues standing prominent on the ridge of the world" (Woolf [1928] 1967, 180).

This primordial setting affords Giles and Isa their first authentic encounter of the day. Once Bartholomew and Lucy go up to bed, the darkness strips Giles and Isa of their own "little badges," including the domestic and public roles that separate them and the various representations of Englishness foisted upon them by the pageant. "Alone," the narrator explains, "enmity was bared; also love. Before they slept, they must fight; after they had fought, they would embrace. From that embrace another life might be born" (Woolf [1941] 1970, 219). Giles and Isa are the present-day iteration of the marriage plots featured in La Trobe's pageant. With the final words—"Then the curtain rose. They spoke."—the entire novel becomes a distended prologue that makes visible the spectacular distance Giles and Isa must traverse and the pseudo-cyclical consciousness that they must shed in order to achieve a single moment of authentic encounter. In this respect, *Between the Acts* parallels Joyce's consolidation of the geographic and temporal separation of Odysseus and Penelope into a single day's experience of the psychological distance that separates Leopold and Molly Bloom. Like Joyce, Woolf takes up Pater's challenge to contemporary artists to leave behind the externalized dilemmas of ancient drama and epic and address the internalized separations that afflict the modern subject.

Certain entries in Woolf's journals and cues within the novel itself lend credence to the view that Woolf wrote *Between the Acts* out of frustration with her society's willful blindness to impending war and the fascist dimension of England's own patriotic impulses. The extent of the critical attention paid to these political concerns, however, risks isolating Woolf's final novel as a grotesque oddity within her oeuvre. As Woolf herself argued in her 1924 essay "Mr. Bennett and Mrs. Brown," "great novelists have brought us to see whatever they wish us to see through some character. Otherwise, they would not be novelists; but poets, historians, or pamphleteers" ([1924] 1966, 326). The characters in *Between the Acts* struggle alongside those in *Mrs. Dalloway* and *To the Lighthouse* to separate reality from representation as they pursue an elusive shared consciousness. Although *Between the Acts* is the only novel of Woolf's in which a pageant is actually staged, Woolf is attentive throughout her fiction to the pageantizing impulse that asserts a collectively experienced "life in time" which clashes with her characters' individual experiences of "life in value."

Consider the fictional biography *Orlando*, for example, in which the title character persists for hundreds of years through successive periods of British history. Woolf literalizes the pageant's logic of a shared national past in which the life of the individual and life of the nation become one. Each chapter of the novel functions as a scene from a pageant that Orlando supposedly inhabits, with Woolf's realist prose laying bare the literary tropes and iconography through which the popular imagination accesses—and fails to access—the lived experience of past ages. Woolf takes these essentialized identities from each era—the visual shorthand of changes in material culture through which pageantry dramatizes the progression of "life in time"—and exposes their insufficiency by restating them within the realist milieu of the novel. Akin to Swithin's heritage tour of Pointz Hall, Orlando furnishes each room in his manor house in the style of a different historical period and spends his days gazing nostalgically upon a museum of his own life. Woolf leaves a page half blank to satirize the transparency of naturalistic prose; La Trobe leaves the stage empty during her experiment with "pure" realism. Just as La Trobe's pageant degenerates into a chaotic echo-chamber in the "Present Day," Orlando experiences a nervous breakdown when her spectatorial distance from the past collapses and she is forced to confront the immediacy and complexity of modern urban life. The image of "ourselves" in *Between the Acts* as a collection of "scraps and orts" that resist assembly into a legible image is prefigured by the falling scraps of white paper to which Woolf compares Orlando's fragmenting visual field as she is driven through modern-day London. One could read Orlando as the mental experience of a single spectator at La Trobe's pageant who initially achieves vicarious identity with the Elizabethans and Augustans, experiences an alienated mix of nostalgia and discomfort with the depiction of Victorians, and is then reduced to a psychotic break upon seeing her own cubist reflection in the mirrors. Like La Trobe's pageant, *Orlando* ends literally in the present moment, with the final words announcing the arrival of "the twelfth stroke of midnight, Thursday, the eleventh of October, Nineteen hundred and Twenty Eight," the date on which the novel was actually published (Woolf [1928] 1956, 329).

Woolf's novel *The Years*, published in 1937 just before she undertook the writing of *Between the Acts*, is structured as a micro-pageant of the aristocratic Pargiter family.[13] Each chapter focuses on moments from a particular year during the 1880s. Like Lucy Swithin and Orlando, Peggy Pargiter takes refuge in her spectatorial relationship to the past as something "so interesting; so safe; so unreal … so beautiful in its unreality" (Woolf [1937] 2008, 333). Pageantry's transformation of lived experience into the consumption of images informs Woolf's account of dons and undergraduates walking around Oxford in their robes "like people dressed up and acting parts" as well as judges and barristers in wigs who "looked like pictures [...] emphatic, cut out, like eighteenth-century portraits hung upon a wall" (74, 109). As in *Orlando* and La Trobe's pageant, the final chapter of *The Years* represents the "Present Day" and functions as a "march past" in which the surviving members of the family gather for a reunion. Similarly to the snippets of conversation that Woolf replays as the audience departs from La Trobe's pageant, North Pargiter engages in a form of realist restatement by repeating phrases to himself that he has overhead among the guests, but "critically, as if he were actor and critic; he listened but he commented" (411). The Pargiter elders form a *tableau vivant* as they bid farewell to their guests. The narrator describes how "the group in the window [...] wore a statuesque look for a moment, as if they were carved in stone" such that "their dresses fell in stiff sculptured folds." Once the public performance of the party ends, however, the statues regain the fluidity of spontaneous life and interact authentically. "Then they moved;" the narrator observes, "they changed their attitudes; they began to talk" (432). This language anticipates the final words of *Between the Acts* through which Woolf signals that the authentic life of Giles and Isa may begin once the pageant-goers have left.

Woolf's reference to T.S. Eliot's play *The Family Reunion* in a journal entry from March 1939 provides further evidence of her broad interest in the pageantizing mindset as a problem of modern consciousness versus targeting particular pageant productions as objects of political satire. The title of Eliot's *Family Reunion* refers to the reluctant return of Harry, Lord Monchesney, to take over the administration of the family estate upon the death of his father. With a forced sense of royal pageantry, Harry's mother assembles his siblings, cousins, aunts and uncles to witness this dynastic transfer of power. She has engaged in a pseudo-cyclical denial of historical change by keeping all the visual trappings of the estate intact since the moment of Harry's departure many years before. As Hardy demonstrates in *Jude the Obscure*, the modern incarnation of the tragic struggle against fate is a sense of lost agency among the spectacle's competing falsifications of reality. Like Giles Oliver, whom Woolf describes as "manacled to a rock" and "forced passively to behold indescribable horror," Harry is a modern-day Prometheus who suffers from the recognition that contemplating dynastic history has replaced participating in lived experience. He describes his relatives as "people to whom nothing has happened" and who have "gone through life in sleep, never woken to the nightmare." Harry is reduced to a "self which persisted only as an eye, seeing," and his relatives form a self-critiquing Greek chorus that denigrates its own voyeurism as "tragic onlookers" and "guilty conspirators, waiting for some revelation when the hidden shall be exposed" (Eliot 1939, 96, 42). Woolf connects Eliot's "experiment with stylized chatter" among the members of his chorus with "a new idea of mine – that I'm evolving in PH [i.e., *Pointz Hall,* her working title for *Between the Acts*] about the drama" (Woolf [1939] 1984, 210). Woolf deploys this "stylized chatter" to portray the audience's response to La Trobe's pageant, which similarly functions as a tragic chorus that articulates the problem of spectacle to Woolf's readers.

Considering Woolf's interest in the persistence of tragic structures and her vision for modern fiction that combines dramatic action with lyric soliloquy, another likely and significant influence on *Between the Acts* was Thomas Hardy's epic dramatization of the Napoleonic wars, *The Dynasts.* Published in three massive, never-to-be-staged segments between 1904 and 1908, *The Dynasts* deconstructs the modern pageantizing mindset by portraying major political and military events alongside their reception in the popular imagination. Closely anticipating Woolf's ideas about literary realism from "Modern Fiction" and "The Narrow Bridge of Art," an early anonymous review of *The Dynasts* describes it as a "poeticizing of the drama of common life" that foregrounds "one way of regarding [...] common things" rather than "the things themselves" (Anonymous [1908] 1993, 351). Hardy employs a chorus of metaphysical "spirits" that comment upon the action, which another early reviewer describes as the "personified moods of the human mind in criticism" (Newbolt [1909] 1993, 357). Each spirit reflects the simultaneous dispositions one could adopt toward the events depicted, much like Woolf's device of the audience's chatter following La Trobe's pageant. The crisis of spectatorship in *Between the Acts* continues the intellectual project of *The Dynasts.* An early critical study of *The Dynasts* observed that Hardy portrays the "agonies of modern self-consciousness," but—just as Forster argues of *Jude the Obscure*—"stops at the point when the challenge of self-consciousness has to be taken up" (Chakravarty [1938] 1970, 99).

A provocative connection between *The Dynasts* and La Trobe's pageant emerges from Newbolt's description of *The Dynasts* as a "chronicle play or historical pageant" in which the theater is the "reader's mind" and "the dramatist had made of us not an audience, but the very theatre itself" ([1909] 1993, 354, 356). What would La Trobe not give to have those same words uttered about her production? This unmediated unity of a play and its audience—the complete overcoming of the alienated distance of spectatorship—with which Newbolt credits *The Dynasts* prefigures La Trobe's fantasy of writing "the play" that transcends the problems of reception. Exhibiting similar concerns as La Trobe regarding the recuperation of his work as spectacle, Hardy initially distanced himself from amateur theater despite his devotion to folk culture in the Wessex novels. Even Parker himself approached Hardy unsuccessfully with ideas for collaboration. Parker notes that he, like Hardy, had at one time "gone about with the monstrous idea of a huge episodical play on Napoleon I" and pitched to Hardy the idea of producing *The Dynasts* as a pageant (Parker 1928, 213; Wilson 1995, 65). Having rejected several requests to permit his novels to be adapted for the stage, Hardy eventually adapted a script from *Tess of the D'Urbervilles* and wrote *The Famous Tragedy of the Queen of Cornwall* (Wilson 1995, 4–5). Against what appears to have been his better judgment, Hardy also permitted *The Dynasts* to be adapted as a pageant, only to see all that was "philosophically speculative" in the original "sacrificed for the requirements of patriotic uplift" (Wilson 1995, 88). With the addition of English heroes and "scenes from Wessex life" that celebrated England's "good-humored endurance and past military glories," the production came to resemble one of Parker's pageants and, to Hardy's regret, made him quite "conventional" (Wilson 1995, 88). Hardy later adapted *The Dynasts* himself, but the constraints of staging led him to eliminate the chorus of the spirits and reduce the play to a succession of "scenes of rural life" held together by a love interest among the minor characters that was not present in the original text (Wilson 1995, 98–9). Thus absorbed into his generic Wessex brand, Hardy's erstwhile pageant of consciousness devolved into the theatrical equivalent of Jude's Christminster cakes.

Through the various self-reflexive portraits of artists in her novels, including La Trobe, Woolf anguishes over this potential for realist consciousness to be recuperated by the very medium in which it is presented. Is whatever consciousness of the spectacle that is produced by reading *Between the Acts* doomed to follow in the footsteps of La Trobe's pageant and promptly dissolve like "a cloud that melted into the other clouds on the horizon" (Woolf [1941] 1970, 209)? Is Woolf—like Swithin—only capable of "laying hold desperately" to a mere "fraction of her meaning" (152–3)? Has she—like Peggy Pargiter—"broken off only a little fragment of what she meant to say" such that "it hung before her, the thing she had seen, the thing she had not said" (Woolf [1937] 2008, 391)? Are we left asking, like the audience of La Trobe's pageant, whether the novel is a failure? Or, as Macherey would argue, is the pageant's apparent cognizance of its own transitory and partial reflection of the real part of the point? By portraying the flawed reception of La Trobe's pageant, Woolf reconditions her readers to be critical of the act of representation and their role as spectators. The pregnant incompleteness of its representation, its "opening out" rather than "rounding off," is what allows *Between the Acts* to restate the experience of spectatorship to the reader without flattening it into a replica for aesthetic consumption. And yet Woolf's realist perspective remains vulnerable to the same false summary that the reporter and the Reverend Streatfield perpetrate against La Trobe's production. I walk a fine line in reconstructing the realism of *Between the Acts* and must avoid pageantizing Woolf's fiction within the finite historical arc of an aesthetic genre. As this study moves past the first half of the twentieth century and turns to Salman Rushdie, Edward Carey and Julian Barnes, I seek to bring Woolf's realism into dialog with more contemporary fiction through their shared ethos of meta-spectacle.

Notes

1. Yoshino (2003), for example, reduces Woolf's character Miss La Trobe to a stand-in for the fascist pageant-master Parker in order to argue that *Between the Acts* is primarily a satire of the stated democratic and patriotic ideals of revived folk pageantry.
2. Miller (1998), for example, focuses exclusively on Woolf's desire to contribute to the war effort by unmasking native fascism, particularly in the imperialist and military aspects of Church- and state-sponsored pageantry dating from the Renaissance. Contrary to Yoshino, Miller draws no connection between the novel and Parker's contemporary neo-folk pageants.
3. See Mitchell (1994) and Helsinger (1994). A shared affinity for the practice of landscape painting has been noted among military and imperial leaders such as Ulysses S. Grant, Winston Churchill, Adolf Hitler, Francisco Franco, Dwight D. Eisenhower, Prince Charles and George W. Bush (Munro 2014).
4. The spectatorial distance introduced by the geological timescales and galactic distances articulated by modern science suggest a connection between Woolf's Lucy Swithin and the character Swithin St. Cleeve in Hardy's *Two on a Tower* ([1882], 1993), whose alienated perspective stems from his pursuit of astronomy. In his 1895 preface to *Two on a Tower*,

Hardy explains his intent to "set the emotional history of two infinitesimal lives against the stupendous background of the stellar universe."

5. See Birmingham (1994) regarding the depiction in art of emerging transient populations in industrial England.

6. Even when what Withington calls "real history" begins to appear in British pageantry in the mid-fifteenth century, historical figures such as William the Conqueror, Edward IV, Henry VIII and Charles V are represented alongside characters from Arthurian legend, "the mythical rulers of England, the giants Corineus and Gogmagog, Roland and Oliver," and other personas who are "as romantic as they are historical" (1963, vol. 1, 79).

7. Withington identifies the first instance of ideological pageantry as the Lord Mayor's Show of 1605, titled "Triumphes of Reunited Britannia," which adopted a nationalist sensibility "due to the fact that James had to be complimented" (1963, vol. 2, 28–9). He notes the subsequent appearance of pageant floats celebrating industrial progress. For example, a pageant in 1677 included a float titled "The Temple of Time" in which a personified figure of time was surrounded by four attendants representing the seasons, who in turn were surrounded by six figures representing various degrees of measurement, namely "a Minute, an Hour, a Day, a Week, a Month, and a Year" (74). The agrarian tradition of cyclical time represented by the seasons is thus visually inscribed within the precise increments of linear time. It is also at this point that representations of "trading interests" begin to emerge within the processions, such as a float portraying the Continent of India filled with "all manner of spice-plants and trees bearing odour" and topped with a figure representing India who was called the "Queen of Merchandise" (75). Three attendants dressed like merchants surrounded this "Queen" with names of "Commerce, Adventure, and Traffic" and were followed by other trade-related figures such as "Negroes, Indians, sea-captains, and sailors" (75). Pageant-cars on the themes of trade and imperialism become more frequent during the Victorian and Edwardian eras. A float titled "England and Her Heroes" from a pageant in 1896 displayed men wearing "various army uniforms of different epochs" (128). Other shows in 1901 and 1902 included displays concerning "the trade and commerce of London in the twelfth century," "the Commonwealth of Australia," "the methods of weighing in use from earliest times," and "the rise and progress of the British Navy" (130). One of the more elaborate floats provided "an allegorical representation of Great Britain and Japan, with a background of Japanese scenery" on which "a boat in the foreground typifies the commerce between the two countries" (130).

8. Noting that Parker would often engage in a year or more of research before staging his pageants, Withington refers to an exhibit of "costumes,

weapons, armor, horse-trappings, carriages, etc." that was available for public viewing several weeks before a pageant in York as "a remarkable museum of real historical value" (1963, vol. 2, 201).

9. Although Marder (1988) alludes in passing to a connection between La Trobe and Brecht, he does not explore this relationship. Other critics suggest that La Trobe attempts to alienate her audience in a manner that is reminiscent of Brecht. However, Balkin's concept of "active spectatorship" attributes intentionality to the disruptions of La Trobe's production (2008, 448), when in fact La Trobe, far from planning these disruptions, deplores them. Westman examines a "narratorial shuttling between mediation and its erasure" that suggests a self-deconstructing production along the lines of Brecht, although she locates this phenomenon not in La Trobe's pageant, but in Woolf's treatment of written texts within *Between the Acts* (2006, 2).

10. Parker's 1908 pageant titled "The Press, the Poets and the Musicians from Chaucer to Milton" and 1910 pageant portraying popular characters from the plays of Shakespeare asserts a reflexivity between literature and history that Withington describes as "literature viewed through the eyes of history" and "history seen through literary spectacles" (1963, vol. 2, 146). Further possible influences on Woolf include the "Pageant of English Literature" presented by Emma Swann and Eva Whitmarsh at Oxford in 1914 (which approached the present day as far as Addison and Steele) and the Colchester pageant of 1909, a meta-pageant that incorporates three genres of popular entertainment in historical progression: a mummer's play in honor of the Lord Mayor's Day circa 1400, a courtly masque from the Renaissance, and a Commedia dell'arte farce from the Georgian period (Withington 1963, vol. 2).

11. Ames (1998) argues that La Trobe's reiteration of marriage plots in each act of the pageant demonstrates her attempt to liberate the pageant from its modern role as an agent of the state. Dynastic progress is replaced by comic romance, with the spontaneity of love triumphant over social constraints and historical contingency.

12. Pageant programs from Bath (*Bath* 1909), Colchester (*Colchester* 1909), Chester (Hawtrey 1910) and Berkhamsted (*Berkhamsted* 1922) each indicate a finale in the form of a tableau containing all the performers or a march past of all the characters. The march past at Colchester involved 3000 performers.

13. Woolf connects the two works in an entry in her journal from January 1939, commenting that in writing the "barn scene" in *Between the Acts*, she has "learnt something from *The Years*" ([1939] 1984, 199). The "barn scene" refers to Manresa's attempt to enact the "democratic principle" of Parker's pageants by mingling with the servants during the intermission,

which is prefigured in Delia Pargiter's desire "to mix people; to do away with the absurd conventions of English life" (Woolf [1937] 2008, 398). Manresa encounters difficulty in convincing the servants to serve themselves first at the reception in the barn during the pageant's intermission. Delia's brother similarly questions her success in breaking down class barriers, noting that Delia has omitted "the Sweeps and the Servers" and "the seamstresses and the stevedores" from the guest list for her party at the end of *The Years* (404).

REFERENCES

Ames, Christopher. 1998. Carnivalesque Comedy in *Between the Acts. Twentieth Century Literature* 44 (4): 394–409.

Anonymous. (1908) 1993. Edinburgh Review CCVII (April 1908). Review of *The Dynasts*, by Thomas Hardy. In *Thomas Hardy: Critical Assessments*, vol. I, The Contemporary Response, ed. Graham Clarke, 351. East Sussex: Helm Information.

Balkin, Sarah. 2008. Regenerating Drama in Stein's *Doctor Faustus Lights the Lights* and Woolf's *Between the Acts. Modern Drama* 51 (4): 433–457.

Bath Pageant. 1909.

Benjamin, Walter. (1939) 1969. What Is Epic Theater? In *Illuminations*, trans. Harry Zohn, 147–154. New York: Schocken.

Berkhamsted Pageant. 1922. Berkhamsted: T.W. Bailey and A.E. Coosley.

Birmingham, Ann. 1994. System, Order and Abstraction: The Politics of English Landscape Drawing Around 1795. In *Landscape and Power*, ed. W.J.T. Mitchell, 77–102. Chicago: University of Chicago Press.

Brecht, Bertolt. (1929) 1964. A Dialogue About Acting. In *Brecht on Theatre: The Development of an Aesthetic*, ed. and trans. John Willett, 26–29. New York: Hill & Wang.

Chakravarty, Amiya. (1938) 1970. *The Dynasts and the Post-War Age in Poetry: A Study in Modern Ideas.* New York: Octagon.

Colchester Pageant. 1909. Norwich/London: Harrold & Sons.

Debord, Guy. (1967) 1995. *The Society of the Spectacle.* Trans. Donald Nicholson-Smith. New York: Zone Books.

Eliot, T.S. 1939. *The Family Reunion.* New York: Harcourt, Brace and Company.

Forster, E.M. (1908) 1986. *A Room with a View.* New York: Signet.

———. (1927) 1954. *Aspects of the Novel.* New York: Harcourt, Brace & Company.

———. 1940. *England's Pleasant Land: A Pageant Play.* London: Hogarth.

Hardy, Thomas. (1882) 1993. *Two on a Tower.* Ed. Suleiman M. Ahmad. Oxford/New York: Oxford University Press.

———. (1895) 1965. *Jude the Obscure.* Riverside Edition. Boston: Houghton Mifflin.

Hawtrey, G.P., ed. 1910. *Chester Historical Pageant*. Chester: Phillopson and Golder.

Helsinger, Elizabeth. 1994. Turner and the Representation of England. In *Landscape and Power*, ed. W.J.T. Mitchell, 103–126. Chicago: University of Chicago Press.

Henley, Ann. 1989. 'But We Argued About Novel-Writing': Virginia Woolf, E.M. Forster, and the Art of Fiction. *Ariel* 20 (3): 73–83.

Hopkins, Gerard Manley. (1877) 1953. Pied Beauty. In *Gerard Manley Hopkins: A Selection of His Poems and Prose*, ed. W.H. Gardner, 30–31. Baltimore: Penguin.

Jameson, Fredric. 1981. *The Political Unconscious: Narrative as a Socially Symbolic Act*. Ithaca: Cornell University Press.

Marder, Herbert. 1988. Alienation Effects: Dramatic Satire in *Between the Acts*. *Papers on Language and Literature* 24 (4): 423–446.

Miller, Marlowe. 1998. Unveiling 'the Dialectic of Culture and Barbarism' in British Pageantry: Virginia Woolf's *Between the Acts*. *Papers on Language and Literature* 34 (2): 134–162.

Mitchell, W.J.T. 1994. Introduction to *Landscape and Power*, ed. W.J.T. Mitchell, 1–4. Chicago: University of Chicago Press.

Munro, Cait. 2014. From Jimmy Carter to Hitler, 10 Politicians Who Tried Their Hands at Art. *artnet news*, April 25. http://news.artnet.com/art-world/politicians-who-had-brushes-with-art-11291. Accessed 17 Nov 2014.

Newbolt, Henry. (1909) 1993. Review. Review of *The Dynasts*, by Thomas Hardy. *Quarterly Review*, January 1909. In *Thomas Hardy: Critical Assessments*, vol. I, The Contemporary Response, ed. Graham Clarke, 193–209. East Sussex: Helm Information.

Parker, Louis Napoleon. 1928. *Several of My Lives*. London: Chapman and Hall.

Powys, John Cowper. (1932) 1987. *A Glastonbury Romance*. Woodstock: Overlook Press.

Quiller-Couch, Sir Arthur Thomas. 1911. *Brother Copas*. New York: Scribner.

Westman, Karin. 2006. 'For her generation the newspaper was a book': Media, Mediation, and Oscillation in Virginia Woolf's *Between the Acts*. *Journal of Modern Literature* 29 (2): 1–18.

Wilson, Keith. 1995. *Thomas Hardy on Stage*. New York: St. Martin's.

Withington, Robert. 1963. *English Pageantry: An Historical Outline*. New York: Benjamin Blom.

Woolf, Leonard. 1927. The Pageant of History. In *Essays on Literature, History, Politics, Etc.*, 125–148. New York: Harcourt, Brace and Company.

Woolf, Virginia. (1924) 1966. Mr. Bennett and Mrs. Brown. In *Collected Essays*, vol. I, ed. Leonard Woolf, 319–337. London: Hogarth.

———. (1925) 1984. Modern Fiction. In *The Common Reader*, ed. Andrew McNeillie, 146–154. San Diego: Harcourt Brace & Company.

———. (1927) 1966. The Narrow Bridge of Art. In *Collected Essays*, vol. II, ed. Leonard Woolf, 218–229. London: Hogarth.

———. (1928) 1956. *Orlando: A Biography*. San Diego/New York/London: Harcourt, Brace & Company.

———. (1928) 1967. The Sun and the Fish. In *Collected Essays*, vol. IV, ed. Leonard Woolf, 178–183. New York: Harcourt, Brace & World.

———. (1937) 2008. *The Years*. Orlando: Harcourt, Brace & Company.

———. (1939) 1984. *Diary of Virginia Woolf*, vol. V: 1936–41. Ed. Anne Olivier Bell. London: Hogarth.

———. (1941) 1970. *Between the Acts*. San Diego: Harcourt, Brace & Company.

Yoshino, Ayako. 2003. *Between the Acts* and Louis Napoleon Parker – The Creator of the Modern English Pageant. *Critical Survey* 15 (2): 49–60.

CHAPTER 5

"Pressed against the screen"— Cinema and Photography as Spectacle in Salman Rushdie's *Midnight's Children*

Because the experience of the colonized is bound up in the process of industrialization, resistance to colonization in many respects involves resistance to the dynamics of spectacle. Edward Said identifies an unprecedented link between industrial transformation and colonial control as the distinguishing trait of modern European imperialism, one that led not only to the "extraordinary and sustained longevity of the disparity in power between Europe and its possessions," but also to the "massively organized rule" that "affected the detail and not just the large outlines of life" (1990, 71). Realist fiction's portrayal of spectatorial distance and the illusion of agency as forms of dispossession are well suited to restating the manner in which the industrial-age colonizer refashions the visual culture of the colony in its own image, exhibits the colony to the West, and marginalizes the colony within Eurocentric history. Achieving political independence, however, does not necessarily resolve the problem of spectacle for the colonial subject, for whom the spectacle's degradation of consciousness through architectural revival, cultural tourism and the pageantizing mindset that I have explored in the preceding chapters remains particularly poignant. The post-colonial environment can be as inauthentic, alienating and uninhabitable as the occupation that preceded it, particularly when the zeal of the colonized to assert independence leads them to deny the cultural and historical hybridity introduced by the colonial relationship. Albert Memmi, French-educated Tunisian novelist and influential sociologist of human oppression, describes the "Great Disillusion"

© The Author(s) 2018
E. Barnaby, *Realist Critiques of Visual Culture*,
https://doi.org/10.1007/978-3-319-77323-0_5

115

116 E. BARNABY

that often follows colonial independence once "the slogans of national unity, heard at a time when everyone felt as if they were members of the same family, have been extinguished" (2006, 3). Any attempt by the colonized to re-inhabit a pre-industrial nationalist purity participates in the pseudo-cyclical consciousness that Debord describes in *Society of the Spectacle* and is subject to critique within realist fiction.

Rushdie's novel *Midnight's Children* presents this dual manifestation of spectacle in post-colonial society by depicting both the imperialist chauvinism of the British Raj and the "optimism epidemic" that plagued the nationalist movement after the Raj's withdrawal (Rushdie [1981] 2006, 39). Saleem Sinai's auspicious birth on the midnight of India's independence thrusts him into the battle for hegemony between a collapsing colonial ideology and the equally surreal nationalist fiction that supplanted it. Rushdie traces the distorting influence of these competing visual discourses on Saleem's consciousness of the real. Portraying the manner in which imperial architecture, Haussmann-inspired urban design, neoclassical portraiture, Eurocentric maps, Western photographic and cinematic practices, mass communication and corporate advertising transform Saleem into a marginalized spectator of the real, Rushdie reveals the spectacle's role in suppressing and overwriting indigenous cultural memory during the British occupation. The novel's full consciousness of spectacle, however, lies in Rushdie's portrayal of how these same dynamics were then perpetuated by India's own nationalist movement, thus replicating the very logic of colonization in order to advance the concept of a politically unified sub-continent. The Bombay that had been architecturally transformed with "roseate edifices of power" by that "race of pink conquerors" is made unfamiliar to Indian eyes once again through an influx of Western commerce (74). Populations once displaced by the East India Company are scattered anew by state-sponsored modernization and urban beautification projects, exiled from the Bombay of their childhoods by their own nationalist government just as their ancestors were first driven from Bombay by European colonizers.

Saleem is transformed into spectacle by the nationalist movement at the very moment of his birth. Swaddled in the colors of the Indian flag and photographed by journalists, he receives a letter from Nehru declaring that the nation will watch over his life as a "mirror of our own" (Rushdie [1981] 2006, 139). Saleem's dehumanization as an image of India's political unity reflects Rushdie's broad concern about iconicity and false consciousness in contemporary society. This issue surfaces repeatedly in

Rushdie's essays, as when he condemns a media campaign for Apple computers which captioned a photograph of Mahatma Gandhi with the company's tagline "Think different." Rushdie laments that Gandhi's complex revolutionary perspective—one which opposed the industrialization of India—had been reduced to a two-word slogan for marketing consumer technology. He criticizes the ad for rendering Gandhi "abstract, ahistorical, postmodern, no longer a man in and of his time but a free-floating concept, a part of the available stock of cultural symbols, an image that can be borrowed, used, distorted, reinvented, to fit many different purposes" (2002, 166). This appropriation of Gandhi's image contributes to the engineered ignorance and generalized amnesia that Debord associates with the mass production and consumption of images in post-industrial society.

Like Hardy, Forster and Woolf, Rushdie regards realism primarily as an ethic that compels an artist to "attempt to respond as fully as possible to the circumstances of the world in which the artist works" (1991, 210). He reports modeling *Midnight's Children* after the Dickensian novel, in which "details of place and social mores are skewered by a pitiless realism, a naturalistic exactitude."[1] It is, in Rushdie's words, "against a scrupulously observed social and historical background – against, that is, the canvas of a 'real' India" that he replays the alienated discourses of political ideology and romanticized historical consciousness for his readers (2002, 64). This enables Rushdie to trace the effect on individual consciousness of the countless visual cues of the Empire's presence that linger post-independence. A print of Millais' painting *Boyhood of Raleigh* (itself an ambiguous hybrid of imperialist fantasy and post-colonial sensibility) hangs above Saleem's crib.[2] His family lives in a cluster of neo-classical mansions named after European palaces, purchasing one cheaply from a departing British industrialist on the condition that the Victorian furnishings of the house remain intact. Saleem's disproportioned facial features—the product of an affair between his Indian mother and an Englishman—combine with various scars and injuries inflicted upon him during childhood so that his face becomes a living map of the Westernized, partitioned and conflict-ridden modern India. Saleem exemplifies Lukàcs' realist hero as the site upon which social forces are made visible and brought into conflict on a human scale. At the same time, Saleem embodies what Jameson describes as the fundamental subject of realism, namely, "a society torn between past and future in such a way that the alternatives are grasped as hostile but somehow unrelated worlds" (1975, 158).

In spite of the context provided by Rushdie's essays, the critical response to *Midnight's Children* has struggled to comprehend Rushdie's motivations and often suggests that the novel contributes to an exotic spectacle of India. Certain post-colonial theorists accuse the British-educated expatriate of casting an imperialist gaze upon India, while others have indicted Rushdie's participation in a capitalist publishing industry that exoticizes Anglo-Indian writers (Barnett 1989; Huggan 2001). Some have questioned whether fictional critiques of imperialism are even capable of prompting an ethical response from the reader or simply reinforce the spectacle of empire (Rosaldo 1993; Aijaz 1992). Graham Huggan, for one, acknowledges Rushdie's attempt to parody colonial chauvinism, yet dismisses this gesture as "vulnerable to recuperation" insofar as the uncritical reader could be drawn into "rehearsing a continuing history of imperialist perceptions of an 'othered' India" (2001, 81).

In order to evaluate Huggan's contention that *Midnight's Children* lacks "oppositional power," clearer definition is needed as to what exactly the novel opposes. Rushdie's concern is not merely to critique imperialism, but also the post-industrial visual culture that persisted after independence and continued to suppress historical consciousness. Anuradha Needham observes that it is typical for writers of a diaspora to advance "reconstructions [that] contest and/or call into question the truth of the dominant, colonial histories of their 'homelands'" (2000, 15). Because Saleem's narrative straddles the transfer of power from the British to the Indian nationalists, the dominant discourse that Rushdie contests undergoes a similar shift during the course of the novel from the colonial vision of India held by the Raj to the vision of a unified modern India advanced by the independence movement. By replaying both discourses for the reader, Rushdie demonstrates how the nationalist discourse replicates the experience of spectacle that was initiated under colonial rule. Saleem struggles to live authentically among these competing un-realities.

Nationalism, like Debord's concept of spectacle, is an alienated form of consciousness that, in Terry Eagleton's words, collapses the "particularity of an individual life into collective anonymity" (1990, 23). Eagleton contends that the temporary indulgence of an alienated nationalist identity which objectifies the "needs and desires" of a "unitary subject known as the people" is necessary in some instances, if only to make visible on a mass level the "sheer fact that these desires are repressed" by a colonial power (28). This nationalist identity—like social class for the proletariat—is a crucible through which the colonized must pass in order to take own-

CINEMA AND PHOTOGRAPHY AS SPECTACLE   119

ership of the false consciousness that has been imposed on them by the colonizer. However, Eagleton observes, it must be "left behind as soon as it is seized" and eventually "dismantled" in order to transcend the reductive binary of the colonial relationship and allow the former subject to "discover and live one's own particular difference" (28, 30). Edward Said similarly regards nationalism as an "insufficient and yet [...] absolutely crucial first step" toward authentic liberation from the spectacle of imperialism (1990, 76). He criticizes "nativism" for reproducing the "divisions imposed [...] by imperialism itself" through "compelling but often demagogic assertions about a native past, history, or actuality that seems to stand free not only of the colonizer but of worldly time itself" (82). In other words, nationalism reproduces the dynamics of spectacle and leaves the overall movement toward liberation vulnerable to recuperation. Debord recognizes this risk in his discussion of the "Proletariat as Subject and Representation." He describes how this provisional identity initially catalyzed social mobility and consciousness for the working class, but eventually became objectified as a permanent condition and as an icon separated from its historical moment, much like Gandhi in Apple's ad campaign. The need to shed nationalist identity after it has successfully disrupted the colonial relationship is akin to Brecht's abandonment of his alienation effects after they began to assume the stability of a theatrical genre.

Exclusively post-colonial readings of *Midnight's Children*, however, are prone to interpret Rushdie's criticism of the nationalists as sympathy for the colonizers. Memmi has noted the doubly tenuous position of the post-colonial writer who not only continues to use the language of the colonizer, but also turns his critical lens on his peers to "depict the incompetence, the egotism, the profitable complicity of the ruling classes, [and] the pressures from his own government" that persist during the process of decolonization. The once-welcomed realism that exposed the ideology of the colonizer is shunned by nationalists seeking to canonize the independence movement with "praise for politicians and religious leaders, bland folkloric tales, [and] reminders of a supposedly glorious past that will help people forget the mediocrity of the present" (Memmi 2006, 37). Literary realism, however, is non-partisan. As Lukàcs, Rahv and Macherey have argued, realist fiction makes visible to the reader any aspect of false consciousness in which they are immersed. Observing that "the power of governments to manipulate images and information is so immense and the reservoir of the cultural semiotic so deep," David Price credits *Midnight's Children* in particular and realist fiction in general with constructing "an entire narrative in opposition to [...] unidimensional, simplistic, reductive, slogan-laden messages" (1994, 105). All governments—colonial and nationalist alike—possess such power, and no authentically realist text that treats the transfer of this power can critique the abuses perpetrated by the former while remaining silent regarding those perpetrated by the latter.

As with the other novels treated in this study, Rushdie's realist gesture is susceptible to an overly literal reception that reinforces an uncritical encounter with spectacle. Under such circumstances, the novel functions as what Jameson calls a "containment strategy" that naturalizes the experience of post-industrial capitalist culture (1981, 193). Haunted by Jameson and often paraphrasing his ideas, certain Rushdie apologists have categorized *Midnight's Children* as magical realism in order to insulate it against claims that it reinforces the Western imperial perspective. Peter Brigg, for example, reads *Midnight's Children* as a fantasy that Rushdie constructs in order to subvert the self-legitimizing rationalism of colonial ideology with a more mythical and anthropomorphic view of history told by an individual (1987, 127). It is true that from the moment Saleem is thrust at birth into the bureaucratic history of the state he becomes obsessed with reconciling the cyclical experience of mythical time and the irreversible experience of dynastic time. Saleem, however, does not succeed, as Brigg suggests, in restoring history to an individual human scale, but instead drives himself to the brink of insanity by attempting to embody the historical scale as an individual. Saleem theorizes his relationship to the real as various combinations of "active" or "passive" and "literal" or "metaphorical" encounters with history (Rushdie [1981] 2006, 272–3). He conflates individual experience with collective memory in the attempt to embody an ideology. Saleem does not achieve empowerment over Western rationalism, but instead exhibits the hyper-rationalist pathology that Debord associates with the spectacle.

The attitude of "freshness" and "childlike" innocence toward the world that Wendy Faris identifies as traits of magical realism smacks of a primitivist fantasy that is at odds with Rushdie's critique of spectacle in *Midnight's Children* (1995, 176–7). Faris locates this freshness and innocence in the novel's opening description of Saleem's grandfather, Aadam Aziz, surveying a pristine mountain landscape on a brisk spring morning (177). As winter snows retreat and vegetation re-emerges, Saleem declares that "the world was new again," noting that "apart from the Englishmen's houseboats on the lake, the valley had hardly changed since the Mughal Empire, for all its springtime renewals" (Rushdie [1981] 2006, 4–5). Faris accepts at face value Saleem's romanticism of the landscape as a timeless, cyclical permanence, when in fact his casual reference to the houseboats raises the specter of colonial occupation and industrialization within that superficially pristine landscape. (Recall that the narrator of Woolf's *Between the Acts* similarly glosses over industrial transformation by nonchalantly substituting the tractor for the plough while asserting that little had changed at Pointz Hall from 1839 to 1939.) Saleem disrupts his own mock-pastoral reverie even more explicitly by reflecting prophetically on the scars of war and military occupation that would be visited upon the Kashmir landscape in the years to come. He further explains that his grandfather's "travelled eyes" perceived the landscape as provincial and stifling after his return from five years of medical training in Germany (5). Far from cultivating a relationship of magical innocence between Aadam and the natural environment, Rushdie anchors his critique of the spectacle in these opening pages by replaying the trope of landscape description in the nineteenth-century novel and then immediately deconstructing the imperialist dynamics embedded in the conventions of the picturesque.

The supernatural elements of magical realism are supposed to be "admitted, accepted and integrated into the rationality and materiality of literary realism" (Zamora and Faris 1995, 3). Even Saleem's least fantastic assertions, however, are undercut by overt references to his unreliability as a narrator, including lapses in judgment, misremembered facts, outright lies and failing sanity. Each of his forays into the fantastic are quickly reined in by Saleem's companion Padma, whose impatience for the abstract and improbable has been described as the "realistic and tangible foil so necessary to keep the narrative to the ground" (Parameswaran 1984, 44). Faris points to Saleem's ability to hear the voices of other children in his head as evidence of the novel's magical traits of "verbal magic" and literalized metaphors. This reading ignores outright both the physiological explanation for this phenomenon that Rushdie establishes in the text and Saleem's own admission later in the novel that his imagined conversations with the other children of midnight were merely a game conjured by a lonely child. Rushdie himself once explained to a BBC director charged with adapting the novel for the screen that "many of the novel's apparently 'magical' moments had naturalistic explanations" and that "however highly fabulated parts of the novel were, the whole was deeply rooted in the real life of the characters and the nation" (2002, 72). The voices in Saleem's head are symptomatic of his alienation within the spectacle and not the manifestation of an authentic mythical consciousness. Referencing Joseph Gabel's work on false consciousness and reification, Debord notes that "the abnormal need for representation" of the sort that Saleem brings with him from childhood into adulthood "compensates for a torturing feeling of being at the margins of existence" ([1967] 1995, 219). Rushdie affirms that "the idea of placing Saleem center-stage in so many political events came to him because a child usually sees himself center-stage" (Parameswaran 1984, 40). The problem is that this need for attention persists into Saleem's adulthood as a desperate attempt to maintain historical agency on the spectacle's alienated terms.

In this light, qualifying the realism of *Midnight's Children* as "magical" places generic limitations on the text that inscribe it within the very terms of otherness and exoticism that Rushdie attempts to expose. Stephen Slemon, for one, warns against oversimplification at the hands of "centralizing genre systems" like magical realism that provide "a single locus upon which the massive problem of difference in literary expression can be managed into recognizable meaning in one swift pass" (1995, 408). In his introduction to the twenty-fifth anniversary edition of the novel, Rushdie observed in hindsight that "in the West people tended to read *Midnight's Children* as a fantasy, while in India people thought of it as pretty realistic, almost a history book" (Rushdie 2006, xiii). Had Rushdie, in fact, adopted the perspective of magical realism, one could more readily accuse him of stereotyping Eastern mysticism within a Eurocentric realist medium for consumption by Western readers. Instead, the irreconcilability of the mythical and realist perspectives are openly debated within the novel. *Midnight's Children* performs "the secularization of the magical religion of fate into the realistic science of psychology" that Jameson identifies with the generic shift from romance to realism (1975, 144). Saleem summarizes the central conflict of the novel in these very terms, explaining to the reader that the children of midnight "can be seen as the last throw of everything antiquated and retrogressive in our myth-ridden nation, whose defeat was entirely desirable in the context of a modernizing, twentieth-century economy; or as the true hope of freedom, which is now forever extinguished; but what they must not become is the bizarre creation of a rambling, diseased mind." Saleem's struggle to reconcile mysticism and historicism does not end in the triumph of a magical perspective, but the blandly rational compromise that "reality can have metaphorical content; that does not make it less real" (Rushdie [1981] 2006, 230).

CINEMA AND PHOTOGRAPHY AS SPECTACLE   123

If there is magic in Rushdie's realism, it is akin to the "form of madness" that Debord identifies in the post-industrial subject who is "condemned to the passive acceptance of an alien everyday reality" in which "all directly lived truth" is repressed by the "organization of appearances." It is only "by resorting to magical devices," Debord explains, that the spectator can conjure the "illusion that he is reacting to this fate." Debord points to the "recognition and consumption of commodities" as being "the core of this pseudo-response" to spectacle ([1967] 1995, 219). Each of the characters treated in this study turns at some point to producing and consuming images as a false means of overcoming the alienation of spectatorial distance. Jude Fawley restores Gothic stonework as a means of participating in feudal culture, and Sue Bridehead buys statues of pagan idols to recover a pre-Christian Hellenic perspective. Lucy Honeychurch breaks free from the pension to experience the "real" Florence, only to end up buying postcards of neo-classical art. Lucy Swithin gives tours of Pointz Hall to forge a connection with dynastic history and thanks the pageant-master for making her feel like she could have been Cleopatra. To these we add Saleem's belief that he can shape the real by inscribing it in cinematic conventions and that being photographed makes one visible and consequential to Western eyes.

Declaring early on in his narration that "nobody from Bombay should be without a basic film vocabulary," Saleem mines the director's lexicon of cutaways, fade-outs, zooms, long-shots and close-ups throughout the novel to reassert agency in an environment in which he has been sidelined as a spectator (Rushdie [1981] 2006, 30).[3] He uses spectatorial distance as both a defense mechanism and a false means of control over events. When Saleem follows his mother to a restaurant and discovers that she is having an affair, he describes observing her with her lover through the "cinema-screen window" of the Pioneer Café. At one point he narrates an "extreme close-up" on the minute details of a pack of cigarettes on the table in order to avoid looking at his mother's face (248). Saleem walks out on "the movie" altogether after the lovers begin to engage in techniques of sublimated eroticism commonly employed by filmmakers to outwit Bombay's censors. He similarly objectifies the mechanics of vision in order to evade responsibility for his voyeurism when he becomes trapped in a hiding place in his mother's bathroom after she enters. Saleem explains in a clinical voice how "unblinking pupil takes in upside-down image of sari falling to the floor, an image, which is, as usual, inverted by the mind"

(184). It is as if he, like Christopher Isherwood, is merely a camera that records the images brought before him with no intentionality.

Saleem's illusion of participating in the real through cinema is shared by others in the novel. Members of the working class routinely flock to the Pioneer Café to be cast as extras in the latest Bollywood studio effort, exhibiting the dysfunctional desire to self-actualize by being transformed into an image for distribution and consumption. They return to the same café in the afternoon to attend meetings of the Communist party, pursuing what Saleem characterizes as merely "a different set of dreams" (Rushdie [1981] 2006, 258). The connection Rushdie draws between these alienated impulses to reassert a sense of agency through the film industry and political organization recalls Debord's critique of various socialist movements that replicate capitalism's consumerist logic. Debord argues that these movements contributed to the spectacle by generating a utopian image of reality that was disjoined from the "historical struggle" of lived experience. He calls this image "the proletariat as subject and representation" ([1967] 1996, 59), and it aptly describes the regulars at the Pioneer Café. As film extras in the morning and extras in the Communist party in the afternoon, they participate in the spectacle's collapse of materialism and idealism into a state of "total ideology" that offers them nothing more than what Debord describes as "a false way out of a generalized autism" ([1967] 1995, 218).

The screenwriting career of Saleem's uncle, Hanif Aziz, further reinforces this connection between the film industry and socialism as forms of spectacle. Having achieved great success producing exotic romances, Hanif experiences a conversion to socialist realism late in his career. He forsakes Bollywood's "temple of illusions" and attempts instead to rouse the consciousness of Indian audiences that had been "dreaming for five thousand years" (Rushdie [1981] 2006, 279). Hanif blames mainstream cinema for perpetuating stereotypes of Indian culture—the very same stereotypes that Rushdie would later be accused of perpetuating in *Midnight's Children*. Hanif commits himself instead to writing scripts that feature "ordinary people and social problems" and which portray "work, not kissing" (277, 280). His final film project features a chutney factory run by women and includes lengthy scenes detailing the pickling process. Reminiscent of Woolf's critique of Bennett, Hanif's work as an "arch-disciple of naturalism" yields a dehumanized simulacrum of lived experience (279). Hanif confuses realism with an amoral, quasi-journalistic naturalism that is characterized by "matter of fact descriptions of the outré and bizarre, and their reverse, namely heightened, stylized versions of the everyday." Saleem observes that while such fiction bears a material resemblance to reality, it reproduces "a picture of the world of startling uniformity" whose "terrifying, nonchalant violence"—like the pulp fiction novel *No Orchids* that Orwell critiques—is incapable of eliciting an ethical response (250).

At one point, however, Rushdie deconstructs the physical space of the movie theater in order to make the dynamics of spectatorship visible to the reader. For a moment the "temple of illusions" becomes a site of re-embodied vision and authentic consciousness. Saleem describes the spectator sitting in the back row of the movie theater in much the same way that Jonathan Crary describes the observer stationed inside a *camera obscura*. In each case, experiential knowledge of the world is replaced by rational separation from the world and contemplation of an objective, disembodied projection of the real. Saleem explains, however, that the movie-goer can shed this purely spectatorial stance and puncture the spectacle's illusion of objectivity by "gradually moving up, row by row, until your nose is almost pressed against the screen." With this collapse of focal distance, "the stars' faces dissolve into dancing grain" and "tiny details assume grotesque proportions" (Rushdie [1981] 2006, 189), just as the aesthetic unity of historical representation is disrupted by La Trobe's pageant in *Between the Acts* when it ventures too close to the present day. Saleem's gesture of pressing the spectator's nose up to the screen parallels the novel's function as meta-spectacle, which similarly confronts the reader with the mechanisms of spectacle through which an objectified image of the real comes to be accepted as reality itself.

This same ambiguity with which cinema reinforces and resists the dynamics of spectacle at various moments in *Midnight's Children* extends to Rushdie's treatment of photography. The photograph is a complex assemblage of technology, social practice and critique of social practice. It functions in the novel simultaneously as a product of industrial transformation, an expression of the power to observe and document the colonial subject, a site of resistance to empire through which a nationalist iconography is reclaimed, and the point of departure for a postmodern ethics of seeing. One can trace Debord's influence on Rushdie through references in *Midnight's Children* and Rushdie's essays to critiques of photography by Susan Sontag and John Berger that draw heavily upon the concept of *détournement*. Recall that Debord describes *détournement* as the process whereby the "despotism of a fragment imposing itself as the pseudo-knowledge of a frozen whole" is restored to "its context, its own movement and ultimately the overall frame of reference of its period" ([1967] 1995, 208). Susan Sontag describes the photograph similarly as a "fragment," a "quotation [...] open to any kind of reading," falsely regarded as a "piece of reality" (1977, 71, 74). Just as Debord critiques the spectacle for naturalizing a socially conditioned way of seeing, Sontag writes that "photographs have become the norm for the way things appear to us, thereby changing the very idea of reality and of realism" (87). Through photography, Sontag concludes, "history is converted into spectacle," "people become customers of reality," and—as with Hanif's naturalism—"every subject is depreciated into an article of consumption [and] promoted into an item for aesthetic appreciation" (110). Berger invokes the process of *détournement* when he argues that photography must be represented in a "radial system" of words and other images as a contextual aid to social and political memory so that individual images are not ascribed positive meanings or substituted for memory in a fascist manner (2001, 292–3).

Further reflection on the connotation of photography in the colonial context is essential to comprehend the full resonance of Rushdie's critique of spectacle and to avoid misreading *Midnight's Children* as magical and exotic. Why, for example, does Saleem's grandmother Naseem react so violently when her husband Aadam commissions a photographer to take portraits of their family? At first glance, the epic proportions of her resistance read like a tall tale through which Saleem rehearses a quaint and amusingly backward oral culture. It is tempting to regard Naseem as a superstitious native whose role is to provide a bit of local color and elicit a patronizing smirk from the Western reader. One can imagine Eleanor Lavish from *A Room with a View* jotting down notes about this figure known as the "Reverend Mother" as part of her "calculations in realism" for the backdrop of a romance set in Bombay.

Naseem's refusal to sit for a photographer, however, participates in the broader tension in the novel between her traditional Indian upbringing and the Western attitudes toward science, sex and politics with which Aadam returns from Heidelberg. In spite of the fact that Aadam leaves Germany because he is uncomfortable with the ethnocentrism of his European acquaintances, his partial acculturation to the West leaves him culturally homeless. Emblazoned with the word *Heidelberg*, Aadam's medicine bag becomes a divisive metonym for the infiltration of his rural village by Western technology. Aadam is first introduced to Naseem by her father, who commissions Aadam to perform various medical examinations of Naseem, but insists that Aadam's observations be mediated by a "perforated sheet" for the sake of propriety. Like the aperture of the *camera obscura*, the hole in the sheet inserts a clinical distance between Aadam and the disembodied physical fragments of Naseem. At the same time Aadam comes to fetishize a false knowledge of Naseem through his eventual accumulation of partial views of her body that leads him to fall in love with her and accede to her father's proposal of their marriage. Their courtship mirrors the explorer's gaze that both objectifies and exoticizes the native, and Aadam later replicates the violent exposure of the colonial subject (and anticipates the continued violence of modernization under Indira Gandhi) when he burns Naseem's veils in order to force her to abandon the purdah and become a sexually liberated "modern Indian woman" (Rushdie [1981] 2006, 32). Aadam's impulse to photograph his family emerges in this context as further evidence of his deprecation to European practices, just as his blind father-in-law purchases a neo-classical oil painting of Diana the Huntress because he is "a lover of culture" (14). In this context, the Reverend Mother's stance as "an ironclad citadel of traditions and certainties" is not humorous hyperbole, nor does her turbulent marriage to Aadam Aziz serve as a timeless domestic farce (40). Their relationship pits the very integrity of India's cultural tradition against European imperialism, restating this conflict of social forces on a human scale in precisely the manner for which Lukàcs praises classic realism.

Instead of provincial ignorance or naïve suspicion, Naseem's behavior is most accurately understood as a defensive response to Aadam's desire to be photographed, which she regards as welcoming the colonizers into their own living room to document their domestic life. Sontag critiques this imperialist aspect of the photographer as both a "supertourist" and an "extension of the anthropologist" who is perpetually "visiting natives and bringing back news of their exotic doings" in the attempt to "colonize new experience" (1977, 42). Photography was first introduced to India by the British shortly after its invention in 1839 for the imperialist purpose of topographical surveying (Pelizzari 2003a, 13). Such photographs made their way into British travel guides that extended the Grand Tour through the far reaches of the Empire and rendered India accessible to Western tourists (Pelizzari 2003b, 29–31). By the time of the Calcutta International Exhibition in 1883, the colonial counterpart to London's Great Exhibition at the Crystal Palace three decades earlier, photography had come to play an important role in the colonial government's ability to catalog all aspects of Indian society (Hoffenberg 2003), including the exhibition of its "indexical power" to "order reality" for the colonized population (Pinney 2003, 266–7). Photography came to be associated in India with the Raj's "intoxication with precision and exactitude both descriptive and spatial" and was viewed as complicit in the dehumanizing scientific "efficiency" of colonial rule (Pinney 2003, 269).

Sontag observes that people in non-industrialized countries often resist being photographed as if it were "some sort of trespass, disrespect, or sublimated cultural looting," whereas people in industrialized countries where the spectacle holds sway tend to feel that they are "made real by the photograph" and "incorporated into the historical record" (1977, 161). Rushdie embodies this cultural divide in the conflict between Naseem and Aadam. Tainted by spectacle during his stay in the West, Aadam exhibits the taxidermic impulse of the colonizer in his desire to display his wife and children as "life-sized blow-up photographs" on the wall of his living room. Naseem regards this exposure and objectification as an extension of Aadam's burning of her veils. Saleem observes that she "was not one to be trapped in anyone's little black box" and declares—in triumphant defiance of the panoptical gaze of the European lens—that "there are no photographs of my grandmother anywhere on earth" (Rushdie [1981] 2006, 40). In language that is reminiscent of Sontag's, Rushdie has noted "something predatory about photography" in this scene and compares Naseem's actions to Princess Diana's fatal attempt in 1997 to flee the voyeuristic lenses of the paparazzi (2002, 104, 109–10).

The Reverend Mother's resistance to being photographed is reflected in the Indian government's decision in the 1960s to replace photographs of national monuments in school textbooks with pen-and-ink drawings. Indian artists stripped away the picturesque elements and staged exoticism of the landscape photography that had originally been commissioned by the Raj (Chatterjee 2003, 283). This effected a symbolic reversal of publishing practices a century earlier, in which picturesque elements not found in India's landscapes were added in by English engravers when transferring photographic images to metal plates for use in British travel literature (Falconer 2003, 161). The photography-free textbooks were intended to undermine the seeming objectivity of photographic realism and its suggestion that the spectator enjoys authentic access to or possession of a geographical space and its history (Chatterjee 2003, 283; Sontag 1977, 9). Ironically, however, the elimination of any geographical or social context in the drawings of the monuments merely traded the romanticism of the colonial vision for an equally romantic nationalist vision. The picturesque antiquarianism of the state-sponsored photography of the Raj suggested the need for British stewardship of India's heritage as a set of ancient ruins, while the nationalists' idealized portrayal of Indian architectural monuments concealed the historical reality of India's contemporary political and economic disarray. In both cases, images function as an opportunistic quotation of reality taken out of context to affirm a particular ideology. For this reason Rushdie beseeches his readers to experience sites like the Taj Mahal in person instead of allowing the "million million counterfeits" in textbooks, postcards and advertisements to substitute for lived experience (2002, 172).

These contested photographs of India's architectural monuments feature in Rushdie's depiction of Lifafa Das' traveling "peepshow." Lifafa peddles a montage of photographs among rural villages throughout India, exploiting the touristic impulse to be connected with the cosmopolitan center through his enticement to "See the whole world, come see everything!" (Rushdie [1981] 2006, 81). This "world" is composed entirely of photographs, principally those of famous sites such as the Taj Mahal, the Meenakshi Temple and the Ganges River. To avoid insulating his audience from the "not-so-pleasant features of his age," Lifafa introduces an element of social realism to his show by incorporating occasional images of contemporary political figures, poverty and social protest (82). Any political consciousness in his selection of photographs, however, is undermined by the commodified voyeurism of the exhibition. Lifafa's inclusion of a publicity photograph of film star Carmen Miranda points to the latently pornographic aspect of his "peepshow," which is consistent with the common use of the stereoscope in Europe by the end of the nineteenth century to view erotica (Crary 1990, 127). Like bacchants swept into a destructive frenzy, children swarm Lifafa while clamoring to view his images. As Lifafa attempts to pacify them, a young girl notices some political graffiti painted on the wall behind him and accuses Lifafa of being a Hindu, whereupon a riot ensues.

Although Rushdie has been faulted for "collapsing cultural politics into ethnic spectacle" in his novels (Huggan 2001, 67), he launches a pointed critique of that very process in his depiction of Lifafa's peepshow. Lifafa's photographs themselves—even the socially conscious ones—do not elicit an ethical response. The riot is ignited instead by the incidental presence of a religious symbol in the midst of a crowd driven mad by its insatiable desire to view the images and partake in the spectacle's illusion of totality. Rushdie pairs Lifafa's manipulation of the spectators with Saleem's decision to narrate the scene from a "foreshortened" aerial perspective, which provides the reader with a global view of the events that parodies the claims of the peepshow itself. Saleem's visual composition of the scene recalls the groundless perspective of many nineteenth-century European landscape paintings, an imaginary panoptical vantage point that has been associated with the imperialist gaze (Helsinger 1994). The last one hears of Lifafa is that he has become obsessed with adding more and more photographs to his collection in the quixotic pursuit of a literal and total reproduction of the real. Echoing Sontag's critique of photography as falsely conveying "the sense of holding the whole world in our hands as an anthology of images" (1977, 3), Saleem expresses concern that Lifafa's "urge to encapsulate the whole of reality" is an "Indian disease" that will infect Saleem's own narrative (Rushdie [1981] 2006, 82).

Like influenza or smallpox inflicted by settlers on an indigenous population, however, this disease is by no means of Indian origin, but is rooted in the "museumizing imagination" that emerged in Europe during the nineteenth century (Pelizzari 2003b, 37). Ethnographic studies of India commissioned by the British East India Company to optimize colonial administration, scholarly studies of Indian civilization that legitimized British intervention, and travel literature that commodified India for consumption by British tourists relied heavily upon the photograph's apparent capacity to replicate reality and render it portable (Guha-Thakurta 2003, 121; Hoffenberg 2003, 191). At that time the photograph enjoyed an aura of objectivity that was not heavily scrutinized, as it appeared—in comparison with landscape painting—to be a relatively scientific means of reproducing reality (Bann 2003, 64–5). One encounters praise of photographs for their "picturesque" potential and historical "legibility," as in James Fergusson's 1848 volume titled *Picturesque Illustrations of Ancient Architecture in Hindostan*. Exemplifying Sontag's critique of the photograph's "surrealist abbreviation of history" (1977, 68), Fergusson constructs a romanticized historical narrative of Indian architectural styles. He undertakes this study based entirely on photographs years after returning from his field work in India, a dubious methodology that participates in a growing trend at the time whereby images and their textual descriptions displaced the authority of direct site observation (Guha-Thakurta 2003, 123). This reliance on photographs as an objective historical record becomes even more problematic in light of the nationalist movement's appropriation of photographs originally commissioned by the Raj. For example, the very same photographs taken by the British in the aftermath of the Sepoy

Rebellion in 1858 to document the Indians' uncivilized savagery were eventually incorporated into nationalist Indian history textbooks and merely re-captioned to vilify the British occupiers (Gupta 2003, 238).

An opportunistic use of images lies at the center of a more recent controversy surrounding criticism of Azar Nafisi's 2003 memoir titled *Reading Lolita in Tehran* about her experiences as a female student and faculty member in the aftermath of the Islamic Revolution of 1979. The front cover of the book jacket features a photograph of two young Iranian women in full headscarves looking down below the margins of the image at what one assumes to be a text. One of them appears to be smiling coyly, as if poring over a particularly taboo passage. Hamid Dabashi, a prominent scholar of Iranian culture who was highly critical of Nafisi's memoir, eventually determined that in the original photograph the women were taking pleasure in a newspaper article about the victory of the reform candidate in a recent election. Dabashi writes, "Cropping the newspaper, their classmates behind them, and a perfectly visible photograph of President Khatami – the iconic representation of the reformist movement – out of the picture and suggesting that the two young women are reading *Lolita* strips them of their moral intelligence and their participation in the democratic aspirations of their homeland, ushering them into a colonial harem"—a gesture that Dabashi regards as emblematic of the exoticism of Nafisi's memoir itself (Byrne 2016, A16). Like Rushdie, Nafisi has been accused of participating in both a "Zionist conspiracy and U.S. imperialism" and chastised for "washing [her nation's] dirty laundry in front of the enemy." Also like Rushdie, Nafisi has found herself elevated as a cultural icon by the mass media in a manner that complicates the reception of her work. She agreed to participate, for example, in a marketing campaign for Audi titled "Never Follow" because of the exposure it could bring to her ethical objectives, but which also found her mingling with celebrities and pursued by paparazzi at posh Manhattan receptions and subject to unlikely captioning, as in the comment of one Audi executive that "Azar is to literature what Audi is to cars" (Salamon 2004).

Rushdie illustrates this fluidity of photographic evidence within the spectacle during Saleem's extended reflection on his "memories of a mildewed photograph" that was allegedly taken of the leaders of an underground pro-independence organization. Co-founded by his grandfather Aadam Aziz, the Rani of Cooch Naheen, Mian Abdullah (an entertainer and activist also known as the Hummingbird), and Nadir Khan (the Hummingbird's personal secretary and a poet), the "Free Islam

Convocation" attempted to attract factions away from the Muslim League, a Pakistani group which the Rani describes as "landowners with vested interests to protect [...] who go like toads to the British and form governments for them" (Rushdie [1981] 2006, 46). Saleem pairs specific visual details from the photograph with vignettes of dialog from the conversation among those pictured. In each instance, however, the visual details either fail to support or directly contradict the substance of the conversation that Saleem reports. According to Saleem, for instance, the Hummingbird boasts of his physical conditioning to Aziz and dares Aziz to punch him in the stomach, yet Saleem notes that the "folds of a loose white shirt conceal the stomach, and my grandfather's fist is not clenched but swallowed up by the hand of the ex-conjurer." Saleem observes that the Rani "was going white in blotches," a visual effect that is plausibly explained by the mildew on the photograph, an overexposed negative or even an actual pigment deficiency known as vitiligo. Saleem then extrapolates this ambiguous visual detail from the fading photograph into a metaphorical symptom of Anglicization, "a disease which leaked into history and erupted on an enormous scale shortly after Independence." He claims that the Rani described herself to the others as "the hapless victim of [...] cross-cultural concerns" and her skin as "the outward expression of the internationalism of my spirit." Finally, Saleem recounts how Nadir Khan coyly described his dabbling in poetry to the others, assuring the reader that Nadir's feet "would be shuffling in embarrassment" if they were not "frozen by the snapshot" (45).

There is no mention of who took this photograph, why it was taken, the circumstances under which Saleem once saw it, or how he came to have such an intimate knowledge of the substance of the meeting, which occurred before he was born. There is no indication in the photograph that a conversation transpires, as each character wears a "foolish, rigid smile" within the photograph's "still, immobile scene" (Rushdie [1981] 2006, 45). Saleem refers to the four figures as consummate *ventriloquists* whose non-moving lips he must attempt to read, which might explain why the characters curiously end up debating the merits of social realism in modernist poetry despite having convened to discuss the future of India. Just as the photographs of the Sepoy Rebellion were commandeered to validate both colonial and nationalist historical accounts, Saleem appears to have re-captioned this photograph to serve his own rhetorical strategy in *Midnight's Children* and focus the reader on issues of realist representation. The ambivalence of Saleem's ekphrastic account of this fictional photograph dramatizes Sontag's critique of photography in general as being "open to any kind of reading" as well as her argument that "only that which narrates can make us understand" (1977, 71, 23).

It is improbable that the participants in a clandestine meeting of a subversive political organization would ever have posed for such a photograph. Not even the more significant event of Mian Abdullah's assassination shortly after this meeting is preserved in the public record, having been suppressed by British authorities and perpetuated only in local lore. Saleem most likely invents this photograph in order to endow these marginalized figures with the aura of historical legitimacy. By placing them in a photograph, Saleem makes them real within the spectacle and invests them with the value accorded by Western society to the staged political photo-op. Saleem's "memory" bears close resemblance to propaganda shots commissioned by the British East India Company of the leaders of various puppet governments and theater states of the very sort that the Rani criticizes. Photographs like those taken by Company photographer Linnaeus Tripe in the mid-nineteenth century exemplify Debord's concept of the "immobilized spectacle of non-history" ([1967] 1995, 214). One stages the Raja with his assembly in a hall that is decorated—much like Saleem's childhood home—in a conspicuously British Victorian style. In another, the Raja is seated at his desk while signing an official order "under the watchful gaze of a Brahman bureaucrat and the colonial state" (Dirks 2003, 212). In spite of their role in overturning colonial rule in numerous instances, nationalist movements are problematic for Said insofar as they are typically "led by bourgeoisies that were partly formed and to some extent produced by the colonial power" such that "one simply gets the old colonial structures replicated in new national terms" (Said 1990, 74). The stiff, forced aspect of Rushdie's photo of the leaders of the Free Islam Convocation parodies the spectacle of propagandistic photography in colonial India, but also reminds the reader that that the nationalist movement would later stage its own spectacles.

Like the socialist movements that Debord critiques for failing to transcend the logic of capitalism, Saleem's own Midnight's Children Conference resembles his grandfather's Free Islam Convocation as an ineffective bureaucracy that loses touch with the "historical struggle" and degenerates into ideology. The Midnight's Children Conference is the culmination of Saleem's desperate attempts to demonstrate that he is "inextricably entwined with [his] world" and "symbolically at one with history." Of the various combinations of active, passive, literal and metaphorical connections to history that he attempts to establish, Saleem concedes that the Conference never achieves "the first, most significant of the 'modes of connection,'" noting that "the 'active-literal' passed us by" (Rushdie [1981] 2006, 273). The remaining three modes—"passive-metaphorical," "passive-literal" and "active-metaphorical"—each participate in the spectacle's illusion of encounter. Saleem explains that although he was "no more than a tourist, a child peeping through the miraculous peepholes" of the equivalent of Lifafa Das' box of images, "the feeling had come upon me that I was somehow creating a world; that the thoughts I jumped inside were mine, that the bodies I occupied acted at my command; that, as current affairs, arts, sports, the whole rich variety of a first-class radio station poured into me, I was somehow *making them happen*." Reflecting as an adult on this experience, he concludes in hindsight that "the spirit of self-aggrandizement which seized me then was a reflex, born of an instinct for self-preservation" against the "flooding multitudes" and their "massed identities" (199). Just as the Pioneer Café brings movie extras and Communists under one abstracted roof, the voices of "All-India Radio" that resound in Saleem's head and his telepathic conference with the other midnight's children link mass media and political organizing as the driving forces that suppress individually lived experience beneath the spectacle of a unified India.

By the conclusion of the novel, Saleem recognizes the alienating spectatorial distance created by the privileging of vision within the post-industrial world. He comes to associate visual experience with the perspective of occupiers and tourists. Rushdie contrasts the symmetry of the "new city" built by "a race of pink conquerors" to the "houses in the narrow lanes" of old Bombay. The original dwellings "leaned over, jostled, shuffled, blocked each other's view of the roseate edifices of power," and their occupants preferred to "look inwards into [...] screened-off courtyards" as if in refusal to gaze upon the imperialist spectacle (Rushdie [1981] 2006, 74). Whereas the inhabitants shun the view, one camera-toting tourist seeks instead to exclude all sensory experience but the visual, touting how much beauty there is to consume in India if only one did not also have to eat the food (478). One is reminded once again of the tourist's panoptical view of Florence from inside the glass-enclosed tram that Lucy Honeychurch contemplates from the balcony of her "room with a view," a scene that enacts the same foreshortened aerial perspective of the imperial gaze.

As a corrective for an "amnesiac nation," Saleem shifts his spectatorial paradigm for historical consciousness away from the visual framework of the movie screen and photograph to engage the senses of smell and taste through his "chutnification of history" and "pickling of time" (Rushdie [1981] 2006, 529). Saleem comes to realize that camera angles, cuts and splices, cropping and captioning produce the selective memory of ideology and engineered ignorance, whereas one cannot un-pickle something that has come into contact with brine. This metaphor of marinating in history captures the true hybridity of the post-colonial situation—the cultural and political brine of empire that continues to flavor the experience of modern India. The melding of flavor among the components of chutney participates in Pico's syncretizing perspective and dispels the pageantizing mindset that falsifies experience through its artificial linear divisions of time. While Hanif's naturalistic cinema reproduces the technique of the pickling process with dry literality, Saleem allows the ethos of pickling to inform the realism of his narrative. Saleem performs the recalibration of "life in value" and "life in time" that Forster attributes to realist fiction by heightening certain flavors of experience "in degree, but not in kind" to show how the past resurfaces subjectively within our understanding of the present. He models authentic historical consciousness for the reader by comparing each chapter of the novel to a pickle jar that possesses "the authentic taste of truth" because it participates in the organic function of memory and understanding regardless of its chronological accuracy (531).

A critique of "image-saturated times" that authentically transcends the logic of spectatorship requires just such a turning away from the visual (Rushdie 2002, 172). Forster intuits this when he compares Henry James' fiction to the "rounded off" experience of looking at a painting or sculpture versus the symphonic "opening out" of the consciousness produced by realist fiction. Returning to the Pension Bertolini in Florence for their honeymoon at the end of *A Room with a View*, Lucy and George turn away from the windows and allow the sounds of indigenous city life and the river Arno to enter the room. Swithin's epiphany at the fish pond at the end of *Between the Acts* is sparked by a breeze that restores her sense of tactility and allows her to recognize her immersion, like the fish, in a medium that had become invisible to her. It is not until Saleem's parents trick him into undergoing an operation to clear his sinuses that his voyeuristic and spectatorial relationship to the Midnight's Children Conference is displaced by the sense of smell that had been suppressed throughout his childhood.

Saleem is reduced at birth to an image—the mirror of the life of the nation—and struggles throughout the novel to regain his tactility as a fully dimensioned individual. Said credits the Irish nationalist poet William Butler Yeats with the ability to "rise from the level of personal experience to that of national archetype, without losing the immediacy of the former or the stature of latter" (1990, 92). When Saleem achieves this stature at the end of novel, however, he develops cracks and fissures all over his body under the strain of embodying the spectacle of nationalist unity. The realist ethic of meta-spectacle is accompanied, perhaps, by a burden from which the lyric poet is spared. Although Saleem considers several possible endings for his narrative that would spare him annihilation, he recognizes that each partakes of an aesthetic unity that would falsify the real. Instead, Saleem is ultimately atomized into dust in the final lines of the novel by a massive crowd comprising of millions of individuals who constitute the authentic diversity of lived experience in India. He experiences the process through which the spectacle "erases the dividing line between self and world" such that "the self, under siege by the presence/absence of the world, is eventually overwhelmed" (Debord [1967] 1995, 219). Saleem cannot cohere as a unified embodiment of the nation without resorting to the illusions afforded by spectacle. Rushdie's realist ethic demands that the reader witness Saleem's destruction so that an ideologically flattened character can be revivified and re-dimensioned through tactile experience.

Notes

1. Reed seeks to exclude Dickens from the realist canon, regarding Dickens instead as a hyperrealist in light of his "ability to convey a sense of the everyday world while at the same time almost magically transforming it" (2010, 4). Reed explicitly rejects the application of "magical realism" to Dickens' fiction and points instead to "something much more insidious that is rooted in style, not content," which explores the effect of the imagination on the real in a manner that one expects to find in lyric Romantic poetry (2, 4). Rushdie's self-comparison to Dickens suggests a shared quality in their fiction that participates in Reed's sense of the hyperreal and which has perhaps mutually complicated their critical reception as realists.
2. For further discussion of Rushdie's allusion to Millais' *Boyhood of Raleigh*, see Kortenaar (1997) and Trussler (2000).
3. See Chowdry (2000) for additional discussion of the narrator's use of technical film vocabulary in *Midnight's Children*.

REFERENCES

Aijaz, Ahmad. 1992. *Theory: Classes, Nations, Literatures.* London: Verso.

Bann, Stephen. 2003. Antiquarianism, Visuality, and the Exotic Moment. In *Traces of India: Photography, Architecture and the Politics of Representation, 1850–1900*, ed. Maria Antonella Pelizzari, 60–85. New Haven: Yale University Press.

Barnett, Anthony. 1989. After Nationalism. In *Patriotism: The Making and Unmaking of British National Identity, Volume I: History and Politics*, ed. Raphael Samuel, 140–155. New York: Routledge.

Berger, John. 2001. *Selected Essays.* Ed. Geoff Dyer. New York: Pantheon.

Brigg, Peter. 1987. Salman Rushdie's Novels: The Disorder in Fantastic Order. *World Literature Written in English* 22 (1): 119–130.

Byrne, Richard. 2016. Peeking Under the Cover. *Chronicle of Higher Education*, October 13, A16.

Chatterjee, Partha. 2003. The Sacred Circulation of National Images. In *Traces of India: Photography, Architecture and the Politics of Representation, 1850–1900*, ed. Maria Antonella Pelizzari, 276–292. New Haven: Yale University Press.

Chowdry, Prem. 2000. *Colonia India and the Making of Empire Cinema: Image, Ideology and Identity.* Manchester: Manchester University Press.

Crary, Jonathan. 1990. *Techniques of the Observer: On Vision and Modernity in the Nineteenth Century.* Cambridge: MIT Press.

Debord, Guy. (1967) 1995. *The Society of the Spectacle.* Trans. Donald Nicholson-Smith. New York: Zone Books.

Dirks, Nicholas B. 2003. Colonia Amnesia and the Old Regime in the Photographs of Linnaeus Tripe. In *Traces of India: Photography, Architecture and the Politics of Representation, 1850–1900*, ed. Maria Antonella Pelizzari, 196–215. New Haven: Yale University Press.

Eagleton, Terry. 1990. Nationalism: Irony and Commitment. In *Nationalism, Colonialism and Literature*, 23–42. Minneapolis: University of Minnestoa Press.

Falconer, John. 2003. Pattern of Photographic Surveys: Joseph Lawton in Ceylon. In *Traces of India: Photography, Architecture and the Politics of Representation, 1850–1900*, ed. Maria Antonella Pelizzari, 154–173. New Haven: Yale University Press.

Faris, Wendy B. 1995. Scheherazade's Children: Magical Realism and Postmodern Fiction. In *Magical Realism: Theory, History, Community*, ed. Lois Parkinson Zamora and Wendy B. Faris, 163–190. Durham: Duke University Press.

Guha-Thakurta, Tapati. 2003. The Compulsions of Visual Representation in Colonial India. In *Traces of India: Photography, Architecture and the Politics of Representation, 1850–1900*, ed. Maria Antonella Pelizzari, 108–139. New Haven: Yale University Press.

138   E. BARNABY

Gupta, Narayani. 2003. Pictorializing the 'Mutiny' of 1857. In *Traces of India: Photography, Architecture and the Politics of Representation, 1850–1900*, ed. Maria Antonella Pelizzari, 216–239. New Haven: Yale University Press.

Helsinger, Elizabeth. 1994. Turner and the Representation of England. In *Landscape and Power*, ed. W.J.T. Mitchell, 103–125. Chicago: University of Chicago Press.

Hoffenberg, Peter H. 2003. Photography and Architecture at the *Calcutta International Exhibition*. In *Traces of India: Photography, Architecture and the Politics of Representation, 1850–1900*, ed. Maria Antonella Pelizzari, 174–195. New Haven: Yale University Press.

Huggan, Graham. 2001. *Postcolonial Exotic: Marketing the Margins*. Florence: Routledge.

Jameson, Fredric. 1975. Magical Narratives: Romance as Genre. *New Literary History* 7: 135–159.

———. 1981. *The Political Unconscious: Narrative as a Socially Symbolic Act*. Ithaca: Cornell University Press.

Kortenaar, Neil ten. 1997. Postcolonial Ekphrasis: Salman Rushdie Gives the Finger Back to the Empire. *Contemporary Literature* 38 (2): 232–259.

Memmi, Albert. 2006. *Decolonization and the Decolonized*. Minneapolis: University of Minnesota Press.

Needham, Anuradha Dingwaney. 2000. *Using the Master's Tools: Resistance and the Literature of the African and South Asian Diasporas*. New York: St. Martin's.

Parameswaran, Uma. 1984. Handcuffed to History: Salman Rushdie's Art. *ARIEL: A Review of International English Literature* 15 (1): 34–45.

Pelizzari, Maria Antonella. 2003a. Introduction to *Traces of India: Photography, Architecture and the Politics of Representation, 1850–1900*, ed. Maria Antonella Pelizzari, 13–18. New Haven: Yale University Press.

———. 2003b. From Stone to Paper: Photographs of Architecture and the Traces of History. In *Traces of India: Photography, Architecture and the Politics of Representation, 1850–1900*, ed. Maria Antonella Pelizzari, 20–59. New Haven: Yale University Press.

Pinney, Christopher. 2003. Some Indian 'Views of India': The Ethics of Representation. In *Traces of India: Photography, Architecture and the Politics of Representation, 1850–1900*, ed. Maria Antonella Pelizzari, 262–275. New Haven: Yale University Press.

Price, David W. 1994. Salman Rushdie's 'Use and Abuse of History' in Midnight's Children. *ARIEL: A Review of International English Literature* 25 (2): 91–107.

Reed, John. 2010. *Dickens's Hyperrealism*. Columbus: Ohio State University Press.

Rosaldo, Renato. 1993. *Culture and Truth: The Remaking of Social Analysis*. London: Routledge.

Rushdie, Salman. (1981) 2006. *Midnight's Children*. New York: Knopf.

———. 1991. *Imaginary Homelands: Essays and Criticism, 1981–1991*. London: Granta.

———. 2002. *Step Across This Line: Collected Nonfiction 1992–2002*. New York: Random House.

———. 2006. Introduction to *Midnight's Children*, ix–xvi. New York: Knopf.

Said, Edward. 1990. Yeats and Decolonization. In *Nationalism, Colonialism and Literature*, 69–98. Minneapolis: University of Minnesota Press.

Salamon, Julie. 2004. Author Finds That with Fame Comes Image Management. *New York Times*, June 8. http://www.nytimes.com/2004/06/08/books/author-finds-that-with-fame-comes-image-management.html?_r=0. Accessed 10 Sept 2016.

Slemon, Stephen. 1995. Magic Realism and Postcolonial Discourse. In *Magical Realism: Theory, History, Community*, ed. Lois Parkinson Zamora and Wendy B. Faris, 407–426. Durham: Duke University Press.

Sontag, Susan. 1977. *On Photography*. New York: Farrar, Strauss & Giroux.

Trussler, Michael. 2000. Literary Artifacts: Ekphrasis in the Short Fiction of Donald Barthelme, Salman Rushdie and John Edgar Wideman. *Contemporary Literature* 41 (2): 252–290.

Zamora, Lois Parkinson, and Wendy B. Faris. 1995. Introduction: Daiquiri Birds and Flaubertian Parrot(ie)s. In *Magical Realism: Theory, History, Community*, ed. Lois Parkinson Zamora and Wendy B. Faris, 1–14. Durham: Duke University Press.

CHAPTER 6

"The law of white gloves"—
The Museum as Spectacle in
Edward Carey's *Observatory Mansions*

In each of his first two novels, *Observatory Mansions* and *Alva & Irva, The Twins Who Saved a City*, British playwright, author and illustrator Edward Carey depicts characters that have been reduced to spectators of a visually abstracted world and warped by the spectacle's psychological separations. Reviewers describe *Observatory Mansions* as a "gently surreal novel" (Koning 2000) and compare *Alva & Irva* to the "illuminated dreams of Borges and Calvino" in its use of "the fantastic [...] to evoke the true and the terrible" that lurks behind the quotidian (Harrison 2003; Greenland 2003). As with *Midnight's Children*, one sees an immediate and seemingly irresistible impulse to explain away the depiction of spectacle in fiction as magical realism. And yet, like Rushdie, Carey's postmodern sensibilities co-exist with his commitment to the realist critique of false consciousness within an everyday reality that is recognizable to the reader.

Indeed, these same reviewers cite details that link Carey's novels to classic realism. Observing the utter lack of "ordinary people" in Carey's novels, one reviewer applauds the fact that his characters are nevertheless drawn with such "sympathy and acute observation" that instead of degenerating into a "grotesque" collection, they inhabit a coherent "microcosm" and exhibit an "admirable [...] resistance to the forces of conventional reality" (Koning 2000). Carey himself refers to the characters in *Observatory Mansions* as "pure people," "concentrated people," or "how everyday people would be if they were subtracted from work, friends, family and all the motions of life which we are told we should take part in." While they are

© The Author(s) 2018
E. Barnaby, *Realist Critiques of Visual Culture*,
https://doi.org/10.1007/978-3-319-77323-0_6

141

"bizarre creatures who seem to have walked out of strange, dark fairy tales," Carey contends that they are nevertheless "real enough, they are about, they are to be found amongst cities [...] with the rest of us" (2000, 7). Another reviewer notes that Carey strips the cities in his novels of geographic particularity in the manner of Beckett's *mise-en-scènes*, but still describes these cities with such material detail that each exists as "a credible place" (Eve 2003). The city of Entralla in which *Alva & Irva* is set "has the features of an all-purpose European metropolis, with examples of Gothic, Renaissance, Baroque and classical architecture, a ruined medieval castle at its summit and Napoleon Street as its central thoroughfare – not far from the golden arches of McDonald's" (Harrison 2003). While it is more a "generalized, if northerly, Mitteleuropa" than the Paris of Balzac or the London of Dickens, Carey's Entrella participates in the realism of the novel by invoking a recognizably contemporary urban environment that shapes the consciousness of his characters.

A central feature of Debord's *Society of the Spectacle* is that the spectacle "elevates the human sense of sight to the special place once occupied by touch" ([1967] 1995, 18). Carey tackles this phenomenon head-on in his debut novel *Observatory Mansions*. A debilitating spectatorial distance alienates Carey's protagonist, Francis Orme, from the city he struggles to inhabit and instills in Francis a pathological aversion to tactile experience. Carey punctuates the novel's largely undifferentiated cityscape with a wax museum, a public park and an apartment house, laying bare the postmodern urban environment as a space in which authentic encounter has been replaced by acts of exhibiting and viewing. Francis functions as a professional art object within the tourist industry, working as a stand-in human dummy at the wax museum and as a performance artist impersonating statues in the park. He has thoroughly internalized the curatorial impulse, compulsively donning clean white gloves at all times and maintaining a clandestine "Exhibition of Myself" that consists of discarded objects which he collects during walks through the city and steals from his neighbors. The novel's title "Observatory Mansions" refers to the Orme family's dilapidated manor house that has been subdivided into an apartment complex. Along with his parents, other fallen aristocrats and various recluses, Francis dwells in this cabinet of curiosities where the inhabitants are exhibited to each other, but otherwise sparingly interact. Francis is held at arm's length from a reality upon which he is permitted to look, but not touch—that is, at least, until a blind woman named Anna Tap leases a unit in the building and reasserts a non-visual perspective that makes Francis conscious of the spectacle that envelopes him.

Archaeologist Ken-Ichi Sasaki attributes visual knowledge of an urban space—its skylines, monuments and landmarks—to the superficial domain of the visitor, whereas inhabitants are privy to a more tactile and embodied knowledge of the city ([1997] 2000, 36). Sasaki describes this tactile knowledge as "the sum of accumulated experiences" that comprehends the city's genuine *atmosphere*, which is located beyond the predetermined routes and places of interest mapped out for the tourist to consume (42). The inhabitable *atmosphere* of the post-industrial built environment evaporates when it is transformed into an image for consumption, prompting movements like the Situationists to re-inhabit urban space through the practices of psychogeography and *dérive* that I have described above. The city Carey depicts in *Observatory Mansions*, however, lacks any capacity to produce this sort of tactile knowledge. It resembles the contemporary "Generic City" which Dutch architect and urban theorist Rem Koolhaas describes as "a sketch which is never elaborated" and to which "the idea of layering, intensification, completion are alien" (Koolhaas and Mao 1995, 1263). There are no inhabitants of such a city—only permanent tourists. Francis' plight recalls Jude Fawley's imaginary interactions with the statuary of Christminster, as well as the Reverend Eager's delusion that rehearsing Ruskin's appraisal of the frescoes in the Santa Croce establishes him as a resident of Florence. This shift from tactile to visual experience is a form of dispossession that is naturalized within the society of the spectacle as a state of perpetual spectatorship which philosopher Richard Kuhns calls "the museum as habitation" (1991, 261).

Sasaki points to Georges-Eugène Haussmann's modernization of Paris in the mid-nineteenth century as an example of this conversion of the inhabitant's relationship with the built environment from a tactile one to a visual one ([1997] 2000, 38). While Haussmann ostensibly sought to address industrial-era concerns of population growth, public health, traffic flow and commercial development, architectural historian Spiro Kostof argues that Haussmann's vision of "broad, elegant boulevards and vistas artfully focused on monuments also became a model for something else – for urban life as a work of art, an esthetic experience, a public spectacle *sans pareil*" (1992, 266). Haussmann's urban aesthetic was widely imitated in industrializing cities across Europe and its colonies. As portrayed in *Midnight's Children*, sometimes it was imposed on the colony by its occupiers, while in other cases it was self-inflicted by nationalist governments seeking to refashion themselves in the image of the modern West. Haussmannization placed inhabitants on a par with tourists insofar as "straight lines were drawn over the twisted streetscapes of history" and deeply rooted cultural practices were ignored, such as when houses were reoriented to face the street (Kostof 1991, 274). To borrow Benjamin's formulation, Haussmann exchanged the "cult value" of the city (the lived experience of urban space accumulated by its inhabitants) for "exhibition value" (the visually legible summary of the city that is sought out and consumed by tourists).

Long before contemporary critiques of Haussmann, and more than a century before Paris inspired Debord's critique of the city as image, Victor Hugo had already grasped the implications for the city of this modern visual turn. Hugo recognized that the alienating aspects of the industrialized city stemmed not from its rapid growth in population or geographic expansion into the rural countryside, but the fact that a tactile and organic relationship between the built environment and its inhabitants was being replaced by an experience of the city as a visual collage. Recounting in *Notre Dame de Paris* how fourteenth-century Paris "burst its four belts of wall" like a "growing child splitting last year's clothes," Hugo portrays urban growth not only as natural and healthy, but also as a liberating act of defiance against monarchical attempts to control the city commercially and bureaucratically ([1831] 1978, 132). Evolving urban formations supplanted one another over time, so that each age—from the Gothic and Romanesque down to Paris' early Roman and Celtic roots—lay in legible strata beneath the emerging Paris of the Renaissance (148). The "ever more foolish and grotesque fashions" that Hugo attributes to the nineteenth century, however, revive the visual discourses of past ages as cultural commodities and displace historical consciousness with the pseudo-cyclical consciousness of spectacle (128). What Debord would later describe as the bourgeoisie's self-legitimizing appropriation of historical iconography and the emergence of a culture industry ([1967] 1995, 144, 180), Hugo visualizes in the novel as the transformation of Paris from an archaeological dig into a gallery of views.

Hugo's insight helps to pinpoint Carey's nuanced critique of spectacle in *Observatory Mansions*. Carey, like Hugo, distinguishes between the urbanization of the countryside during the industrial era and the truly alienating aspect of the spectacle, namely, its aestheticization of the built environment. The physical expansion of cities does not, in itself, produce the conditions of spectacle and the experience of the "museum as habitation." Louis Wirth, a leading figure of the Chicago School of urban sociology in the 1930s, warned against conflating logistical issues posed by urban growth with more fundamental social transformations wrought by industrial capitalism, noting that it is not merely growing numbers of people, but "a state of interaction under conditions which make their contact as full personalities impossible" that leads to an alienating "segmentalization of human relationships" in modern culture ([1938] 1996, 98–9). In his study of literary treatments of London, Julian Wolfreys has similarly criticized Friedrich Engels for mistaking the modern metropolis as the source of anxiety for the capitalist subject instead of regarding both the city and the individual as alienated products of the same dysfunctional economic system (1998, 120). Far from the city destroying the countryside, Debord argues, the post-industrial economy has "abolished both of these poles" ([1967] 1995, 175). Reconstituted as a cultural commodity for consumption, the post-industrial pseudo-city is a "negation of life" that has, in Debord's words, "invented a visual form for itself" (10).

Debord devotes a chapter of *Society of the Spectacle* to "environmental planning," which he describes as an attempt to "refashion the totality of space" in a capitalist *décor* in order to keep the masses "isolated together" ([1967] 1995, 169, 172). He contends that planned environments stage essentialized modes of social interaction which exacerbate the very sense of alienation that the planners purport to address. Urban historian Robert Fishman identifies this common thread among the work of Ebenezer Howard, Frank Lloyd Wright and Le Corbusier. Though stylistically distinct, each of them attempted to realize utopian visions of urban order through the regulation of space (Fishman 1977). Political historian Judith Shklar critiques this "historical optimism" of social engineers who attempt to establish the "non-places" and thought experiments of classical utopian literature as political realities achieved through reason ([1973] 2000, 291–2). Their competing impulses toward historical preservation and avant-garde futurism flatten the tactile dimensions of urban space into an uninhabitable image that renders the inhabitants homeless in Debord's psychogeographic sense. In this respect, Forster's terminology in *Aspects of the Novel* once again proves useful. Preservationism—like the pageantizing mindset in *Between the Acts*—risks overemphasizing the experience of "life in time" by cultivating a false collective consciousness based on the spectacle of immobilized history. Futurism, on the other hand, risks overemphasizing the experience of "life in value" by razing the historical landscape and, as Henri Lefebvre suggests, reducing "social space and physical space" to a solipsistic "epistemological (mental) space—the space of discourse and the Cartesian *cogito*" (1991, 61, 65). Koolhaas similarly points to urbanists' "belated discovery of the virtues of the classical city at the moment of their definitive impossibility" as an instance of ideology's "fatal moment of disconnection" (Koolhaas and Mao 1995, 963). Severed from the organic accretion of an archaeological site, the built environment is alternatingly reduced to a collection of material objects and a collection of abstract concepts—the very same extremes of pseudo-cyclical consciousness that Debord associates with the triumph of "total ideology" which has achieved material form ([1967] 1995, 214).

Urban planning—like realistic fiction itself—reinforces the spectacle when it fails to integrate the inhabitants' experience of "life in time" and "life in value." Carey substantiates this connection through his efforts to understand how the spaces he narrates in his novels influence the consciousness of his characters. Having built a plasticine model of the fictional city in which his second novel is set, Carey (n.d.) explains that the process of researching architectural guidebooks and building designs in order to construct a fictional city in miniature suggested to him certain parallels between the novelist and city planner, particularly the "responsibility there is to the people who would have to live with, and in, the decisions you make." Carey deliberately flattens the cityscape in *Observatory Mansions* to illustrate the conditions of spectacle through which the contemporary city has become objectified as a collection of views. At the same time, Carey avoids engaging in a realistic reproduction of space through textual description. Instead, with a sensibility that echoes Gaston Bachelard's phenomenological study of architecture in *The Poetics of Space*, Carey's novel advances a realist restatement of space that foregrounds its own limitations as an uninhabitable image.

The figure of the *flâneur* is particularly suited to dramatizing this visual abstraction of the city. The solitary urban walker who catalogs endless observations of the city's burgeoning industrial-era material culture has become emblematic—particularly for Walter Benjamin—of the displacement of the modern subject's tactile proximity to the real by spectatorial distance. Indeed, it is the spectatorial distance provided by the *flâneur*'s anonymous embeddedness in the urban crowd that makes the sensory overload of the modern metropolis tolerable (Lauster 2007, 142). In his essay "A Berlin Chronicle," Benjamin laments the evolution of his visceral experience of Berlin as a child into his more exclusively visual experience of Berlin as an adult. He describes how the material culture of the cityscape recedes into the background as the mere "décor and theater of [his] walks" because his "gaze has brushed them too often" ([1932] 1978, 26).

THE MUSEUM AS SPECTACLE   147

I have noted elsewhere in this study that any realist restatement of the conditions of spectacle is liable to collapse into mere reinforcement of the spectacle if it is received literally or uncritically by the reader. Although certain critics have identified the trope of the *flâneur* as a locus of consciousness in realist fiction toward the act of seeing (Rignall 1992, 2), fiction that replays the observations of the *flâneur* with naturalistic objectivity nevertheless risks inscribing the reader within the *flâneur*'s spectatorial distance. Such fiction is particularly susceptible to Jameson's critique of realism as a containment strategy that reifies the capitalist order. However, Carey does not use Francis to catalog the visual presence of the city for the reader, but instead scrutinizes Francis' very impulse to catalog as an alienated curatorial stance toward reality. Carey presents Francis as overtly dysfunctional and critiques the very social conditions from which his anti-tactile compulsions emerge. His museumized relationship to objects, his habit of wearing white gloves and even his father's addition of the observatory to the manor house are prefigured in several of Benjamin's reflections on post-industrial visual culture in "One-Way Street." Francis thus functions as a post-Benjaminian meta-*flâneur* within Carey's realist critique of spectacle.

Just as the tragic drama must evoke the emotions of pity and fear before they can be purged, Carey's account of the transformation of Tearsham Park into Observatory Mansions initially invites the reader to feel nostalgia for agrarian feudal life and to blame urbanization—and not urbanism—for the alienating effects of the spectacle. The narrator describes how the city had siphoned away younger generations of workers from the estate until a shortage of farmhands forced the Ormes to sell parcels of land to developers. Eventually only the house remained, trapped within a traffic island and a circular wall that the Ormes built as an antagonistic declaration that "this was as far as the city would get" (Carey 2000, 4). They auctioned off family heirlooms to finance the conversion of the manor house into flats, where they are forced to live alongside their tenants. The four columns adorning the neo-classical mansion stand covered in graffiti. Occasional visits from demolition experts maintain a constant threat of annihilation at the hands of city planners. Mother and Father Orme have made a mental escape into the past, lying in self-protective comas in their beds. A melancholy yearning for the pastoral that is mediated by the picturesque landscape tradition informs Carey's descriptions of plain painted walls that were once adorned with "hunting prints" and windows that once opened onto "a parkland filled with nonchalant cattle" (26).

Long before Tearsham Park was subsumed by urban sprawl, however, Father Orme commenced a spectatorial retreat from reality that culminated in his construction of an astronomical observatory on the rooftop of the manor house. The true transformation of "Tearsham Park" into "Observatory Mansions" precedes the urban reorganization of space and reflects instead an epistemological shift in industrial culture from an emphasis on tactile, embodied knowledge of the world to an abstract, predominantly optical one. The first word Father Orme utters upon awakening from his coma is "plough," which Anna Tap misinterprets as his longing for the revival of agrarian society, but which Francis correctly identifies as an astronomical reference to a constellation (Carey 2000, 177). Father Orme's seclusion within his observatory is but the latest phase of his lifelong obsession with observing the world through visual apparatuses that began in his early childhood when he was given a microscope as a gift. His parents attempted to wean him from this condition by replacing his microscope with a series of magnifying glasses of decreasing strengths in order to recalibrate his vision to a life-sized scale. Even after they finally remove the weakest lens from the magnifying glass altogether, he remains dependent on its empty circular frame to focus his attention. As a young man Father Orme discovers binoculars and, as an adult, the telescope, at which point he builds the observatory in order to spend his nights gazing upon the stars and his days contemplating astrological charts.

Beginning with Father Orme's receipt of the microscope (which, Francis notes, "coincided with his absence from the outdoors") and concluding with his retreat to the observatory, the manor house takes on the aspect of a *camera obscura* (Carey 2000, 178). This optical device, which first appeared in the sixteenth century at the same time as the fictional Tearsham Park itself, consisted of a dark room in which the observer was sequestered and which was perforated only by a small aperture that cast images onto its rear wall. Art historian Jonathan Crary recounts that the *camera obscura* was initially credited with overcoming the subjectivity of observation by enabling one's "withdrawal from the world" in order to "regulate and purify one's relation to the manifold contents of the now 'exterior' world." Crary notes, however, that the *camera obscura* was ultimately criticized for contributing to a modern "metaphysics of interiority" that transformed the observer into "a privatized subject confined in a quasi-domestic space, cut off from a public exterior world" (1990, 39). Crary points to Vermeer's 1688 painting titled *The Astronomer* as a

THE MUSEUM AS SPECTACLE   149

poignant example of this dynamic (46). Father Orme resembles the painting's solitary figure, whom Vermeer portrays in the act of consulting various charts, maps and globes while averting his eyes from the window opening out onto the world from his small chamber.

By suppressing the observer's tactile relationship to the environment, the *camera obscura* produces "decorporealized vision" to which Crary attributes the illusion of an uncontaminated, mechanically produced "pregiven world of objective truth" (1990, 39–40). Martin Jay's study of post-Enlightenment visual culture similarly points to the proliferation of the looking glass, microscope, refracting telescope and *camera obscura* in the sixteenth century as part of an intensifying epistemological reliance upon the visual faculty during the early modern era. Like Crary, Jay argues that this emphasis on visual technologies contributed to a sense of "modern individualism, the depersonalization of the external world and the glorification of observation as the only valid way of knowing the world," as well as the "confusion of real and simulacrum that is so much a part of contemporary visual experience" (1993, 65–7, 123). In a brief *pensée* titled "To the Planetarium," Walter Benjamin similarly criticizes modern astronomy for encouraging solipsistic tendencies like Father Orme's that stem from its "exclusive emphasis on an optical connection to the universe" ([1928] 1978, 92). The effects of decorporealized vision extend beyond Father Orme's seclusion in his observatory to afflict the other reclusive residents of Observatory Mansions. Their consciousness of the real is transformed from a tactile encounter with a world that they inhabit into a spectacle that is "seen via different specialized mediations" (Debord [1967] 1995, 18).

One tenant named Mad Lizzy exhibits a compulsion to capture the "essence of city existence" on film. Francis explains that Lizzy photographs the city in order to "feel somehow a part of it," yet she grows "more distanced" from the city with each picture she takes. Instead of participating in the lived experience of the city as an inhabitant, Lizzy heightens her sense of detachment as an observer who is "unable ever to pin the city down" as new people and new events continuously emerge (Carey 2000, 217). Crary argues that the *camera obscura* had a similar effect on eighteenth-century paintings of urban life. The traditional bird's eye perspective which provided a "synoptic and totalizing apprehension of the city as a unified entity" was replaced with a ground-level vantage point which portrayed "a city that is knowable only as the accumulation of multiple and diverse points of view" (Crary 1990, 52–4). The act of photographing the city reduces Lizzy from an inhabitant to a tourist, who must cobble together her sense of place from a series of disconnected glimpses, much like the children clamoring for their turn at Lifafa Das' peep show in the attempt to "see the whole world." As in my discussion of Rushdie's novel, Mad Lizzy's quest is similarly subject to Sontag's critique of photography for providing the false impression of "holding the whole world in our hands as an anthology of images" (1977, 3). Sontag questions the knowledge to be gained from decorporealized vision, maintaining that photographs are not so much "statements about the world" as they are mere "pieces" of it (4). Just as Lifafa Das' audience will never "see the whole world" no matter how many images he adds to his show, Lizzy will never comprehend the city as an inhabitant from behind the lens of her camera.

Mother Orme and another tenant named Lord Pearson frame their reality as museum exhibitions. Their curatorial relationship to objects and people exemplifies Kuhns' critique of the post-industrial city as "the grand container of our time" (1991, 261). For Kuhns, the city has come to function as both a meta-museum in which life is displayed rather than lived, as well as a home to discrete sub-collections of cultural objects that are themselves formally identified as museums. Mother Orme's bedroom, to which Francis refers as the "Exhibition of Mother," is a gallery of personal artifacts with which she surrounds herself so as to maintain a state of continual meditation on her past. Francis notes that "Mother never opened her eyes to a person, only to objects, those certain objects collected in her room" (Carey 2000, 33). Lord Pearson exhibits himself to his neighbors in the manner of a docent. Before relocating to Observatory Mansions, he had tried to preserve his family's estate by charging admission for guided tours. He was eventually forced to turn the house over to a trust, which replaced him with a staff of historians and architects who had been "professionally trained" within the heritage industry to "entertain the public." Pearson's commentary on his apartment features an even balder exaltation of quotidian detail than Lucy Swithin's tour of Pointz Hall in *Between the Acts*. He historicizes his present reality in the past tense: "This is the drawing room where Lord Pearson sat and watched television. This is the bathroom where Lord Pearson washed himself with lemon-smelling soap. This is the kitchen and at this table Lord Pearson sat and sipped his consommé soups." In the note that accompanies his eventual suicide, Lord Pearson refers to himself in the parlance of museum catalog copy as "a stately relic dating back to the beginning of the century," indicating his complete spectatorial separation from the real (201).

One could argue that Carey borders on the allegorical or magical in this literalization of the "museum as habitation" were it not for the advent in recent years of certain urban residential towers that are clothed entirely in glass and which architectural designers have described as "a dialogue between voyeurism and exhibitionism." These structures reconceive their individual dwelling units as "stages for people to perform on in some way" by allowing residents "to see and be seen by passers-by on the street below" and through "peekaboo features" between rooms. They are expressly designed to "frame and exhibit the intimate details of life" as "aesthetically pleasing" through the use of shades and scrims that "tune[e] the privacy of each room [...] as you would change the aperture of a camera" (Green 2007).

Francis, too, maintains what he calls an "Exhibition of Myself" in the basement of Observatory Mansions. However, as opposed to Lord Pearson's tours and the "Exhibition of Mother," Francis stages an anti-exhibition in order to subvert museum culture. The "Exhibition of Myself" originated as a childhood collection of discarded shopping receipts, empty containers and broken glass that young Francis recovered during walks through the city streets. Benjamin associates this impulse to save objects of no apparent value with the child's instinctual desire to liberate objects from their "place within the bourgeois order," particularly by stealing and collecting (Gilloch 1996, 86). Benjamin regards these transgressive acts, when pursued by a child, as participating in a sense of *renewal* rather than *possession* because they typically proceed as a series of "haphazard acquisitions" and a "motley agglomeration of random finds" (Gilloch 1996, 89). The child's focus on objects that have been discarded by the culture of commodity is thus distinguishable from adult collectors, who manifest what Debord describes as the "mystical self-abandonment to the transcendent spirit of the commodity" in their antiquarian urges and faddish pursuit of items "that have recently been manufactured for the sole purpose of being collected" ([1967] 1995, 67).

As Francis matures, however, the initial naïveté of his collection gives way to a self-conscious critique of the post-industrial consumerism. Unable to recover every abandoned object in the city that crosses his path, Francis establishes a requirement that any object he collects must bear some evidence—such as a child's teethmarks—that "their former owner prized them above his or her other possessions, that they are originals, that they are irreplaceable" (Carey 2000, 43). This criterion reflects Francis' desire to identify and preserve instances of authentically tactile relationships with objects, an increasingly rare phenomenon within a society dominated by mass production and reproducibility. His impulse to preserve such traces of tactility contrasts sharply with the conservation efforts at the wax museum, which Francis describes as a "virtual washing machine of history" that strips artifacts of "all the various pieces of autobiography" that give them a tactile context, such as "sweat, lipstick, food, mud, wine, blood, semen and many other memories besides" (Carey 2000, 102). Francis' collection even takes a vengeful turn during his adolescence. For example, Francis steals a ruler that his tutor uses to discipline him and which the tutor had inherited from his own father. Francis also confiscates a volume of the Orme family history that Father Orme often reads instead of spending time with Francis. Bearing out Benjamin's description of the childlike instinct to subvert the social order, the ruler and book of genealogy embody for Francis a bourgeois concern for institutional authority and family lineage against which he rebels.

However, with the evolution of Francis' curatorial rationale, the emergence of his alienated spirit and his rhetorical shift from "collection" to "exhibition," Francis' acquisitions can no longer be considered "haphazard" nor his finds "random" in Benjamin's sense. By concealing his exhibition from public view "down below where the carpet stopped, where nothing was on display for the residents," Francis might seem to have eluded the spectacle of museum culture (Carey 2000, 47). On the contrary, the fact that his exhibit is visible and legible only to him as "owner, archivist, attendant and public" suggests a mood of solipsism more than a spirit of play (48). In *The Poetics of Space*, Bachelard identifies the attic and the cellar as archetypal figurations of rationality and irrationality, contrasting the geometric design and transparent functionality of the rows of rafters against the formless obscurity of the dark, subterranean vault (1964, 18). Although Francis' gesture of locating his exhibition in the cellar could be read as a corrective to the abstract rationalism of Father Orme's attic observatory, these spaces in fact share a common separation from the main domestic space of the house where the authentic tactility of human encounter and an embodied relationship to the real are possible. Father Orme's and Francis' respective withdrawals to the attic observatory and basement exhibition manifest their mutual condition as disembodied spectators whose tactile engagement with the world has been supplanted by visual mediations. They dwell at the simultaneous extremes of abstraction and materialism that Debord associates with the "total ideology" of the spectacle.

THE MUSEUM AS SPECTACLE   153

Francis wades even deeper into spectacle when he asserts that history is "encoded" in his exhibition of post-industrial detritus "like layers in a rock face" from which he can allegedly distill positive historical knowledge of "the life of the city, changes in taste, in fortune, in its people" (Carey 2000, 48). Carey's geological metaphor parallels Hugo's account of the sedimentary layers of Parisian architecture and Benjamin's figure of the urban archaeologist. Unlike Francis, however, Benjamin's archaeologist pursues his task with an attitude of "fruitless searching," keeps no "inventory" of his finds, and proceeds without an "excavation plan." For Benjamin, the archaeologist must not "proceed in the manner of a narrative," but instead "assay its spade in ever-new places, and in the old ones delve to ever-deeper levels," suggesting a tactile and open engagement with the entire field of material culture ([1932] 1978, 26). Francis violates Benjamin's principle of "genuine reminiscence," which is informed by the same sense of play that Benjamin associates with the subversive behavior of the child. He accumulates objects for his exhibition according to an historicist logic that is more akin to a curator than Benjamin's disinterested "man digging."

Like the historical pageants that Woolf critiques in *Between the Acts*, Francis' exhibition mimics the museum's objectified collective experience of "life in time" by providing him with a false sense of access to his past through chronologically ordered objects. Francis explains that "all time was there in that tunnel, neatly documented" in the form of objects that each "indicated a year of existence." He carefully numbers the items in the exhibition as he adds new ones, but continually moves one artifact—known definitively as "The Object"—to the end of the exhibit. This, coupled with Francis' claim that he sees "the city retreating through history" as he walks through the exhibition in reverse, indicates that he has inscribed his exhibition within an historical narrative in precisely the manner that the Benjamin of "A Berlin Chronicle" would reject (Carey 2000, 302). Ironically, Benjamin's translator Edmund Jephcott has noted that Benjamin's reflections on childhood in "A Berlin Chronicle" in 1932 are "far more restless and profound" than those in his 1938 piece titled "Berlin Childhood Around the Turn of the Century," in which "individual memories are neatly ordered in a static if not mannered way" (1978, xvi). Perhaps Benjamin himself failed—at least temporarily—to maintain "genuine reminiscence" in his relationship to material culture and succumbed to the same curatorial abstraction that plagues Francis.

Francis' "Exhibition of Myself" is subject to Debord's critique of the culture industry for attempting to "offer a coherent account of the social totality" ([1967] 1995, 182), as well as Leonard Woolf's faulting of cultural materialists in his essay "The Pageant of Civilization" for inscribing and concealing historical transformation within the trivial residue of commodity culture (1927, 131). A similarly problematic reading of material culture is evident in the work of Camilo José Vergara, a self-described "archivist of decline," who has conducted photographic studies of a number of American inner cities during the past four decades, including the transformation of the Harlem streetscape from the aftermath of the 1960s' race-riots to its emergence as "another of New York City's globalized districts, joining Tribeca, Wall Street and Times Square." Vergara locates "a people's history – their accomplishments, failures and aspirations" in "the material world in which they lived and which they helped to shape." Vergara's study over time of specific buildings and street corners records the displacement of "local organizations [...] that served to link residents with life in the rural South or even the Caribbean" by "mainstream franchises." The Harlem Vergara encounters in the 1970s was a "tough, even militant place," which he describes as "a run down version of Paris, whose life was lived outside, on the streets." Contemporary Harlem, according to Vergara, boasts an entirely different street life in which "the level of alienation and anger appears to have ebbed dramatically" as inhabitants and tourists—indeed, "all humanity"—stroll like latter-day *flâneurs* down 125th Street as "part of a joyous parade to see and be seen in." Vergara writes of "sexy black youths" who "proudly show themselves off wearing baseball caps, T-shirts, sneakers and gold chains" to Japanese, Dutch and Spanish tourists who "feel comfortable here and want to see and be a part of everything."

Remarkably, Vergara is able to conclude that "Harlem is still about the African-American experience" and "that on its streets and in its neighborhoods, the visitor still feels far away from America." But what is this "far away" feeling? For Vergara, the Harlem of the 1970s was "disconnected from mainstream America" by its derelict buildings and public spaces, his own "constant fear of being mugged," and perhaps, too, his very act of photographic documentation (Vergara 2007). The separation Vergara now feels as he walks through New York's latest "global district" is the spectatorial distance through which this "run-down Paris" and its own *esprit de '68* have been transformed into a piece of performance art for consumption. Like Vergara, Francis undertakes the quest of Walter Benjamin's urban archaeologist only to find, as Koolhaas writes, that the "archaeology" of the modern "Generic City" consists merely of the "documentation of its evaporation" by "an archaeologist without finds, or a site even" (Koolhaas and Mao 1995, 1263).

Confronted with mass culture's industrialized reproducibility, Francis' last resort for individuation is to assemble a unique configuration of commonplace objects. Wolfreys identifies a parallel phenomenon in the relationship between various Victorian authors and the cities in which they set their novels. He coins the term "citephobia" to describe the authors' desperation to assert the "subjective ego of the narrator" within the "leveling civic identity" of the industrial city (1998, 102). Like Francis, Dickens uses "lists of seemingly random elements" of urban material culture in order to construct and portray an original experience of London. This "architextural" list, as Wolfreys calls it, restates a series of chance encounters with objects of interchangeable descriptive value, but distinguishes the narrator's particular experience of the city from the endless permutation of objects and images that one could have encountered in the same city at the same time (146, 149). Zuzanna Jakubowski detects a similar anxiety within contemporary object studies in reaction to the "digital media and their rendering virtual of almost every aspect of daily interaction" (2013, 125). She analyzes two novels published in 2008 and 2009 that relate love stories through annotated museum and auction catalogs comprising hundreds of photographed lots and "brief prosaic descriptions, complete with measurements and pricing" (137). For Jakubowski, the realism of each text derives not from the literality with which it invokes actual objects, but from the "circulation of reference" among those objects that constitutes the real for the characters (131, 132). Jakubowski suggests that these novels portray the possibility for objects to mediate—or at least preserve the trace of—authentic human encounter. Francis, however, fetishizes the object's capacity to mediate or memorialize the experience of love into an illusory capacity to transmit love. By stealing and amassing objects loved intensely by others, Francis hopes to extract from these objects and experience for himself the love that had been bestowed upon the object without needing to endure the intimacy of authentic encounter.

Francis' desire to maintain curatorial distance from reality within the post-industrial "museum as habitation" is epitomized by his constant wearing of white gloves. Francis is first forced to wear white gloves during a childhood bout with obsessive scratching. By the time the treatment ended, however, he had become psychologically dependent on the protective rational distance that the gloves provided. Francis explains that "wearing gloves, monitoring everything you touched, was like floating above the world, watching everybody in it, watching all the suffering, always observing it, but never touching it" (Carey 2000, 311). The gloves transmute all tactile experience into visual traces on their white cotton and allow him to regulate his encounters with the physical world. His self-imposed "law of white gloves" dictates that he must maintain the purity of his gloves at all times. When they become soiled, he must cease to use his hands until he can replace the dirty gloves with clean ones. This process is governed by an elaborate ritual whereby he archives his used gloves in boxes, separating each pair with a layer of tissue and recording the explanation of how they came to be dirty in a notebook he calls his "glove diary" (32). In other words, Francis reduces the entirety of his tactile experience to a chronology of captioned images.

When Anna Tap expresses interest in a physical relationship with Francis, he commissions a sculptor at the wax museum to create a bust of her based on pictures that he pays Mad Lizzy to take. Francis explains the need for these dual acts of mediation as enabling him to "touch her and be sure that my gloves would remain unharmed" (Carey 2000, 256). At one point Anna asks if she can hold Francis' hands, but instead he gives her the hands from a dummy at the wax museum that were modeled after his own (274). Francis' use of artificial body parts to mediate social relationships takes Debord's concept of the illusion of encounter within the spectacle to its logical extreme. In a reflection titled "Gloves," Benjamin identifies tactility as humanity's closest connection to nature and, thus, the greatest threat to its sense of individuality ([1928] 1978, 66). As with Saleem's telepathic conference of mythologically gifted children, Francis' declaration that "glove people are a magical people" exemplifies Debord's observation that "the individual, though condemned to the passive acceptance of an alien everyday reality, is thus driven into a form of madness in which, by resorting to magical devices, he entertains the illusion that he is reacting to this fate" ([1967] 1995, 219). Like Saleem, Francis believes that he has transcended the flattening effects of mass culture and is blind to the psychologically internalized separations wrought by the spectacle.

As with the attempts by Dada and the Surrealists to repudiate the spectacle through art, Francis' anti-exhibition, his "art of stillness" and his "law of white gloves" remain inscribed within the logic of spectatorship. Nevertheless, these gestures play an important role in Carey's realist restatement of the problem of spectatorship by making visible the generalized condition of "museum as habitation" that both inspires Francis' acts of resistance and recuperates them as spectacle. Roland Barthes observes that "the values of civilization are gathered and condensed" in the urban center in the form of churches, banks, offices and stores ([1970] 1982, 31). It is telling that a wax museum is the only such institution in the novel that Carey distinctly identifies within the "city center," which is conspicuously devoid of inhabitants and overrun with tourists (Carey 2000, 12). This wax museum is part of a national cultural bureaucracy that is overseen by "the largest of all the wax museums in the capital city" (15), a concept that seems less far-fetched if one considers that Madame Tussauds now boasts locations in Hollywood, Las Vegas, New York, Orlando, San Francisco and Washington, D.C., as well as major cities across Europe and Asia. A "Committee of Wax Museums" determines which public figures will be memorialized in each of the nation's museums, regulating the rise and fall of celebrity value like a currency exchange (139). As anthropologist and noted socio-cultural geographer David Harvey observes, urban planners must identify "symbolic" or "cultural capital" that will draw "monopoly rents" from tourists in spite of the reality that most urban environments have come to resemble one another through the presence of global brands and reproducible cultural experiences (2001, 411). Forster taps into this same reality when he portrays Lucy Honeychurch's disappointment with the English trappings of her hotel in Florence and the advice she receives that there is no point in venturing outside the hotel when the galleries are closed.

Francis fancies himself capable of achieving an authentic relationship with material culture that is independent of the commodity value conferred by museum authorities. As a recluse with little knowledge of popular culture, he is not susceptible to the wax figures' lure as idols within the cult of celebrity. Although not in so many words, Francis exhibits a Debordian sensibility toward "media stars" as being "spectacular representations of living human beings" and "a semblance of life [...] which is intended to compensate for the crumbling of directly experienced [...] productive activity" (Debord [1967] 1995, 60). He scoffs at tourists who pay to have their pictures taken with mere effigies and indulge the illusion of being "so close to fame" as to "touch it" (Carey 2000, 139). As absurd as the novel reveals that premise to be, it informs the actual marketing campaign for Madame Tussauds, whose web site (*Madame Tussauds* n.d.) poses the question "Who do you want to meet?" and then promises the pseudo-tactile opportunity to "get close enough to hug your heroes and take the perfect photo with wax figures of the world's most famous faces."

Francis appears at first to have established a subjective relationship with objects that stands outside of the logic of commodity. Francis relates numerous anecdotes from his youth in which he attempts to experience "what it could be like to be an object" and continues to channel that impulse toward a rigorous and disciplined "art of stillness" (Carey 2000, 14). He even distinguishes between the "outer stillness" of one who adopts the pose of an object versus the "inner stillness" through which one achieves complete ontological unity with object-ness. This could be taken to suggest that Francis is able to maintain into adulthood the naïve relationship to objects that Benjamin associates with the perspective of the child. In his reflection titled "Construction Site," Benjamin describes children as ignorant of objects' use-value in the adult world and thus able to recontextualize objects within a "new, intuitive relationship" during liberated moments of play ([1928] 1978, 69). Museum culture, in contrast, fosters a fetishized commodity relationship with objects by validating the curatorial impulse to "preserve, restore, protect, squabble over, and even adore" certain objects and—as Kuhns notes—by training children to "respect" them (1991, 261). Much like Debord's gesture of *détournement* in which an object is resituated outside of its conventional associations and meanings, Benjamin attempts to re-inhabit his naïve relationship with objects of his childhood in order to reflect on the abstract value of commodities in post-industrial society.

Francis' "art of stillness," however, like his "Exhibition of Myself," is not a liberated moment of play, but an iconoclastic negation of the museum dynamic that ultimately replicates the same spectatorial and commodified relationship to material culture. Instead of fetishizing the wax figures within the cult of celebrity, Francis fetishizes them as aesthetic feats of naturalism that participate in a pseudo-tactile illusion of encounter. He theorizes the waxworks as a "people museum" of the "wonderful ordinariness of mankind"—a place to "study in minute detail the human form." Noting that "even the most uninhibited person becomes coy when intensely stared at," Francis regards the wax museum as the only place where the "human being [can] be really, truly examined" (Carey 2000, 140). Francis, however, goes so far as to allow his interaction with wax dummies to mediate and, in the case of the wax bust of Anna, replace human interaction. Furthermore, he exploits his art to secure employment in the wax museum as a human dummy. He is stationed among the mannequins to underscore how realistic they are by occasionally shocking the patrons with his own movements. After being laid off due to the

THE MUSEUM AS SPECTACLE   159

advent of more cost-effective automatons, Francis reaps money from tourists as a performance artist by posing as a human statue on an empty pedestal in the park. When anyone drops a coin in his cup, Francis begrudgingly opens his eyes and blows a soap bubble for them, acknowledging that "if people part with money they demand some compensation," even if that compensation is ironic (13–4). His ability to "achieve such inanimacy" as if he were "half-flesh, half-object" is merely another form of alienated labor and embodies the "freezing of life" and "generalized autism" that Debord associates with the false consciousness of the spectacle (Carey 2000, 17, 13; Debord [1967] 1995, 170, 218).

The graffiti that is found on the walls of Observatory Mansions and throughout the city serves as a similarly ambivalent site of resistance to spectacle. Typically regarded as a form of subversive behavior, whether criminal, artistic or political, graffiti was often used by Situationists to disrupt the glossy veneer of consumer culture and make their marginalized perspective visible within the spectacle's built environment. At the beginning of the novel, Francis notes that the phrase "and even you can find love" has been spraypainted on the façade of Observatory Mansions (Carey 2000, 3). Foreshadowing Francis' ultimate liberation from spectacle, this gesture reads initially like a rallying cry for alienated city-dwellers to transcend the dehumanizing commodified relationships to which they had become inured. Toward the end of the novel, however, Francis meets the graffiti artist, one Mark Daniel Cooper, and learns that this phrase and others that Mark has tattooed across the city are actually advertising slogans. Mark explains that he took up graffiti out of loneliness due to the severe stutter that deterred people from communicating with him. At first he would write down angry comments in notebooks, but he eventually became frustrated because nobody could access them and his ideas "just lay there, useless." Noticing some graffiti on a wall one day, he took to "scrawling his innermost thoughts on the city" and experienced complete relief of his "pain and frustration." Even after running out of commentary to share, Mark could not stop spraypainting words because "it was all that made him feel alive" (270). With nothing original left to say, Mark began to graffiti excerpts from advertisements.

On the surface, Mark's actions resemble the Situationist tactics of pastiche and *détournement* that stripped slogans from their commodified contexts and estranged them as a form of pop art. We are told, however, that Mark finds the "confidence" of the advertising slogans inspiring and that he derives a sense of community and self-worth from them. He believes, for example, that the "Coca-Cola signs in the city, which had been there for as long as he could remember, made us worth something" and that "with them here we truly belonged to the world." Mark's fetishized relationship to advertising jingles that promise "the softest skin," "the whitest teeth," "the freshest breath," the ability to "turn back the clocks" and "say goodbye to your wrinkles [...] because you're worth it" gives concrete form to the spectacle's illusion of tactile encounter and its falsification of time (Carey 2000, 270–1). The spectacle is similarly operative in Saleem's childhood encounter in *Midnight's Children* with a billboard advertising Kolynos toothpaste, except that the confident smile of the "Kolynos Kid" does not inspire Saleem, but reinforces his own insecurities and sense of marginalization. Rushdie deconstructs the ad from Saleem's adult perspective as being "one-dimensional" and "flattened by certitude" (Rushdie [1981] 2006, 175). Mark's sincere (as opposed to ironic) advertising graffiti speaks instead to the constant recuperation of Situationist gestures which finds referent in contemporary corporate branding campaigns that adopt the aesthetic of graffiti as a visual identity to reach new markets while discarding its ethical premise. However, even when Mark was spraypainting his own angry comments about the city, it is not clear whether he was engaged in authentic social dialog or merely voicing a series of "negations" of the spectacle that merely replicate its alienated one-way discourse. Francis notes that throughout their interaction Mark cannot bring himself to look Francis in the eye and ends their conversation by spraypainting "goodbye" on a wall and running away.

At the end of the novel, Observatory Mansions is demolished by developers to make way for a high-rise apartment complex named City Heights. After the house has been evacuated, Francis sneaks back to the basement to save his exhibition. The initial detonation leaves him trapped under piles of rubble. Insofar as the "law of white gloves" forbids Francis from using his hands when his gloves have become soiled, Francis is forced to choose tactile engagement over curatorial distance in order to climb out from under the debris and save his own life. Making an unprecedented exception to his regimen, he decides to free himself and abandon the hundreds of objects that he has collected, taking only "The Object" itself. At this point Carey reveals "The Object" to be the skeleton of Francis' elder brother who died in childhood. This elder brother originally held the name Francis in the tradition of the Ormes' first-born sons. Carey literalizes the spectacle of cultural revival in revealing that the "Francis" who narrates the novel was originally named "Thomas" at birth and was subsequently renamed "Francis" after his deceased brother. Kostof observes that "the urge to preserve certain cities, or certain buildings and streets within them, has something in it of the instinct to preserve our family records; something of the compulsion to protect a work of art" (1991, 305). Like the neo-classical façade of the manor house that has been internally subdivided to accommodate the conditions of the industrial age, Thomas is called upon to maintain a façade of feudal primogeniture while suffering the attendant internal divisions of the spectacle's pseudo-cyclical consciousness. Standing at this convergence of preservationist impulses, Thomas is reduced like Lord Pearson to an art object in his family's own cottage heritage industry.

With this revelation, Carey definitively locates the source of spectacle in the preservationist logic that establishes the museum as an organizing principle for urban life. The trauma of his brother's death and the subsequent merging of their identities—not the loss of agrarian society—is what sends Thomas on his pathological quest for individuation. Forced by his father to inhabit the image of a first-born son, Thomas is dispossessed of his tactile relationship to the real and must mediate his identity through an exhibition that culminates in the skeleton of his dead brother. Thomas clings to material objects as a source of tactile reality because his personal history has become abstract, so much so that he doubts his ability to "remain Francis Orme" were the exhibition to be destroyed (Carey 2000, 302). Once again Carey's novel directly echoes Benjamin's observations in "One-Way Street," in this case Benjamin's note titled "Cellar." Much like Thomas' exhibition in the basement of Observatory Mansions and his highly ritualized archival practices and glove changing, Benjamin's figure of the "cellar" portrays human memory spatially as a "horrible cabinet of curiosities" in which "the deepest shafts are reserved for what is most commonplace" and "enervated, perverse antiquities" are "interred and sacrificed amid magic incantations" ([1928] 1978, 62). Recounting a dream about an old schoolfriend, Benjamin describes how he awoke to realize that what his memory had summoned "like a detonation" was merely the "corpse of that boy, who had been immured as a warning: that whoever one day lives here may in no respect resemble him" (63). When Thomas' own exhibition falls prey to dynamite, he experiences this same rupture of the past into the present and the same breaking of the spectatorial illusion of dynastic continuity afforded by images and objects from the past.

The novel concludes with Anna and Thomas taking a flat in City Heights. The demolition of both the house and the "Exhibition of Myself" frees Thomas to pursue authentically lived experience. Unable to carry them all out of the basement before it collapses, Thomas is forced to let go of the nearly one thousand objects through which he had curated his own illusory spectacle of individual significance and purpose as "guardian of all that love" (Carey 2000, 302). Thomas returns his brother's remains to the family crypt, explains to Anna that he has literally and symbolically "run out of gloves," and allows her to put her hands on his face (315). Tactility is restored and spectatorial distance bridged in the figure of Thomas' and Anna's daughter, who is described as having tiny hands that "grip and won't let go" and "absolutely no understanding of inner or outer stillness" (324).

Philosopher Karsten Harries describes the ethical function of architecture as allowing individuals to "experience ourselves as essentially incomplete, in need of others, in need of community" and locates this in homes that are built to house successive generations so as to place the individual in a shared experience of time (1997, 264). This ideal is achieved and frustrated in unexpected ways within the country house and the urban apartment complex that Carey depicts in the novel. The preservationist will read into Carey's novel a narrative of decline in which the manor house is enveloped by the encroaching city and ultimately replaced with a dehumanized hive out of one of Le Corbusier's sketches. Instead, Carey provides a counter-narrative in which the subdivision of the neo-classical country house into apartments punctures Father Orme's rationalist retreat from society and aristocratic denial of historical change. The conversion of mansions into apartments in post-revolution Paris produced a highly cognizant moment in urban history insofar as "one class succeed[ed] another in the same buildings" (Kostof 1991, 292). By renovating Tearsham Park and bringing in new residents from the city, Thomas' mother takes the first step in breaking the pseudo-cylical gaze of the family portrait gallery—a chronological totem pole five heads high of ancestors all bearing the name "Francis Orme"—that paralyzes Father Orme within a dynastic narrative which requires that he transform Thomas into an iconic replica of his deceased brother (Carey 2000, 194). Anna Tap continues the job by weaning the alienated residents of Observatory Mansions from their memory-suppressing fetishes and restoring them to authentic human interaction—a painful and sometimes fatal process for them. Carey reverses Bachelard's idea that memory and identity are threatened when the organic space of the house is replaced by the repetitious geometry of the modern apartment complex (Bachelard 1964, 8, 9, 26). It is ultimately in his generic contemporary apartment building that Thomas achieves authentic encounter and participates in the life of "successive generations," as Harries would say, by raising his daughter.

As Forster suggests in *Aspects of the Novel*, realist authors avoid reducing their characters to static art objects by tempering their sense of participating in a collective "life in time" with individual consciousness of their own "life in value." Kostof argues similarly that society must circumscribe its desire for "historical purity" and a "scientific approach to urban conservation" within the broader goal of continuing to treat cities as "live, changing things" (1991, 305). Kuhns also warns against extremes in historical practice that vacillate between an antiquarian "greediness to amass" and Futurist "fantasies of destruction." He contends that "complex urban reality" and "the domain of objects" must be treated with greater subtlety than "either avant-garde manifesto or the museum curator can recognize" in order to derive "an album of our cultural passions and actions, a map of our deepest feelings" (1991, 266)—that is, to derive what Debord would call an authentic psychogeography. Why do we cringe at the demolition of the Ormes' Arcadian manor? Why does Sue Bridehead prefer Corinthian ruins over Gothic ones? Why does Lucy Honeychurch seek the real Italy in Ruskin's commentary on the frescoes of the Santa Croce? Why does Aadam Aziz purchase a replica of the Sanssouci Palace in which to raise his family? Shklar critiques the "claim upon our imagination" enjoyed by classicism, "not only as a set of political values and memories, but as a legacy of words, conceptions, and images" which caption us with an alienated discourse that renders us unable to "bring order to what we know" ([1973] 2000, 296). At the same time, Koolhaas has suggested that the abandonment of urbanism in the wake of the "fallout from modernization" has left the contemporary city with an accumulation of architecture that offers individuals no means of "encoding civilizations on their territory" (Koolhaas and Mao 1995, 967).

As with other instances of meta-spectacle that I have examined, Carey's realism successfully navigates these extremes. Carey does not reduce the realist perspective to an ideological manifesto that pretends to solve the problem of spectacle, nor does he simply indulge a Dionysian "fantasy of destruction" by portraying the demolition of Observatory Mansions as the eradication of spectacle. The act of demolishing the manor house is immediately recuperated in the novel as spectacle by media coverage and crowds of onlookers who photograph the event and scavenge the remains of the house for souvenirs of the eccentric Orme family (Carey 2000, 312). Chronic soap-opera addict Claire Higg—who had been unable for many years to relate to anyone other than the stars of her favorite shows—catches her own image on one of the news monitors that had been set before the crowd and promptly dies of a heart attack. Just as the audience of La Trobe's pageant experiences shock and disgust at the end of *Between the Acts* when the actors reveal their unspectacular everydayness and their lifeless role as spectators, Higg cannot abide this "moment of high consciousness" when she is made real to herself through the medium of the television screen (320). The novel concludes with Thomas painting his new apartment white and occasionally dipping his hands in the paint with nostalgia for the insulating rationalism of his white gloves (324). Neither utopian nor dystopian, Carey provides a realist restatement of the individual's ongoing struggle with the alienating rational distance that the social conditions of spectacle continuously produce.

Observatory Mansions enacts a provocative inversion of Diderot's famous thought experiment concerning the experience of a blind man whose sight is restored, which Carey recasts as the experience of an exclusively "visioned" man whose tactility is restored. In each case, the individual must learn to apprehend the world and construct meaning through a previously unknown medium, a struggle that can render him both exiled from his former understanding of the world and paralyzed in his attempt to encode a new understanding of it through an alternate sensory language. Carey allows his readers to begin to imagine the process, however faltering, of re-inhabiting our own social environment that has been stripped of tactility and flattened into an image. Enacting Lefebvre's distinction between a realist "representational space" as opposed to a naturalistic "representation of space," *Observatory Mansions* does not contribute another layer of mediation to the spectacle, but produces consciousness of the spectacle by portraying how lived experience and its distorted reproductions co-exist in reality. Carey provides his readers with what architect Edward Robbins has called a true "spatial realization" in which destruction and creation, imprisonment and liberation, spectacle and history, visual distance and tactile experience are each possible (Robbins 1996).

REFERENCES

Bachelard, Gaston. 1964. *The Poetics of Space*. Trans. Maria Jolus. New York: Orion.

Barthes, Roland. (1970) 1982. *Empire of Signs*. Trans. Richard Howard. New York: Hill and Wang.

Benjamin, Walter. (1928) 1978. One-Way Street. In *Reflections: Essays, Aphorisms, Autobiographical Writings*, trans. Edmund Jephcott, 61–94. New York/London: Harcourt Brace Jovanovich.

———. (1932) 1978. A Berlin Chronicle. In *Reflections: Essays, Aphorisms, Autobiographical Writings*, trans. Edmund Jephcott, 3–60. New York/London: Harcourt Brace Jovanovich.

Carey, Edward. n.d. Interview with Edward Carey. In *Harcourt Books*. http://www.harcourtbooks.com/authorinterviews/bookinterview_carey.asp. Accessed 25 Feb 2005.

———. 2000. *Observatory Mansions*. New York: Vintage Books.

Crary, Jonathan. 1990. *Techniques of the Observer: On Vision and Modernity in the Nineteenth Century*. Cambridge: MIT Press.

Debord, Guy. (1967) 1995. *The Society of the Spectacle*. Trans. Donald Nicholson-Smith. New York: Zone Books.

Eve, James. 2003. Dual Purposes. Review of *Alva & Irva, The Twins Who Saved a City*, by Edward Carey. *The Times (London)*, March 22. Accessed 1 Feb 2016.

Fishman, Robert. 1977. *Urban Utopias in the Twentieth Century: Ebenezer Howard, Frank Lloyd Wright and Le Corbusier*. New York: Basic Books.

Gilloch, Graeme. 1996. *Myth and Metropolis: Water Benjamin and the City*. Cambridge: Polity.

Green, Penelope. 2007. Yours for the Peeping. *The New York Times*, November 4. http://www.nytimes.com/2007/11/04/weekinreview/04green.html. Accessed 10 Sept 2016.

Greenland, Colin. 2003. Small World. Review of *Alva & Irva, The Twins Who Saved a City*, Edward Carey. *The Guardian*, May 16. https://www.theguardian.com/books/2003/may/17/featuresreviews.guardianreview22. Accessed 1 Feb 2016.

Harries, Karsten. 1997. *The Ethical Function of Architecture*. Cambridge: MIT University Press.

Harrison, Carey. 2003. One Word: Plasticine. Review of *Alva & Irva, The Twins Who Saved a City*, by Edward Carey. *The New York Times*, March 23. https://www.nytimes.com/2003/03/23/books/one-word-plasticine.html. Accessed 1 Feb 2016.

Harvey, David. 2001. *Spaces of Capital: Towards a Critical Geography*. Edinburgh: Edinburgh University Press.

Hugo, Victor. (1831) 1978. *Notre-Dame of Paris*. Trans. John Sturrock. New York: Penguin.

Jakubowski, Zuzanna. 2013. Exhibiting Lost Love: The Relational Realism of Things in Orhan Pamuk's *The Museum of Innocence* and Leanne Shapton's

Important Artifacts. In *Realisms in Contemporary Culture: Theories, Politics, and Medial Configurations,* ed. Dorothee Birke and Stella Butter, 124–145. Berlin/Boston: De Gruyter.

Jay, Martin. 1993. *Downcast Eyes: The Denigration of Vision in Twentieth-Century French Thought.* Berkeley: University of California Press.

Jephcott, Edmund. 1978. Introduction to *Reflections: Essays, Aphorisms, Autobiographical Writings,* vii–xliii. New York/London: Harcourt Brace Jovanovich.

Koning, Christina. 2000. Strangely Normal. Review of *Observatory Mansions,* by Edward Carey. *The Times (London),* March 11. Accessed 1 Feb 2016.

Koolhaas, Rem, and Bruce Mao. 1995. *S, M, L, XL.* Ed. Jennifer Sigler. New York: Monacelli Press.

Kostof, Spiro. 1991. *The City Assembled: The Element of Urban Form Through History.* Boston: Little, Brown & Co.

Kuhns, Richard. 1991. The Last Manifesto. In *City Images: Perspectives from Literature, Philosophy and Film,* ed. Mary Ann Caws, 261–269. New York: Gordon and Breach.

Lauster, Martina. 2007. Walter Benjamin's Myth of the 'Flaneur'. *Modern Language Review* 102 (1): 139–156.

Lefebvre, Henri. 1991. *The Production of Space.* Trans. Donald Nicholson-Smith. Cambridge: Blackwell.

Madame Tussauds. n.d. https://madametussauds.com. Accessed 31 May 2015.

Rignall, John. 1992. *Realist Fiction and the Strolling Spectator.* London/New York: Routledge.

Robbins, Edward. 1996. Thinking Space/Seeing Space: Thamesmead Revisited. *Urban Design International* 1 (3): 283–291.

Rushdie, Salman. (1981) 2006. *Midnight's Children.* New York: Knopf.

Sasaki, Ken-Ichi. (1997) 2000. For Whom Is City Design? Tactility Versus Visuality. In *The City Cultures Reader,* ed. Malcolm Miles, Tim Hall and Iain Borden, 36–47. London: Routledge.

Shklar, Judith. (1973) 2000. The Political Theory of Utopia: From Melancholy to Nostalgia. In *The City Cultures Reader,* ed. Malcolm Miles, Tim Hall and Iain Borden, 289–298. London: Routledge.

Sontag, Susan. 1977. *On Photography.* New York: Farrar, Strauss & Giroux.

Vergara, Camilo Jose. 2007. An Archivist of Decline. *The Chronicle of Higher Education,* June 8, B14–B15.

Wirth, Louis. (1938) 1996. Urbanism as a Way of Life. In *The City Reader,* ed. Richard T. LeGates and Frederic Stout, 97–105. London/New York: Routledge.

Wolfreys, Julian. 1998. *Writing London: The Trace of the Urban Text from Blake to Dickens.* New York: St. Martin's.

Woolf, Leonard. 1927. The Pageant of History. In *Essays on Literature, History, Politics, Etc.,* 125–148. New York: Harcourt, Brace and Company.

CHAPTER 7

Epilogue: "Those old *soixante-huitards*"— Debord as Spectacle in Julian Barnes' *England, England*

Debord's articulation of the problem of spectatorial distance illuminates a fundamental concern of realist authors that persists throughout the twentieth century and across the stylistic innovations of modern and postmodern novels. My Debordian gloss on the realism of fiction by Hardy, Forster, Woolf, Rushdie and Carey opens up a new dimension to readings of earlier British fiction by Thackeray, Trollope and Gissing, as well as the continental tradition. The concept of meta-spectacle frames a distinctive ethos of realism that will inform readers of novels to come. The disorientations wrought by architectural revival, tourism, pageantry, photography, cinema and urbanism that I have discussed in this study are being succeeded by new sites of disembodied vision and illusions of encounter, including social media, virtual technologies and the post-human.

Equally important, however, is Debord's analysis of various attempts to critique the spectacle that have been neutralized by their transformation into commodities by the culture industry. *Society of the Spectacle* does not propose a definitive solution to the problem of spectacle. It does, however, identify the insidious conditions of industrial society that continuously erode historical consciousness. The techniques of *dérive* (urban "drifting") and *détournement* (liberating objects from their conventional meanings and value) are specific options for pursuing this critique of everyday life that were practiced by Debord's "Situationist" collective of artists, social theorists and political revolutionaries in the 1950s and 1960s. These practices in and of themselves are not an objectified state of

© The Author(s) 2018
E. Barnaby, *Realist Critiques of Visual Culture*,
https://doi.org/10.1007/978-3-319-77323-0_7

167

authentic consciousness, but function—like Brecht's alienation effects—as provisional gestures to restore consciousness and must be discarded before their ethical force is recuperated aesthetically as a genre. For this reason, Debord dissolved the Situationist International in 1972 at the point that it had degenerated, in media theorist McKenzie Wark's estimation, into "collective celebrity" and "part of the spectacular consumption of 'radical chic'"(2008, 10). The Situationists themselves had become yet another instance of the phenomenon that Debord describes as "The Proletariat as Subject and Representation" ([1967] 1995). Like other organized oppositions to capitalism, the Situationists had shifted from authentically intervening in history to contemplating history from a position of ideological detachment.

Literary realism's capacity to function as meta-spectacle similarly relies on the novel's performance of an ethical gesture. However, I do not wish to suggest that realist fiction is reducible to a Situationist manifesto. Realist fiction does not summarize or theorize authentic consciousness, but allows the reader to experience instances of individual consciousness in negotiation with the world. The recognition of spectacle evoked by the performance of this gesture fades with the performance itself and must be renewed through a subsequent performance, just as the insight prompted by La Trobe's pageant immediately recedes like "a cloud that melted into the other clouds on the horizon" (Woolf [1941] 1970, 209). Criticism of the realist novel—this present study included—must cultivate the reader's susceptibility to these realist gestures without simply captioning them. To this end, Debord's awareness in *Society of the Spectacle* of the limits of a critical method that is constantly threatened by recuperation proves particularly useful.

Literary realism enacts the workings of consciousness for the reader as an intersection of verbal discourses and the visual perspectives, or what Gilles Deleuze calls the "statements" and "visibilities" that constitute a "way of seeing and saying" in a given time and place (1988, 49). There is chronic tension, Deleuze suggests, between the captioning power of the statement and the visible self-evidence of the world, each laying claim to truth and resisting the totality of the other (50). As an enunciation of what is possible to express and what is possible to recognize as self-evident at a specific moment, realist fiction is uniquely capable of depicting both the struggle of individual consciousness to ascribe legible meaning to the world and the resilience of the world toward the inherently reductive statements made about it. This tension is the hallmark of the *realist* perspective, which degenerates into a merely *realistic* perspective when a novel reproduces diction and images as objective phenomena instead of re-performing statements and visibilities that emerge and evolve amid changing social conditions.

The distribution of statements and visibilities—what is possible to express and to observe—shifts over time and produces an observable experience of historical difference. Deleuze, elaborating upon Foucault, compares this phenomenon to the strata of sedimentary formations that comprise an archaeological site and which can be excavated and interpreted. To the extent that realist fiction traces the particular discourses and visibilities circulating within society at a given moment, the evolution of these "ways of seeing and saying" can become visible cumulatively across many novels. However, one must resist reducing the material culture inscribed in works of fiction to fossils from which to extract historical consciousness. Textual descriptions of objects and sights do not necessarily reveal the conditions that delimit or enable certain ways of seeing. Similarly, one must resist deriving a positivist historical narrative out of changes in literary style. Such alterations in the aesthetics of prose and diction do not necessarily reveal the conditions that allow certain parties to enunciate certain discourses while other parties and discourses are silenced. As Leonard Woolf argued in his essay on the "Pageant of Civilization," the work of the archaeologist is to understand the relationship between the individual and the world at a certain moment in history, not merely to reconstruct a replica of that moment's material form. This claim informs my own distinction between the *realist* restatement of a social context versus a *realistic* reproduction of a time and place.

Deleuze discerns in Foucault's archaeological metaphor for knowledge the troubling assertion of a "third agency"—a seemingly objective vantage point from which the archaeologist comments upon the significance of the various distributions of statements and visibilities (1988, 68). This third agency presumes a spectatorial distance through which the archaeologist transcends their own embeddedness in what is possible to express and observe in their own time, as if their analysis were not constrained by the conditions of the present. Deleuze urges us to recognize the subjectivity of the perspective through which historical difference across the strata is observed. There can be no objective or definitive reading of the strata. This plays out vividly in Ruskin's claim in *Stones of Venice* that the historical meaning embodied in architecture can be read like pages in a book, whereas those very same "pages" prompt diametrically opposed "readings" by Walter Pater of the same shift in statements and visibilities that occurs between the Middle Ages and the Renaissance.

Literary realism prevents the reader from losing sight not only of this subjectivity, but also of the false sense of objectivity that the real sometimes assumes. Epitomized by Hugo's critique of the modern Parisian cityscape in *Notre Dame de Paris*, realist novels have elevated the spectacle to consciousness by depicting how post-industrial culture scrambles the legible evolution of statements and visibilities within the surplus commodity culture of industrial society. The Gothic revival in architecture, the repackaging of classical culture within the Grand Tour, the nationalist pageantizing of history, the Empire's taxidermic photographing and captioning of colonial sites, and the conversion of the built environment from a place to inhabit to the exhibition space of the museum are tectonic upheavals wrought by industrial culture that homogenize the historical strata and thus flatten our experience of historical difference. I turn in conclusion to Julian Barnes' novel *England, England*, which synthesizes in one grand scenario the effect of the spectacle on each of the post-industrial visibilities that I have thus far examined separately in this study. Barnes splices contemporary discourses of post-nationalism, deconstruction and even Situationism onto these visibilities to confront his reader with the problem of authenticity as applied to historical consciousness, bringing Deleuze's critique of "third agency" directly to bear on Debord himself.

At one point in *England, England* Barnes explicitly subjects Debord to deconstruction by an unnamed "French intellectual." (Deleuze? Foucault? Derrida? *Qui sait?!*) To paraphrase Orwell's critique of pulp fiction that I cited in the introduction, one could argue that by virtue of their appearance in a mass-market novel, Debord and the deconstructionists have now "reached the outer suburbs" (Orwell [1944] 1981, 147). Orwell's original comment refers disparagingly to the reduction of realism to a nonchalant acceptance of *realpolitik*. Orwell objected to the manner in which popular novelists had stripped fiction of its ethical context and reduced it to conveying naturalistic detail within a violent and amoral "daydream appropriate to a totalitarian age" ([1944] 1981, 146). I have noted Rushdie's similar objection to Apple's abuse of Gandhi's legacy in its "Think Different" campaign. Barnes, however, does not invoke Debord and the "French intellectual" as realistic shorthand to situate his characters in a late-twentieth-century milieu. Instead, he restates these competing discourses within *England, England* to question the legitimacy of Debord's concept of spectacle, suggesting that it posits a pristine, commodity-free era as its founding mythology. Barnes raises the possibility that Debord fetishizes pre-industrial time by suggesting that there was a social moment when life was, indeed, "directly lived." In other words, perhaps Debord himself advances an instance of pseudo-cyclical consciousness. The French intellectual suggests that instead of bemoaning the spectacle out of nostalgia for a utopian authenticity, we should celebrate the reality of the replicas that we are invited to construct from the field of raw historical material.

Like other realist characters treated in this study, Barnes' protagonist Martha Cochrane seeks a realist middle ground between rejecting and embracing the spectacle. The novel follows Martha from her childhood in rural England and her auspicious career as a global marketing executive for an historical theme park to her eventual retreat to a neo-agrarian community. "England, England" is the name of this historical theme park on the Isle of Wight that British developer Sir Jack Pitman builds in order to exploit the Empire's last remaining commodity, namely, the image of its past. Pitman harnesses the dynamics of spectacle to construct a replica of Britishness that, over time, will come to be regarded by consumers as "the thing itself" (Barnes 2000, 63). Martha's experience of her own professional rise and fall alongside the commercial history of the British Empire prompts her to reflect on the relationship between personal memory and collective history, both of which, she comes to realize, rely upon "an element of propaganda, of sales-and-marketing" (7). Grappling with the distinction between authentic and false consciousness, Martha exhibits what Forster describes as a realist "roundness" of character, in that her moments of insight are tempered by various regressions. Like Jude Fawley, Lucy Honeychurch, Lucy Swithin, Saleem Sinai and Francis Orme, Martha experiences no idealized denouement in which the spectacle is defeated, but gradually achieves a realist vigilance toward the spectacle's false consciousness.

Pitman, on the other hand, is what Forster would call a relentlessly "flat" character—an embodiment of the spectacle and ideology itself. Martha's antagonistic relationship with her mentor brings the forces of post-industrial culture into conflict on a human scale in precisely the manner that Lukàcs praises in the historical novel. Pitman functions as an agent of the spectacle's stunted historical consciousness. In a speech to his executive team, Pitman compares his concept for England, England to the industrial transformation of the local landscape that has become concealed over time within the appearance of an unchanging natural world

(Barnes 2000, 62–3). His aspiration for England, England is that his replica will similarly come to be regarded as the authentic experience of England by tourists and inhabitants alike. While the architects of Pitco's headquarters theorize their extensive use of glass walls and ecologically friendly design as part of Pitco's commitment to transparent corporate governance and social responsibility, Pitman's private office is a Victorian-styled heart of darkness ensconced deep in the center of the building that gives visual expression to his actual imperialist aims (29). Pitman preys on consumers like Jude who will pay for the illusion of inhabiting a recreated feudal world picture. Collapsing the false distinction between "genteel 'travel'" and "vulgar 'tourism,'" he packages England for the "Quality Leisure" industry in the same way that Florence, Rome and Athens are packaged for Lucy as part of her Grand Tour (43, 49). Like the famed pageant-master Louis Napoleon Parker, Pitman reduces historical consciousness to a sentimental parade of antique costumes and dialects that glorify the Empire. He hypes the British Empire to developing countries as an idealized image of their future, just as William Methwold does when he sells his furnished European chateau to Saleem's family in *Midnight's Children*. Like the city in which *Observatory Mansions* is set, England, England is a "museum as habitation" designed to level the distinction between inhabitant and tourist.

Pitman rationalizes his degradation of historical consciousness into mass-market kitsch as the revival of an authentic oral culture in which the common man is given a say in constructing the nation's identity. Instead of hiring curators like other heritage parks do, Pitman surveys consumers to determine England, England's attractions. The result is a list of "The Fifty Quintessences of Englishness" within the popular imagination that the theme park will reinforce (Barnes 2000, 86–8). As with Parker's pageants, Pitman portends to facilitate the participation of all classes in the dynastic thread of history. However, far from reviving a pre-literate community bound together by collective memory, his focus groups exemplify the engineered ignorance of the neo-peasantry that Debord associates with the spectacle. The historical understanding demonstrated by even the most educated professionals in the focus groups has barely matured beyond the superficially pageantized account of English history that they first encountered in elementary school (83–5). Barnes satirizes the cultish ritual of "chants" through which children encounter history as a list of dates, personages and events that are distilled into rhymed, mnemonic sound-bites (11–3). Pitman repackages and sells this naïve glorification of empire back to consumers as their collective history. One is reminded of Disney's ill-fated attempt in the early 1990s to construct a theme park inspired by American history in Northern Virginia. Joseph Dewey notes that, "unlike nearby Williamsburg, where restored edifices stand on original foundations, this park would be uncomplicated by actual history, just bits of the American historical imagination"—one might say, *quintessences*—"magically reconstructed amid the Virginia countryside – historic, along Disney's logic, by association" (1999, 253).

The focus group functions as a neo-peasantry that has been sufficiently educated to consume industrial society's increasingly abstract products, but kept sufficiently ignorant of historical process so as not to question Pitman's naturalization of the spectacle's exclusively dynastic—or what Debord calls "irreversible"—experience of time. Barnes' realism makes visible this process through which Pitman presents to the masses their essentialized self-conception as an objective reality. The substitution of Pitman's theme park for collective memory—indeed, the outsourcing of historical consciousness to a corporate venture—epitomizes Debord's description of the triumph of spectacle as "the systematic organization of a breakdown in the faculty of encounter, and the replacement of that faculty by a *social hallucination*" ([1967] 1995, 217). Barnes dramatizes the manner in which capitulation to the commodity as the exclusive basis for all societal interaction leads to the creation of a self-affirming material environment in which particular ideologies no longer function as specific and temporary distortions, but the experience of ideology itself becomes a generalized condition.

As part of his feasibility study for hijacking the British tourist industry from mainland England to his island theme park, Pitman hires a "French intellectual" to deconstruct the distinction between original and replica. Quoting directly from *Society of the Spectacle* during his presentation to the executive team, the French intellectual concedes Debord's insight that directly lived experience is largely replaced in post-industrial society by representations of experience. However, he rejects Debord's vilification of the spectacle as a form of "sentimental and inherently fraudulent" Platonism. The French intellectual contends that to be modern is to abandon the quixotic quest for authenticity and embrace the replica as the only available means to participate in the reality of the original. He characterizes this relationship to the original in imperialist terms, describing the replica as an opportunity to "possess, colonize, reorder [and] find *jouissance*" in the original (Barnes 2000, 57). Acknowledging the vertiginous existential nausea that accompanies one's liberation from the notion of authenticity, the French intellectual repeatedly applauds Pitman's fearless modernity and exhorts his team not to shy away from this precipice as Debord did.

Deleuze advances a similar argument in a chapter of *The Logic of Sense* titled "Plato and the Simulacrum." He explains that the underlying metaphor of Plato's theory of the forms is one of authentic "lineage" that can be used to distinguish false "pretenders" (1990, 254). Pretenders are judged against a founding mythology that establishes their correspondence to an ideal form, producing a hierarchy of copies ranging from those that participate authentically in the model down to the most degraded *simulacrum, mirage* or *counterfeit* that exhibits a mere external likeness, but no "internal resemblance" to the model (255–6). Deleuze describes the difference between a "poor copy" and a "simulacrum" as the categorical shift from a "moral" existence to an "aesthetic" existence (257). The copy alleges a principled relationship to the form that must be judged by an objective standard, whereas the simulacrum is indifferent to the meaning of the original and asserts various subjective intersections with it. This transition from the moral sphere to the aesthetic sphere parallels the process Benjamin describes whereby an object exchanges its "cult value" for mere "exhibition value."

Unlike Benjamin and Debord—and more significantly, unlike Baudrillard's (1994) pejorative use of the term *simulacrum* to describe the degradation of modern consciousness to the point of abandoning the metaphysics of the real itself—Deleuze ascribes no negative connotation to this shift. For Deleuze, the simulacrum is not merely a "degraded copy," but a "positive power" that challenges the very "original/copy" distinction by reasserting a truly cyclical experience of time alongside the dynastic authority of the founding mythology on which authenticity is based (1990, 263). Invoking Nietzsche's concept of the eternal return, Deleuze explains that the simulacrum allows the individual to relive the same "manifest content" while experiencing new meaning and truth in that content each time. Humanity experiencing and re-experiencing itself in this manner integrates the cyclical and linear experiences of time like "a circle which is always eccentric in relation to an always decentered center" (264). By constructing a system of meaning out of dissonant experiences, the simulacrum allows for co-existing perspectives, truths and realities (262). As such, the simulacrum is not simply a negation of the founding mythology that leads to a crisis of meaning or which is easily recuperated within the founding mythology itself. For Deleuze, the simulacrum "joyfully un-founds" objective truths to allow the individual to participate subjectively in the production of new meaning (263). Perhaps this idea of constructing a new founding mythology is another possible reading of the wall-building tableau at the conclusion of La Trobe's pageant in *Between the Acts*. The relationship that Deleuze draws between the simulacrum and the "eternal return" also informs Saleem's question in *Midnight's Children* of whether he would come to the same conclusion if he retold his story from the beginning, or if the very performance of the first telling would lead him to re-experience his own past from an altered perspective.

So is Pitman's theme park a Debordian spectacle or a Deleuzian simulacrum? Martha struggles with this question, asking Pitman's "official historian," Dr. Max, whether or not he thinks that the theme park is "bogus." Dr. Max replies that the project is "vulgar" in its insensitivity to historical difference, "staggeringly commercial" in its aims, and ideologically manipulative (Barnes 2000, 134). In that respect, the theme park exploits its own artificiality as a commodity and is thus a form of spectacle. At the same time, however, Dr. Max refuses to regard the theme park as the betrayal of authenticity implied by Martha's use of the term "bogus." He dismisses the idea that there is a "lucid, polyocular transcript of reality"— an ideal form of Englishness—to which one can be unfaithful, offering up as an example his own queer interpretation of the Robin Hood legend (152). In this sense, the theme park is not a false pretender to English history, but merely constructs new readings of the same raw materials from a contemporary perspective. Dr. Max's explanation, however, projects a spirit of intellectual play onto the concept of the theme park that is belied by Pitman's own view of the project as a means to inherit England's political and economic dynasty.

Another way of answering Martha's question lies in Deleuze's distinction between the "artificial" and the "simulacrum." He explains that the "artificial is always a copy of a copy, which should be pushed *to the point where it changes its nature and is reversed into the simulacrum* (the moment of Pop Art)" (1990, 265). To bring Debord within Deleuze's terminology for a moment, Debord's critique of spectacle is a critique of the "artificial," namely, the proliferation in post-industrial culture of degraded copies and "false pretenders" that insinuate themselves as objective realities. The process that Deleuze describes whereby artifice is exposed through Pop Art corresponds to the process that Debord describes as *détournement*. Each is a form of pastiche that juxtaposes high culture and ideology alongside everyday objects and advertising jingles to make visible the arbitrariness of the founding mythology through which these commodities are ascribed value and to allow them to take on new meanings in relation to each other. The difference between Debord and Deleuze, however, is that Debord's process of *détournement* will ostensibly strip away accrued layers of artificial commodity value to restore an authentic experience of the real that had become obscured by false mediation, whereas for Deleuze the moment of Pop Art reveals that there is no authentic experience of the real that stands outside of the individual act of consciousness itself.

Barnes portrays one moment in which the artificiality of the theme park verges upon Pop Art's liberated consciousness. As the actors evolve from artificial likenesses of historical figures to inhabit a more authentic internal resemblance to the characters that they play, they undergo a corresponding shift from art objects of pure exhibition value to ethical participants in history. Pretend peasants stage an actual revolt, and pretend pirates begin to traffic in contemporary contraband. Dr. Johnson's double unleashes his caustic wit upon unsuspecting visitors, and Robin Hood's reconstituted band of thieves conducts real raids on the faux royal family. Characters across the theme park begin to interact with a simultaneity that cannot be contained by the linear narrative of history into which they were cast. Martha attempts to restore order—political and chronological—by staging a series of military interventions. History is at war with itself as the British army is deployed against the Merrie Men, and Barnes' gesture takes on the Brechtian sensibility of the subversive march past at the conclusion of La Trobe's pageant. The theme park's illusion of authentic Englishness—grounded in the abbreviated dynastic history that is taught to children—appears to have been irretrievably destabilized by a more mature meta-historical consciousness. However, just as the failing aesthetic unity of La Trobe's pageant is reinforced at crucial moments by timely interventions of nature, Pitman's quick-thinking marketing team repackages these disruptions to the accepted course of history as "cross-epoch conflicts" and are pleased to find that they have "strong Visitor Resonance" (Barnes 2000, 238). The threshold of Pop Art is recuperated within the leisure experience, and England, England remains a post-historical commodity for consumption.

The debacle costs Martha her job, and she returns to the mainland, which has depopulated at Pitman's hands into economic collapse. Pitman formally pronounces the sovereignty of his replica of England and declares himself prime minister. The mainland government renames itself Anglia, secedes from the European Union, disbands the United Kingdom and adopts isolationism as the "last option for a nation fatigued by its own history" (Barnes 2000, 261–2). Dialects spread through the land once more, gazettes cataloging local happenings turn a blind eye to global politics and celebrity culture, and numerous rituals connected with the changing of the seasons resume. Martha seeks out this neo-agrarian community to reconnect with a sense of the real that she identifies with her childhood in rural England—the "directly lived" life that predates the spectacle. Anglia, however, provides no simple solution to the question of authenticity. Barnes does not allow the trappings of revived agrarian culture to enable a fantasy of returning to a pre-industrial, spectacle-free way of life. Instead, Martha is left with the task of evaluating whether Anglia itself is a spectacle or a simulacrum. Are Anglians merely nostalgic spectators of an inauthentic copy of pre-industrial life, or as the French intellectual might suggest, do they participate authentically in a post-industrial life that they have constructed as an optimized re-presentation of a pastoral ideal?

Barnes explores the relationship between Anglia and spectacle through the phenomenon of folk culture. Earlier in the novel, Martha's boyfriend recounts the conundrum faced by Russian composers who were commissioned during the post-Stalin era to restore a sense of nationalism by reviving traditional folk songs. They were forced to invent this music for themselves because Stalin had killed all the peasants and erased their traditions from collective memory (Barnes 2000, 68–9). Anglia's folk culture must be similarly reinvented after the suppression of historical consciousness effected by the industrial era. The blacksmith in Martha's village, for example, is an American-born corporate lawyer named Jack Oshinsky who changed his name to Jez Harris upon relocating to Anglia. He fabricates tall tales about the local landscape and fictional ancestors, which he shares—often in exchange for money or a meal at the pub—with eager anthropologists and linguists who have come from abroad to study and document Anglia. The schoolmaster, Mr. Mullin, chastises Harris for counterfeiting folklore for profit and insists that Harris has an obligation to relate stories that have been officially recorded and collected. Mullin offers Harris a collection of local legends and lore, but Harris explains that the academics prefer his made-up stories and plan to publish anthologies of them, thus making them real within the spectacle of the culture industry. Mullin finally concedes that his own collections are no more factual than Harris' contrivances, but clings to the distinction that authentic folklore should at the very least belong collectively to society (252). Like Debord, Mullin remains committed to a mythology of the "original" and the "authentic" that is unadulterated by commodity relationships. Harris' cottage industry, on the other hand, anticipates Pitman's mass-marketing of the past as a commodity. In this respect, Anglians have merely turned back the clock to a proto-industrial moment that is destined to evolve similarly toward the mature conditions of spectacle.

In another example of artificial folk-product, the leaders of Martha's village decide to host a festival based on the tradition of the May Queen. They initially turn to Martha for advice, since she is the only one among them who was actually raised in rural England. She shows them the program from an agricultural fair that she attended as a child, but they are uninspired by its catalog of regulations—the Platonic forms by which ideal specimens of livestock and crops were judged. They decide instead to model their fair on fictional sources. Preferring their replica to the original, they effectively eliminate from the fair all that is actually agrarian. The main event is a costume contest in which six villagers dress up as Queen Victoria, Lord Nelson, Snow White, Robin Hood, Boadicia (a Celtic queen who led a revolt against the Romans), and Edna Halley (a character that the professional folklorist Jez Harris has invented). A debate ensues regarding the eligibility of Edna Halley insofar as she is not a "real person." After much discussion, the judges pronounce that in order to be considered real, a character must have been "seen by someone, been written of in a book, or been believed in by others" (Barnes 2000, 273). Once again Barnes suggests that the Anglians have not transcended the spectacle, but merely returned to a more primitive stage of it. Their festival, like Parker's neo-folk pageantry, is already tainted by the historicism that suppresses the cyclical experience of time beneath the dynastic representation of time. Barnes allows the reader to witness them in the act of establishing the founding mythology that will eventually become naturalized as timeless and unquestioned.

Although the Anglians struggle at a communal level to achieve an authentic experience of cyclical time through their revival of folk culture, Martha negotiates her way beyond the alienation of the spectacle on an individual level. She accepts that the inaugural fair has founded an Anglian tradition through which the community's dynastic historical identity is born. As the debate among the elders about Edna Halley rages on in the background, however, Martha observes that the children are able to enjoy the costume pageant with a "willing yet complex trust in reality" that accepts in carnivalesque spirit the co-existing identities of the characters and the people who play them (Barnes 2000, 273). Martha reflects on the children's ability to see originals and representations simultaneously and hold those categories in productive tension, experiencing reality as a set of reconcilable perspectives without feeling compelled to historicize them— the very capacity that distinguishes Pico della Mirandola as a truly unmodern humanist in Pater's *The Renaissance*. Martha wonders if one can "reinvent innocence" in a way that does not simply turn back the clock and deny the experiences that have shaped one's consciousness, just like the nationalists deny their hybridity in *Midnight's Children*. Martha does not regress to childhood, but seeks to reconnect in Benjaminian fashion with the child's non-museumized relationship to objects that Carey explores in *Observatory Mansions*.

Barnes models a scenario in which this reinvented innocence need not involve false consciousness. As Martha embraces the life and role that Anglia offers her, she adopts attitudes that are indeed "artificial," but at the same time "not specious" (Barnes 2000, 269). The narrator describes her village as "neither idyllic nor dystopic," suggesting that the inhabitants had attained a realist middle ground. The narrator's comment that "if there was stupidity, it was based on ignorance and not knowledge" (265) signals to the reader of Debord that the villagers have reconnected authentically with a cyclical experience of time through a spontaneous provinciality as opposed to the engineered ignorance wrought by mass culture. Whereas outsiders regard Anglia in Gibbon-like fashion as signifying the fall of the British Empire, the narrator points to "quieter changes that eluded them" figured in the detoxification of the natural environment, a resurgence of local farming, revitalized ecological diversity, and reduced light pollution (263). The narrator notes that even "weather, long since diminished to a mere determinant of personal mood, became central again: something external, operating its system of rewards and punishments, [...] self-indulgent in its dominance" (264).

This is not simply a pastoral fantasy, but a post-industrial realignment with what Debord describes as the "old cyclical rhythms" of the "natural order" that have been replaced by industrialization with a "pseudo-nature constructed by means of alienated labor" (Debord [1967] 1995, 150). Think of how the natural seasons have been repackaged as a "cycle of vacations" and punctuated by holiday shopping periods that conflate leisure with consumption. Television viewing seasons and professional sports seasons culminate in hyped rating wars and world championships whose "paltry contests [...] are utterly incapable of arousing any truly *playful* feelings" (62). In Martha's final conversation with Dr. Max before she moves to Anglia, she laments the loss of "seriousness" at stake in this surplus existence wrought by industrialization. She suggests that she would almost prefer the capricious brutality of past ages to modernity's spectatorial insulation from the real (Barnes 2000, 244). Anglia thus provides Martha with relief from the entirely self-fashioned industrial environment that leads the modern subject to internalize the human struggle for meaning and become a spectator of his own reality. This is precisely the condition that Pater calls upon the modern artist to explore in his conclusion to *The Renaissance*.

As I have noted throughout this study, the capacity of the realist novel to generate the critical perspective I have called meta-spectacle is constrained, at least to some extent, by its reception. La Trobe's fantasy of writing a play without an audience notwithstanding, authors cannot eliminate the variable introduced by the subjectivity of the reader. Like the visitors to England, England, consumers of fiction who look to the novel exclusively as a recreational encounter with the familiar are largely indifferent to whether fiction reproduces the real naturalistically or restates it for their critical inspection. I have brought realist fiction into dialog with Situationist theory to redeploy the original gesture of these texts, namely, to disrupt the act of consumption by compelling the reader to respond to these depictions of the real ethically instead of aesthetically. In parallel with Philip Rahv's concept of "proletarian catharsis" and Brecht's non-Aristotelian theater for the "scientific age," the realist novel urges the reader to shed the role of spectator—no longer to observe, but to *interfere* (Rahv [1939] 1978; Brecht [1929] 1964; [1949] 1964, 193). Realism's restatement of characters that struggle to overcome their own false consciousness empowers the reader to respond to the conditions of spectacle both in the text and at large and to engage in what the Situationists called a critique of everyday life.

Commenting that "I trust we are by now far enough along in our consciousness of the narrative structure of historicity that we can forget about hoary old chestnuts about the evils of totalization or teleology," Jameson expresses a desire to move beyond the apparently exhausted field of metahistory, and perhaps rightly so (1998, 73). It is time to shift our focus to the novel's engagement with post-industrial visual culture and its role as meta-spectacle. Acknowledging that "there is some agreement that the

EPEPILOGUE: DEBORD AS SPECTACLE   181

older modernism functioned against its society in ways which are variously described as critical, negative, contestatory, subversive, oppositional and the like," Jameson asks whether postmodern art merely "replicates or reproduces – reinforces – the logic of consumer capitalism" or also achieves moments in which "it resists that logic" (20). As demonstrated by these far from exhaustive examples from across British fiction in the twentieth century, novels and their various "realisms" do not totalize or naturalize the act of representation, but make visible to the spectator the myriad representations that converge to distance them from the real at any given moment.

REFERENCES

Barnes, Julian. 2000. *England, England*. New York: Vintage Books.

Baudrillard, Jean. 1994. *Simulacra and Simulation*. Trans. Sheila Faria Glaser. Ann Arbor: University of Michigan.

Brecht, Bertolt. (1929) 1964. A Dialogue About Acting. In *Brecht on Theatre: The Development of an Aesthetic*, ed. and trans. John Willett, 26–29. New York: Hill & Wang.

————. (1949) 1964. A Short Organum for the Theater. In *Brecht on Theatre: The Development of an Aesthetic*, ed. and trans. John Willett, 179–205. New York: Hill & Wang.

Debord, Guy. (1967) 1995. *The Society of the Spectacle*. Trans. Donald Nicholson-Smith. New York: Zone Books.

Deleuze, Gilles. 1988. Strata or Historical Formations: The Visible and Articulable (Knowledge). In *Foucault*, trans. Sean Hand, 48–69. Minneapolis: University of Minnesota Press.

————. 1990. *The Logic of Sense*. Ed. Constantin Boundas and Trans. Mark Lester. New York: Columbia University Press.

Dewey, Joseph. 1999. *Novels from Reagan's America: A New Realism*. Gainesville: University Press of Florida.

Jameson, Frederic. 1998. *The Cultural Turn: Selected Writings on the Postmodern, 1983–1998*. London/New York: Verso.

Orwell, George. (1944) 1981. Raffles and Mrs. Blandish. In *A Collection of Essays*, 132–147. San Diego: Harcourt, Brace & Company.

Rahv, Philip. (1939) 1978. Proletarian Literature: A Critical Autopsy. In *Essays on Literature and Politics, 1932–1972*, ed. Arabel J. Porter and Andrew J. Dvosin. Boston: Houghton Mifflin.

Wark, McKenzie. 2008. *50 Years of Recuperation of the Situationist International, 1957–2007*. New York: Princeton Architectural Press.

Woolf, Virginia. (1941) 1970. *Between the Acts*. San Diego: Harcourt, Brace & Company.

INDEX[1]

A
Antiquarianism, 14, 18, 21, 46, 47, 60, 61, 69, 85, 89, 93, 151, 163

B
Barnes, Julian, 9, 14, 108
  England, England, 7, 18, 170–181
Benjamin, Walter, 6, 18, 33, 39, 66, 91, 144, 146, 147, 149, 151–154, 156, 161, 174, 179
Brecht, Bertolt, 9, 15, 23n9, 29, 31, 49, 92, 93, 97, 100, 110n9, 119, 168, 176, 180
Built environment, 2, 5, 7, 14, 31, 38, 143, 144, 146, 159, 170

C
Camera obscura, 1, 125, 127, 148–149
Carey, Edward, 14, 108, 141–142, 146

D
Dada, 19, 32, 89, 156
Debord, Guy, 4–5, 22n6, 60, 167–168, 170–171, 173–174
  See also Situationist International; *Society of the Spectacle*
Deleuze, Gilles, 168–170, 174–176
  See also Simulacrum

E
Eliot, T.S., 78n2, 106
  Family Reunion, The, 82, 105–106
Epic theater, *see* Brecht, Bertolt

F
Flâneur, 6, 12, 17, 25n13, 25n14, 146–147, 154

Observatory Mansions, 6, 7, 14, 18, 141–164, 172, 179

---

[1]Note: Page numbers followed by 'n' refer to notes.

© The Author(s) 2018
E. Barnaby, *Realist Critiques of Visual Culture*,
https://doi.org/10.1007/978-3-319-77323-0

184   INDEX

Flâneur (*cont.*)
  See also Benjamin, Walter
Forster, E.M., 8, 13, 20, 82, 90, 95,
  117
  Aspects of the Novel, 57–60, 75,
    78n2, 98, 100, 145, 163
  on Hardy, Thomas, 57–58, 61
  on "life in time" and "life in value",
    59–60, 75, 77, 78n3, 81, 88,
    98, 100, 101, 103, 104, 135,
    145–146, 153, 163
  A Room with a View, 7, 15, 17,
    62–77, 84, 87, 89, 100, 102,
    123, 126, 134, 135, 157, 163,
    172
  on "round" and "flat" characters,
    15, 59, 61, 99, 171

G
Gothic architecture, 17, 18, 31,
  35–38, 41–45, 47–48, 52, 53n2,
  53n3, 53n6, 61, 67, 71, 83, 90,
  102, 123, 142, 144, 163, 170
Grand Tour, The, 7, 62, 64, 70, 71,
  73, 75, 78n1, 83, 127, 170, 172

H
Hardy, Thomas, 19, 31, 57–58, 82,
  83, 90, 107, 108n4
  Dynasts, The, 20, 58, 82, 106–107
  Jude the Obscure, 7, 13, 17, 31,
    33–53, 57, 58, 61, 63, 67–68,
    71–72, 74, 75, 81, 84, 91, 100,
    102, 105–107, 123, 143, 163,
    171, 172
  on naturalism, 8, 31–33, 42, 49, 69
  on realism, 7, 8, 13, 31–32, 44, 50,
    52, 61, 81, 117
  on tragedy and satire, 8, 33, 49,
    52n2

Wessex, 31, 39, 43, 50, 52, 71,
  107
Haussmann, Georges-Eugène, 116,
  143–144
Hellenism, 34, 36, 37, 45–49, 61, 64,
  67, 72–75, 90, 123
Hugo, Victor
  Notre Dame de Paris, 38–39, 144,
    153, 170

J
Jameson, Fredric, 10, 16–17, 24n12,
  33, 38, 51, 84, 85, 117, 120,
  122, 147, 180–181
Joyce, James, 13, 60, 78n2
  Ulysses, 11–12, 103

L
Literary realism, *see* Realism
Lukàcs, Georg, 12, 14, 16, 33, 117,
  119, 127, 171

M
Macherey, Pierre, 12, 20, 51, 59, 70,
  108, 119
Magical realism, 9, 25n13, 120–122,
  126, 136n1, 141, 151
Marxist criticism, 3–4
Medievalism, 34, 36–51, 53n5, 54n6,
  61, 66, 67, 75, 90, 100
Mitchell, W.J.T., 3–4, 34, 53n5,
  108n3
Modernism, 3, 8, 13, 17, 19, 22n6,
  22n8, 23n10, 25n13, 60, 81,
  106, 132, 167, 181
Museum culture, 3, 7, 12, 19, 22n7,
  37, 65, 73, 75, 90, 104, 110n8,
  130, 142–144, 150–153,
  155–159, 161

N

Naturalism, 13, 16, 20–21, 23n11, 31–32, 42, 49, 95, 124, 126, 158
Neoclassicism, 8, 12, 17, 31, 33, 36, 38, 42, 46, 47, 61, 64, 116, 117, 127, 145, 165, 170

P

Pageantry, 18–20, 50, 82–83, 85–86, 89–91, 94–97, 106–107, 108n1, 109n6, 109n7, 110n8, 110n10, 110n11, 110n12, 167, 172, 178
Parker, Louis Napoleon, 19, 82, 89–90, 95–97, 107, 108n1, 108n2, 109n8, 110n10, 110n13, 172, 178
See also Pageantry
Pater, Walter, 17, 31, 72
on Giovanni Pico della Mirandola, 46, 74, 77, 101, 135, 179
on Johann Winckelmann, 47–48, 61, 73
Renaissance, The, 36, 45, 47–50, 58, 82, 97, 103, 170, 180
Photography, 1, 2, 18, 24n12, 31–32, 37, 48, 50, 52n1, 53n4, 68, 116, 123, 125–133, 149–150, 154, 155, 164, 167, 170
Post-colonialism, 17, 18, 20, 115–121, 125–136, 170
Postmodernism, 3, 8, 17, 21n1, 23n8, 25n13, 117, 125, 141, 142, 167, 181
Powys, John Cowper
A Glastonbury Romance, 83, 98

Q

Quiller-Couch, Sir Arthur Thomas
Brother Copas, 83, 94, 96, 98

R

Realism, 2–4, 6–21, 21n1, 22n6, 23n8, 23n10, 24n11, 24n12, 25n13, 25n14, 31–35, 38, 44, 49, 52, 57–61, 69, 70, 75–78, 78n2, 78n3, 81–82, 84, 85, 95, 98–100, 102, 104–108, 115–117, 119–120, 122–124, 126–129, 133, 135–136, 136n1, 141–142, 146–147, 155–156, 163–164, 167–171, 173, 179–181
Rushdie, Salman, 8, 14, 16, 18, 20, 108, 117–118, 128–129, 131, 136n1, 141, 170
Midnight's Children, 7, 9, 14, 16, 18, 20, 59, 116–136, 136n3, 141, 143, 160, 172, 175, 179
Ruskin, John, 17, 31, 52n1, 53n3, 61, 66, 75, 143, 163
Stones of Venice, The, 36, 39–44, 46–48, 54n6, 66, 169

S

Simulacrum, 18, 42, 71, 87, 90, 124, 149, 174, 175, 177
See also Deleuze, Gilles
Situationist International, 4–5, 22n4, 159, 167–168
dérive, 4, 11, 22n6, 66, 143, 167
psychogeography, 5, 11, 22n6, 66, 143, 163
See also Debord, Guy; Society of the Spectacle
Society of the Spectacle
alienated labor, 5, 35, 42–45, 60, 159, 179
culture industry, 5, 6, 8, 9, 19, 32, 35–39, 45, 87, 90, 145, 153–154, 167, 177

186 INDEX

Society of the Spectacle (*cont.*)
  détournement, 11, 36, 59, 66, 75,
    97, 125–126, 158, 167,
    175–176
  history and time, 39, 46, 60, 77,
    78n3, 83–85, 94, 96–97, 116,
    145, 171–173, 179
  ideology, 6, 14, 22n5, 102, 146,
    152
  proletariat as image, 18–19, 44,
    119, 124, 133, 168
  spectacle, 4–7, 40, 51, 91, 117,
    118, 122–123, 136, 142, 149,
    156, 157, 159, 160, 175
  tourism, 65, 69, 157
  urban planning, 5, 145
  See also Debord, Guy; Situationist
    International
Sontag, Susan, 68, 125–128, 130,
    133, 150
Spectacle, *see* Debord, Guy;
    Situationist International; *Society
    of the Spectacle*

T
Tourism, 4, 7, 14, 15, 18, 41, 51,
    62, 64–71, 74–75, 83, 89, 115,
    127, 129, 130, 134, 142–144,
    149, 154, 157, 159, 167,
    172–173

See also Grand Tour; *Society of the
    Spectacle*

U
Urbanism, 6, 7, 14, 146, 147, 163,
    167
  See also Society of the Spectacle

W
Wilde, Oscar, 23n11
  Picture of Dorian Gray, The, 20–21,
    32
Woolf, Virginia, 8, 13, 20, 23n10, 60,
    82, 117, 124
  Between the Acts, 7, 15, 18, 19,
    82–89, 91–108, 108n1, 108n2,
    109n4, 110n9, 110n11,
    111n13, 121, 125, 135, 145,
    150, 153, 164, 168, 175, 176,
    180
  "Modern Fiction", 8, 13, 60, 81,
    82, 106
  "Narrow Bridge of Art, The", 81,
    82, 106
  Orlando, 82, 103–105
  "Sun and the Fish, The", 101, 102
  Years, The, 82, 104–105, 107–108,
    111n13